Song of the

Pearl and Oyster

Bono - Music can change the world because it can change people.

Einstein - I get the most joy in life out of my violin.

Victor Hugo - Music expresses that which cannot be put into words and that which cannot remain silent.

J. Earp - The truth in every myth is the pearl in every oyster.

Dedicated to the memory of Joe Freyre and musicians everywhere.

Song of the Pearl and Oyster 2

1

Part I

Nora
Indianapolis, 1990

She walked across the plush lobby carpeting and paused at the ballroom door. The clink of wine glasses and laughter sounded before she reached for the handle. It didn't surprise her that she'd been invited to arrive late. At first look, the room seemed too large for the number of guests. Her stride was long and the razor-sharp pleat in the back of her skirt opened to accommodate her steps. One familiar face in this black-tie crowd turned and she caught his eye. Her half-brother, taller than nearly everyone, soon found his way to her side.

"She's in the far corner." Asher looked at her with his half-grin. Nora slipped her hand over his arm and looked up, taking him in. The shining eyes were just as confident as her mother's, not Asian and uncertain like hers. He ran his fingers through the waves of his hair, now with strands of steely gray.

"This is it, Asher." It's all that came out, though a thousand questions waited behind that one. She felt the judgment of strangers, a subdued crowd gathered for a momentous occasion. Was it a mistake to come? "Maybe this is enough." She backed away.

"You flew all the way from California just to see me?" He frowned. "After all these years, is this enough?"

Nora breathed deeply to calm herself. How many times had she done this when they were children? When she was six and he was three, they would run to his room, and press their bodies against the door, against his father's anger. Father's voice bellowed threats when Nora placed a spoon on the wrong side of the plate or left a shoe in the hallway. Her un-American face and curious questions were constant sources of torment for Asher's father, until the day when brother and sister were separated.

Hand in hand they moved through the Art Deco-fashioned ballroom toward the corner where a tall white chair with curved lines stood like a throne. Dozens of friends and family members parted to make way for this unknown woman on Asher's arm.

Nora felt her brother's hand tighten. He cleared his throat. "Mother?"

A stylish white-haired woman with laugh wrinkles looked up at Asher from her place of honor. When she saw the woman on his arm, her eyes narrowed and her champagne glass shook before she placed it safely on the glass table beside her.

"Happy birthday, Mother. Happy 75th birthday." Nora tried to steel her voice against the tightness in her throat. Her mother would not meet her gaze, so she looked down at her dress that rippled like cream. Heads turned and she felt the stares from inscrutable faces. Countless times she'd imagined this moment. Why hadn't she prepared what to say to a mother she hadn't seen since she was six years old?

"Did you get my letters? I used to write to you every week."

"Nora...Everyone, this is Nora, my daughter." She looked at everyone except Nora. An uncomfortable silence made the celebration suddenly painful.

"Every week I hoped to get a letter back from you. "Nora's voice tensed in her throat. I imagined you at the little desk in the dining area beside the kitchen door, picking up a pen, writing about Asher, and asking how my classes at school were going, or if I had made friends. I imagined you hadn't really sent me away – "

But then Nora noticed the pearl ring. In her mind, she would shout smothered emotions and vengeful feelings bringing her mother to tears. But there was the ring her mother wore every day, where it had always been, on her still-graceful right hand. Nora's six-year-old self had her heart set on the normal childhood she was sure other kids had. The ring brought forth a distant, ordinary family memory: sitting close together, reading a book with her mother, watching her tuck a wave of her auburn hair behind her ear for a better look at the page. Nora sat on one side of her mother and Asher on the other. Over and over, Mother read a picture book about a little boy who ran away to rescue a baby dragon, in a familiar, rhythmic lilt. Nora knew many phrases by heart and listened as her mother made the character's voices come alive. And always the familiar pearl on the slender hand that reached to turn a page.

"Asher," Nora faced her brother and grabbed his arms. "Do you remember a book about a dragon that Mother used to read to us?"

Asher shrugged, lost in the new direction of the conversation.

"I remember," Mother brightened. "It was *My Father's Dragon*. You would hug that book and pull us to the sofa. You loved to be read to. The book was in tatters by the time – "

Nora didn't listen. Maybe this wasn't a mistake. She softened her grip on Asher's arm. The memory of the dragon book was proof that there was a time in her childhood when her mother cared.

2

Kioshi
Yokohama, 1935

Kioshi and his friend had anchored their small boat and were preparing to dive. "All the other divers are in the shallows," said Isamu. Kioshi was the best diver, fearless among them. He brought back some of the biggest, most beautiful pearls. "Nobody's tried here," Kioshi said. "It might be too deep. Are you afraid?" He raised his eyebrow at Isamu not as a dare, but out of concern for his friend. His parents named him Kioshi, meaning quiet and peaceful, but he had been the noisiest of the neighborhood children since he was born.

Isamu checked the anchor line while Kioshi secured the net to the outside of the boat and tested the other end of the net where the shell basket was attached. He gathered rocks tied individually in a long scarf and secured it to his waist.

"If you think this is best, we'll try." Isamu secured his own rocks around his waist.

"Can I tell you something?" Kioshi said. "I have a feeling. I'm going to find the most beautiful pearl today - for my future wife in America."

"America?" Isamu repeated the fearful word.

"I've saved up. I have almost enough for passage on a steamer." The two young men rubbed oil on their bodies to preserve warmth. "I'll find a woman, confess my love, and ask her to be my wife. When she says yes, I'll give her the most beautiful pearl I found." Kioshi stretched his arms high taking ten quick breaths and one long one. And so it happened, Kioshi dove deep, nearly 40 meters. Isamu watched the time - five minutes, six, then seven. Fearful, he watched the water for air bubbles, willing his friend not to drown. A sudden burst and gasp - Kioshi broke the surface holding a small basket of oysters.

With their boat back on shore, they used their knives and strong, practiced hands to pry the shells open, tossing small ones back into the sea. Isamu found the first pearl. The oyster was big, so he saved it for his family to eat. When all the shells had been cracked open Kioshi found four beautiful pearls, two from the same oyster, perfectly round with a mirror-like luster. He chose the bigger one for his future wife and knew the others would complete his savings for passage to America.

Kioshi was one of the youngest riders on the freight rail cars that traveled around California, from one Japantown to another. The older riders gave him the advice to sleep light and beware of pickpockets. He asked at each stop about his grandfather who had worked on the rails. Holding an old picture, he watched their faces, but people just shook their heads. He picked up work along the way, cleaning here, road building there. Pearl diving was not a marketable skill in America, and he was anxious to establish himself. San Francisco's *Nihonmachi* seemed like a good place.

Hungry and with no place to stay, he knocked on the door of a rooming house. A woman with a broom and no patience answered the door. When he smiled and asked her for a room, she announced an amount of money and held out her hand. Kioshi had only a few coins, but he offered to clean the rooms in her boarding house in exchange for a place on the floor to sleep. She showed him to an empty corner behind the kitchen where food scraps were stored for the chickens. Kioshi was accustomed to sleeping on a mat on the floor, and in his exhaustion, he approached the corner to sit down.

The woman pushed him away with her broom. Three rooms needed cleaning before he would be allowed to rest. She gave him a bucket and rags.

When he finished scrubbing floors and the one shared bathroom, he dragged himself to his corner. There she was again with her broom, admonishing him, reminding him of his mother. He had to learn English now that he was in America. She gave him a pamphlet in Japanese pointing to the places and times for the classes. Kioshi decided it was best to take a class. So many obstacles confronted him in this country, and English was a big one.

3

Ruth
Michigan, 1938

Relief was the first word that came to Ruth's mind during her first year at college. She felt fortunate to earn a scholarship from the local Farm Bureau to attend Michigan State College, an agricultural school near the state capital in Lansing. Every letter from her mother was filled with resentment of the toil she bore because Ruth was not there to do her share of chores. When Ruth bounded down the terrazzo stairs from her third-floor room at the all-women's dorm, Mary Mayo Hall, she checked the tiny glass door in her mailbox, number 327, turning the combination lock anticipating her father's letters. He had always wanted to go to college and his encouraging words warmed her heart. But the past few weeks, she was checking for notes from a young man, one with a wry grin and a sense of confidence that unsettled her.

She first saw Kioshi across Grand River Avenue at the People's Church. In the college paper, the *Michigan State News* mentioned a student group gathering that evening. Tiptoeing in late, she took a seat beside a broad-shouldered young man in the back who was following the speaker with such intensity, he didn't notice her. But she noticed him. Ruth hardly listened to the speaker, who raised his voice about Roosevelt's court-packing and the problem of Germany's takeover of Austria. When the speaker left the stage, the young man beside her stood up, bumping her arm.

"Excuse me miss, I have to get to the front."

"Ruth," she said.

"Kioshi. Ruth."

She locked eyes with him and told herself she would not be the first to look away.

"I hope you will wait here. Could we talk after?"

"I – yes, I'll wait," Ruth said.

"Please. I come right back here. It won't be long, and I'll come right back." He walked up the aisle and she saw him look back to see if she was still there. She noticed he corrected his words as he spoke.

Folding chairs scraped on the wood floor and side conversations continued as Kioshi began to speak. Ruth was annoyed at the noise, but before long, the mood changed. Kioshi kindled a fire with his forceful, plainspoken words. He told stories of immigrants like himself, and Americans who had lived here for generations, hard-working people who just wanted a fair shake. When he finished and left the podium to walk back to his seat, no one reached out to pat his back or shake his hand as with the last speaker. A few students cheered, but one woman who sat in the back was applauding and smiling. It was Ruth.

"You liked my speech," he said.

"You were wonderful." Ruth smiled at him. "Did you hear how everyone quieted down when you spoke?"

"I hope my language is okay. Could they understand my words? Know what my stories mean? "

"I'm sure they understand. I think of your story about the boy who quit school to care for his family. How could – "

"He's here, just down the street. I invited him to the pool tomorrow. I am a lifeguard there and I got him a guest pass. You should come. Meet him."

The next afternoon was cool, and as soon as she left Mayo Hall, Ruth wished she had worn a warmer coat. In the entryway beside the stairs was a portrait of the long-passed Mary Mayo imprisoned in her frame, for whom the dormitory was named. Mayo's eyes seemed to follow her with disapproval as she pushed her weight against the oak front door. She'd told her kitchen supervisor this morning that she wasn't feeling well and wouldn't be able to work her dinner prep shift. Part-time jobs at the college were required of scholarship students. She'd never begged off work before, but the weight of her decision vanished when she thought of Kioshi. and now she was dashing off to see him.

After the student meeting, Kioshi asked her to join him at the Cunningham Drug Store for a Coke. He told her how he had come to America and rode the rails around California looking for his grandfather. He made her laugh with stories about his landlady and her broom.

"How did you come to Michigan?" she asked.

"The English classes I took led to other classes and a diploma. A counselor at the language school told me about a scholarship here if I agreed to major in agriculture."

Ruth had never met anyone from a foreign country. She was fascinated by his independence. "You came from the other side of the ocean. You left your country for one you'd never seen, one where you couldn't speak the language?" Her questions continued after their Coke glasses were empty. Cunninghams was turning off the lights for the night.

"I'd like to walk you home," Kioshi said.

Ruth nodded. Her dorm was just across Grand River Avenue. She wished it was farther. They walked under the trees and lamplight directed their path. "You are the first girl I've ever walked home," Kioshi said. "I never talk so much about myself. Next time I want to hear about you."

With her jacket collar up, she walked around West Circle Drive to the Intramural Circle Pool. A woman with shiny, wet hair pushed the door open and she dashed in, feeling the whoosh of humid air. She changed into her swimsuit in the women's locker room and stashed her street clothes in a locker. "Shower first," the monitor at the door demanded.

Ruth dutifully walked past the lockers to the cavernous tiled women's shower and was finally granted entry after showing her student ID. The six-lane pool held two lap swimmers and Ruth noticed other groups of students talking at the pool's edge. The strong smell of chlorine irritated her throat as much as the echoes of voices bouncing off the walls attacked her ears. The lifeguard tower was centered at the side of the pool, but where was Kioshi? Tossing her towel in a chair nearby, she scanned the pool for a small boy that might have fit the description of the one in Kioshi's story last night.

The men's locker room door opened, and there was the boy, about ten years old, wet hair cut like a curtain. Behind him was Kioshi, and his broad shoulders. Ruth forgot to breathe.

"I'm glad you made it. Lawrence, this is Ruth."

She knew she should say something to Lawrence, but all she could do was nod her head.

Kioshi moved close to her, and she didn't back away. "Ruth, I'm on duty, so I'll head back up the tower. Lawrence is a good swimmer, but maybe you can check in with him now and then to see if he's okay."

Ruth nodded and remembered to breathe. Kioshi carried a towel for Lawrence and she suggested he place it next to her towel on the chair behind them.

"You can check back in with me now and then too." Kioshi winked at her.

Ruth watched him climb up the tower and turned to Lawrence. "Well, what will it be?" she called over the echoes of splashes. "Shallow or deep end?"

"Cannonball!" Lawrence announced. He took a running leap, hugged his knees, and made a spectacular splash.

Ruth shrugged at Kioshi who had been watching them both. She made her own shallow dive and swam her way across the pool with straight strokes, attempting to impress the lifeguard with her style. Close to the deep end, she felt a tug on her ankle and turned. "Race ya to the bottom!" Lawrence said, peering through his curtain of hair.

Feeling Kioshi's eyes upon her, she followed. Hands together like an arrowhead she tucked her head down and swam toward the pool bottom, just as she had learned in her school physical education class. Imagined tailfins replaced her legs and she stretched with the joy of complete control. It wasn't long before she lost sight of him. He couldn't have disappeared so quickly. Once her feet were on the bottom, she blinked her eyes in all directions. A sudden whoosh of bubbles appeared beside her. Strong arms grabbed her waist and she tried to push away, but her arms became a useless tangle. He knew how to hold her so all she could do was give in to her capable rescuer. Their faces broke the surface of the water together.

"What happened? This is four meters deep here." Kioshi's voice was far from calm.

"Lawrence dared me to go to the bottom with him. Where is he? I couldn't find – "

"Here I am!" Lawrence chirped from the side of the pool.

A few students had gathered behind him to see what had happened. Some of the guys were smiling and laughing. Ruth blinked as the students and Lawrence stared at her. Kioshi had to know Lawrence was safe when he dove in. She turned to Kioshi, her furious treading of water making her bounce.

"I'm fine, really." She glared at him and pushed her hair away from her face. " I didn't need your help. I don't know what you were thinking." Ruth's humiliating rescue made her the center of attention. She turned away and swam to the side, slapping the water with each stroke. This was not the man she talked with for hours last night, the one who thankfully didn't ask questions about her life on the farm where the ghost of her brother hovered interminably. Not Kioshi who didn't see the Great Depression as a wallowing quagmire but a stepping stone. How could he possibly think she couldn't save herself? Without a backward glance, she grabbed her towel and left the pool.

A shiver crept up her back as Ruth walked back to her dorm. In her hurry to get away she didn't dry or comb her hair, and it dripped in a cold drizzle down her back. By the time she opened the door and faced Mary Mayo's disapproving gaze, she felt overheated. She could still feel his strong arms wrapped around her deep in the water.

That night, Ruth wrote to each of her parents.

Mother,

The weather is pleasant. No gentlemen are allowed in dorm rooms and dances at the student union require feet to be on the floor at all times. I'm completing my homework. I received a 3.5 on my art history exam.

Papa,

College is such a curious place. Conversations fill my head with ideas I'd never imagined. We're learning about humanities and the Enlightenment and abstract art that doesn't try to look real at all. It's just an expression of the artist's feelings. A professor said the World War and the Depression are so staggering, the artists want to rebel against what is real and create something new, something you can't put your finger on and say exactly what it is. Will anything good come of these hard times?

I attended a church meeting last night and met a man who amazes and infuriates me. He's here from California to pursue an agriculture degree. I think Dan would have done that if he had lived, don't you? I wonder if you and Mama ever felt this way, amazed about each other when you first met?

Today I went swimming at the MSU pool where he is a lifeguard. He pretended to save me and it was all very confusing because I didn't need saving. Don't tell mother, but I often think of Dan and how different it would have been if he was here. He would have been two years away from graduating by now. Sometimes I feel he's watching over me as I walk to my classes. I miss him every day.

The next morning Ruth left her stamped letters at the front desk and found a piece of green paper in her mailbox. She chided herself for hoping the green paper came from that humiliating lifeguard. What was wrong with her wanting to hear from Kioshi again? She worked the combination and saw her name on the folded sheet:

Ruth, I am sorry. You are a good swimmer. You didn't need my help. I could see I caused you hazukashii. That is Japanese for embarrassed shame. Confusion maybe. I like you. Lawrence likes you. We hope to see you back at the pool some afternoon. If not, I understand. Kioshi

Ruth crushed the note in her fist and glared at the painting in its frame, that smug look on Mary Mayo's face. On her way to her class in the home economics building, the foreign word *hazukashii* played in her head. What did he understand? The more she tried to banish Kioshi from her thoughts, the more he consumed them. She arrived early and the lecture hall was still nearly empty. In the back of the room, she pulled at the note-taking desk attached to her seat, its surface rough to the touch with carvings. She swung it up over her lap scowling at the names in hearts, the ones she'd overlooked until now. With a sigh, she opened her fist revealing the crumpled green note. Why did Kioshi upset her so? She'd go back to the pool this afternoon and find out.

4

Nora
Indianapolis, 1946

When Nora and Asher were sent to their rooms, they knew that their parents would argue. Nora was used to making herself scarce when her stepfather returned from work. His cold silence at the sight of her made her learn to tiptoe away from the kitchen instead of bounding up to him to tell him about the day like Asher was allowed to do. But this evening was different. Asher was not allowed to greet his father either. He hopped on the black floor tiles, skipping the alternating white ones, away from his father's stern voice. Mother swirled ice in the two glasses that held their drinks, handing one to her husband.

The children pressed their ears to the door of Nora's room, closer to the kitchen for better listening. Angry words came and went. Mama and Dad must have been moving around, but the words they could hear were hard to understand. "...can't endure Nora any longer," she heard her stepfather say.

"The war is over...job to do...hard enough for a Jew in Indianapolis. People want to forget. Nora - reminds us every day of the war."

Nora tried to understand and explain. She told Asher their father was mad at her because of the war.

"Samuel, she's a child," her mother said.

"Ruth, she has to go...at the store people stare at her. She's a reminder of what we all want to forget. I can't live like this."

Nora grew more fearful but couldn't pull herself away from the door. Asher looked to her for answers.

"Either she goes or...divorce...keep Asher...Nora goes with you!"

Nora had never heard her stepfather so angry. Her mother began to cry. "Tell me," Asher pleaded.

Nora wondered, what was divorce? She explained the part she did understand. "Dad wants me and Mama to go away," she said. "He wants you to stay here with him and mama and me to go away. I don't want to leave you, Asher!" Her arms shook. She put them around her little brother's shoulders. Everything felt upside down.

Her mother had always told her to look after Asher. When he had chicken pox, Ruth worried and waited by his bedside and rinsed the cool cloths for his fevered head. She drew pictures of dogs and cats, snowmen, and jack-o'-lanterns for him and taped them on the walls of his room. It took a long time for him to feel better. Maybe she hadn't been good enough.

They held their breath and tried to be quiet with their ears to the door. "I can buy a bus ticket tomorrow." Nora hears her mother's tired voice. "... my mother and dad, to the farm in Michigan."

"...quick. I want her gone by the company family Christmas party...not going to another event...staring at her...ridicule I put up with at work...hard enough...mocking about a Jap kid..."

Nora heard the ice cubes in the glass and figured her mother would refill it. "I'll take care of it," her mother said. Nora held her brother close but the shaking wouldn't stop.

5

Ruth

Michigan, 1940

Ruth's letters home explained her course of study in art history. Her letters didn't mention the nights that she would sneak out of the basement window after curfew to see the father of her child-to-be. Ruth sat in the front row of the Student Christian Movement when Kioshi was speaking. Neither of them could figure out the group's name since they accepted all beliefs, even atheists. This night Kioshi, drew from a book he had read by Karl Marx, *The Communist Manifesto*. He warned students that Nazis started out with calls to patriotism. They invented an enemy that didn't exist and the Jews became the enemy.

He warned that discrimination could happen here in East Lansing if we weren't careful. After polite applause at the end, a few students asked Kioshi questions about the book. What about the Nazi concentration camps that imprisoned German communists? Kioshi said, "Why should one group of people be held in higher esteem than any other?" He walked Ruth back to the basement window of her dorm, but it had been locked. She couldn't go to the front door and sign in, or she would be given demerits. Shey may lose her scholarship.

"Will you spend the night with me in my apartment?" Kioshi asked.

Ruth walked hand in hand with him all the way to M.A.C. Avenue.

The following week, Kioshi spoke of negroes and immigrants who desired work the same as anyone. To prove themselves, they felt the need to work harder than whites, but people were afraid of them. Just like in Germany, that fear made it easy for whites to see them as less than human, to lash out and try to find ways to keep them from the American Dream, keep them out of the neighborhood. A heckler interrupted. "Why should you get a job? Red-blooded Americans have lived here their whole lives and deserve it more than you"

"Unless you're an Indian, your ancestors came from somewhere else just like me," Kioshi answered. "We all want to work."

Ruth didn't try to get back to her dorm on meeting nights anymore. She knew the way to Kioshi's apartment, but they always walked together. "Your speeches give me ideas and more questions, and then new ideas," she kissed his cheek. "I want so much more than just to be a Hill Road farm girl."

"Ruth, your roots came from the farm, but here you are now in my heart."

Ruth waited as long as she could before she called long-distance to tell her mother about her visit to Olin Health Center on campus. She began by telling her mother how new the center was and how clean and efficient it seemed. When she talked about the kindness of the doctor, her mother grew impatient at the expense of the call and inexorably Ruth's fears tumbled out. "Mother, I'm pregnant and I don't know if I can finish out the term."

She knew her mother would be upset, but she couldn't have predicted the screams and the language her mother was capable of. Her mother had never hung up on her in mid-sentence. The sanctimonious lecture Ruth heard pieced together the part about ruining herself and the family name, the part about leaving before anyone found out, and the part about never setting foot in the farmhouse again. Ruth had imagined what it would be like to introduce Kioshi to her parents. Before the phone call, she thought her mother would object, but she was sure her dad would prevail with his easy-going ways, and his readiness to help out. Now she knew she could never take Kioshi home.

The kindness of the health center doctor surprised her. He ushered her into his office and closed the door. Floor-to-ceiling books on shelves lined one wall. The doctor in his crisp white lab coat sat opposite her on the other side of his desk and began to speak. Her mind landed on the phrase *unwed mother,* a phrase whispered in a circle of young women she sat with on a dorm room floor one night. Shame, humiliation, the sentence of motherhood that slammed the door and locked away dreams confronted her. How could she graduate now?

"Do you have any questions? Is there anyone I can call for you?" the doctor asked.

Ruth shook her head and released her hands where they had been gripping the wooden arms of the chair. She had to get out of there.

"Nurse Wallberg has a pamphlet to give you at the desk. It explains what you can expect over the next nine months."

A few weeks later when Ruth returned from a class, she was shocked to find her parents in her dorm room. The chest of drawers she shared with Betty was open, and they were hastily packing her clothes.

"I asked them if they wanted to wait until you got here," Betty stood in a corner by the window wringing her hands.

"I told her it's a family emergency," Ruth's mother said. "Check for anything we missed. We're leaving."

Ruth looked around the room she had shared with Betty, her empty desk and stripped bed. Betty reached for her with a knowing embrace and wished her well.

Only her coat and books were left to carry. Nearly everything else was already in the truck. Her father carried the last suitcase and Ruth signed out at the front desk. Dad tossed her bag in the truck bed and they were off, Ruth sitting between her parents as if she were a child again.

"Where are we going?"

"We've enrolled you in Antioch College in Ohio. I didn't know who to turn to for this panic, this calamity you put us in. I wrote to Eleanor Roosevelt"

"Oh, Mother. Roosevelt?"

Her mother pulled a letter from her purse and handed it to her.

My Dear Mrs. Gilbert,

I am in receipt of your heartfelt letter. Surely you want what is best for your daughter and family. Rest assured, you are not the first family to experience this quandary. I see you want to be as discreet as possible while allowing the completion of your daughter's educational experience. I am told by the best of resources that Antioch College in Yellow Springs, Ohio is a private Christian college with sound values. I have contacted the admissions office. Following is the information you will need to begin your transition. Best wishes for a hopeful solution for your family.

Regards,
E. Roosevelt
Malvina Thompson, Private Secretary
Eleanor Roosevelt

Ruth returned the letter and her face grew hot with more anger than embarrassment. She was waiting until Kioshi returned from California to tell him about their child. Now she wouldn't be able to say goodbye.

6

Kioshi

California, 1941

On the bus to California, Kioshi thought about what he would say in his speeches. Already his longing for Ruth ate at him. Maybe his passion for justice was what made it more difficult for him to get good-paying jobs, but even with his scholarship, he could barely afford rent and food. He took every carpentry or handyman job he could find, but a promising job sometimes ended for no apparent reason.

His friend from a political science class told Kioshi about a request for rally speakers at a campus in California. Even though it paid only for his transportation, room, and board, he might find it easier to get a job there.

"Kioshi, are you sure it's safe?" Ruth asked. She reached for his hand one last time before he boarded the bus.

"It's a chance," he said. "Out there are more people like me. We need more people to wake up and see that there's more to America." He thought not everyone was free, but he left the words unsaid.

"I wish you wouldn't go," she tucked her head under his chin. "It would change everything. I worry that something might happen to you."

"Another guy on the bus is from MSC, so I won't be alone. The first rally is next week." He held her hand over his heart, feeling its warmth. "This is important to me, Nora."

Days before he left, Kioshi took her to a tiny jeweler's shop over the Cunningham Drug Store on Grand River Avenue across from her dorm. The jeweler had a collection of silver rings and Kioshi asked Ruth to choose one. He watched her cheeks turn pink. Kioshi wanted to make sure Ruth felt secure about his feelings for her. He watched her choose a simple silver ring with two curves that met in the center.

"Kioshi, I love it." Her eyes shined.

He held her hand back, inspecting the ring. "I'm glad you like it, but it needs something," he said. From his pocket, he took a soft cloth pouch that had traveled with him from Japan. He opened it to reveal a beautiful pearl.

"I can mount that for you," the jeweler said, plucking up the pearl from Kioshi's hand and examining it in the light before Ruth had a chance for more than a glance. "That is a rare beauty. The color is matchless - pale off-white." The jeweler seemed lost in thought. He reached for his jeweler's glass.

They made arrangements to pick up the finished ring. Ruth was brimming with happiness and that was all he cared about. Kioshi took her arm and escorted her back to her dorm, revealing the story of the dive for the pearl and how he had brought it from Japan to give to the woman he would marry one day.

Ruth spun around, giddy with excitement. "To think you dove to the bottom of the sea. I can only imagine what it must be like."

"And after all this time, the pearl is right where it is supposed to be."

She held her hand in front of her to look at the pearl once more.

Kioshi couldn't get the smile to leave his face. Hearing the joy in her voice thrilled him.

During the day, he was allowed in the lobby of Mary Mayo Hall. He held the heavy oak door for her and she dashed to meet a friend she saw at the front desk. Kioshi watched as the young women leaned over with their heads together examining the ring, and oohing at the sight of it.

The following week, Kioshi and his MSC friend spoke at Long Beach, his first California campus protest. Preparing for the second speech, he spent his spare time searching for work opportunities. He felt guilty for not being completely honest with Ruth. But he was so sure she'd forgive him if he found work, that he kept searching.

If he found a job where he could support them both, he would send for her. She could pursue her art degree in California and he could work the railroads in a place where more people looked like he did. He took jobs wherever he could find them, the docks, where roughnecks worked, or cleaning floors at Japanese restaurants, which didn't pay as well. Letters between the two passed furiously at first. Ruth often asked when he would return. Suddenly, her letters stopped. Kioshi had changed addresses and figured she hadn't gotten the new one yet. He kept writing as weeks turned into months. As hard as he tried, his life was a struggle. Saving enough for the two of them seemed like a faraway dream.

One day in December Kioshi hauled pallets at the Long Beach docks, back-breaking work, but it was a two-day job and paid well. He was hopeful that it would turn into something more but on his second morning, the men stopped work and gathered around. Pearl Harbor had been hit in a surprise attack. The Japanese used bombs and bullets, smashing through the decks of battleships. The docks closed and workers turned to one another in confusion. They wondered if Long Beach would be next.

On his way from the docks, Kioshi passed a newsstand and glanced at the headlines: War on Japan Declared December 8. He read the headline again and again. The country of his birth and the country he adopted were at war. Suddenly people he loved were now his enemies.

He stopped and another Japanese dock worker ran up to him. "Will they blame us? Are you gonna fight?"

Kioshi thought of his childhood in Japan and tried to make sense of this senseless act. "This is war. I'm going to join the Navy." Kioshi told him. But what if Ruth answered his letter while he is gone?

Days after, Americans who had applied for citizenship like Kioshi were still stunned in disbelief by Pearl Harbor. Kioshi, on an exhausted walk home from a night job, heard a late radio broadcast blaring from a loudspeaker: "Hitler declares war on the US this day, December 11th..." He found it hard to breathe, hard to find his way to the rooming house. President Roosevelt would declare war after Japan and Germany declared war on the US.

Was the US army big enough to stand up to two enemies? He passed his rooming house, unable to stop walking, unable to shake thoughts of harm coming to his new country from the evils of the old one. He passed a woman walking her cocker spaniel. She pulled the dog's leash close and her eyes narrowed when she saw him, a common occurrence now. What if harm came to Ruth? He returned to his room and wrote another letter in hopes that if any of the dozens of letters he wrote would find their way to her, it would be this one. He told her he was joining the Navy to protect her.

The following spring, Kioshi earned a promising job at the Long Beach docks after failed attempts to sign up for the Navy. He planned to make a speech outside after work that included his willingness to fight after being turned away. His speech could jeopardize his ability to work there. When it came to life and death, when it came down to Ruth, there was no decision to be made.

He practiced speaking in his mind as he worked that day, penciling in changes on the notes in his pocket that would grab the attention of the dock workers. With arms aching after lifting a day's worth of heavy pallets, he tried not to look anxious as he stepped on a box outside the docks' gates. The workers stopped to listen, more men than he'd talked to at MSC or the university protests.

"Why lock up Japanese Americans like enemy prisoners? These men want to fight for America!" Kioshi was incensed with a desire to protect his adopted country with all its struggles, and his hopes for the future. His speech was about rights, but also the right to join the war. "Let them see what we're made of. We can show them we're on the right side." He talked about pride in his future citizenship. He ended with the words, "I want to protect my country."

The men responded with some cheering when Kioshi felt a club crack bone across his chest. A searing pain took his breath away. He tried to cry out, but no sound came. An officer grabbed his hands, clicked handcuffs behind him, and dragged him away faster than his heels could land on the pavement. His arms were pulled, his legs purposely tripped beyond his control. One of his captors grabbed him by the scruff of the neck, making it harder to breathe and swallow. Another struck his ribs with a club. He felt something break. Focused on which pain and where the next blow was coming from, Kioshi didn't understand what he had done.

He was pushed into a cell that smelled of cigarette smoke and urine. A crowd of men, many of them Japanese Americans, spent the night with no place to sleep. Kioshi couldn't call Ruth and didn't want to alarm her. A big breath shot pain through his left rib cage, so he breathed in shallow breaths.

The next morning the jailers came to move him but there was no explanation for his charge. Was it against the law for him to try to sign up for the Navy? He was separated and directed into a bus with other Japanese Americans. Kioshi's handcuffs were taken off and he was pushed to sit down in a seat. Every push pulsed in his chest where the officer's club had hit him. There was much confusion and no one knew where they were being taken.

Many hours passed after the bus made its way out of the city. Hour after hour there was nothing to see but filtered daylight and the feel of bumpy, rutted roads. Kioshi heard a mother comfort the girl behind him when she asked if they had done something so bad that people didn't want to look at them. All the windows were papered over. Hearing the girl made Kioshi feel farther away from Ruth than ever before.

By late afternoon the bus slowed at a remote outpost that looked like military barracks. The sign read *Manzanar*. Kioshi watched the driver get out and listened to a disagreement unfold. He couldn't hear the words, but he gathered they weren't staying. Every seat was full and passengers asked in a combination of Japanese and English, where are we? Where are we going? With impatience, the driver stomped on the bus. "Quiet! Shut the hell up."

Someone gave Kioshi a sandwich wrapped in waxed paper. There was no food or bathroom for the passengers. He unfolded the sandwich wrapper and looked down the long dirt road through the windshield ahead.

Hours later in the middle of the night, tired and hungry, dozens of exhausted Japanese Americans filed out of the bus. They saw what looked to be a prison in the middle of the desert. Barbed wire circled the top of a tall fence and then stopped. Rows of rough wood cabins were in various stages of completion. No name or mark of identification could be seen. Outhouses were in the back. Everything was new and unfinished. "This is your home now," the man in charge yelled.

"Everybody works. You'll be assigned to a work crew. They'll tell you what to do."

Whispers traveled through the group and Kioshi learned the name was Topaz. Even if she'd worry, he had to tell Ruth what was happening. What if she changed her mind about him and believed he was the enemy?

Days turned to weeks and although others finally received mail, Kioshi was beside himself that he hadn't heard from Ruth, the only person on this continent who cared about him. In his mind he relived the dive to the bottom of the pool and the way she felt in his arms as they swam to the surface. He volunteered for extra work detail to earn credits for paper and stamps to send more letters to her dorm. Searching his thoughts, he remembered her talk of the farm on Hill Road in Grand Blanc. With no street number, he tried mailing letters to the farm in care of Nora's mother.

7

Ruth

Indiana, 1945

The day Ruth graduated from Antioch began with excitement and pride. The resentment over young Nora was enough to keep her parents from attending the ceremony, and their absence stung. But little Nora and Ruth bathed and dressed with special attention to Nora's pigtails. Their landlady had given her new blue ribbons for her hair and found a blue flowered dress at a thrift shop that fit Nora almost perfectly. Ruth's excitement spilled over to her daughter, who skipped along the sidewalk on their way to the auditorium.

"Mrs. Anders, the dress and ribbons are beautiful," Ruth said.

Nora stopped her skipping and twirled her pigtails. "Thanks, Mrs. Anders."

Ruth watched for the two of them as she walked across the stage, her robe billowing behind her. On their way back to the boarding house after the ceremony, Ruth and the landlady talked about the challenge of taking care of a child and the relief of freedom from deadlines for her course assignments.

Walking up the steps to the boarding house, Mrs. Anders turned to face her. "It's not up to me." She looked troubled and her hands rolled the graduation program tight into a tube. "There are city ordinances about student housing that have to be followed. I could lose my license if you and your daughter continued to stay in your room. Only students are allowed and you are no longer a student."

By the following afternoon, Ruth and Nora gathered their few belongings into a battered suitcase and started walking.

"Where are we going, Mama?"

Suddenly Nora dashed to the neighboring lawn to chase a cat and Ruth dropped the suitcase to grasp her shoulder and corral her back to the sidewalk. "We need to find a safe place to stay, darling."

"Let's go to grandma's farm. You told me stories. She has chickens and we could eat the chicken eggs for breakfast."

The crackling sound of cicadas followed them. The day was heating up and once they reached the end of the street, the shade trees stopped. "No, Nora. We can never go back to Grandma. She is - so angry. She doesn't want to see us. She would never let us in the door."

"Why, Mama?"

Ruth couldn't answer. They walked on for hours beyond the sidewalks and trees, past the paved road, and into the countryside. A car with a big family sped by leaving a dusty cloud that settled on their bodies wet with sweat. Nora cried with exhaustion, her face red, ribbons untied, and feet sore from shoes that were too small. Ruth tried to pick her up but the building heat and heavy, humid air exhausted her. She thought about leaving their suitcase behind, diploma and all. The sun passed overhead and sank lower in the western sky. She was sure anyone would be repulsed by her down-at-the-heel state, a hobo and child. Where could she go? They sat at the side of the road to rest when thunder rumbled. Clouds brought drops of rain that turned into a gusty rainstorm.

"I'm hungry, Mama," Nora whimpered. She barely made it to the side of the road before she sat down in the wet gravel.

A truck barreled down the road behind them and Ruth stood up to wave. He appeared to be turning their way, but her hopeful look at the driver only revealed the scowl of a man in a hurry. His tire hit a puddle and sprayed them with mud. Scanning the farmer's field for shelter, Ruth saw a feed shed on a far hill. She picked up Nora and set her on her feet. "Put your face up to the rain and the mud will wash off," she said.

Nora lifted her face and squinted her eyes closed. More wind made the rain feel like needles against their skin as Ruth gently rubbed the mud from Nora's face. They stepped high, marching through field grass that sawed their bare legs with each step. Despite her misery, Ruth carried the suitcase and Nora up the last rise before they reached the shelter. Once they ducked into the shed, Ruth checked the corners and the floor for any snakes or rats. All she found was the last gray of the day between the boards. The roof leaked occasional drops of rain on their heads. A crack of thunder struck alarmingly close and Nora yelped. The air grew cool and Ruth sat down beside her shivering daughter, holding her close. The half bale of hay propped in the corner could make a barrier on the open side of the shed, so Ruth moved it close to the side where the roof had the fewest holes. She maneuvered the bale until it seemed to offer the best protection from the wind gusts and rain, and they moved to the inside of it.

"I want a drink of water." Nora whimpered.

Angry at herself, Ruth looked up at a spiderweb in the corner, nearly broken by rain and wind. The strands that were left carried shiny water drops in an intricate, geometric puzzle. But it was just another invisible barrier. The spider would repair its web tomorrow, and they would be gone.

The next day the storm had cleared. Ruth tried to loosen Nora's shoelaces, but she winced when Ruth pushed them on her feet. Her heart sank as she looked at her daughter's face. Did Nora believe her mother would protect her and keep her safe? She had a college degree, but she couldn't think through this. If Nora wasn't half Japanese, her grandmother would have probably taken them back to the farm. Why hadn't Kioshi come back? The guilt Ruth felt matched the emptiness in her stomach and she forbade herself to wish Nora was anyone else. The more she tried, the more the thought returned and haunted her. A heavy fog made them both sticky and uncomfortable as they made their way back to the road. Pangs of hunger slowed their progress. In the heat of midday, Nora saw a steep hill ahead and whimpered. She let go of Ruth's hand and sat down at the side of the road, refusing to move.

"Nora, let's stop and think." She didn't have the strength to scold, and rest might do them both good. She looked back where they had come, and then up at the top of the hill. Dizziness overtook her as she sat, and leaned on her suitcase. Nora's head dropped into her lap.

"We'll take some deep breaths," she said, shaking her own head to clear her mind. Reluctantly, Ruth looked up the steep road ahead of them. Near the highest point, she saw a tree with a chimney top behind it. "Look up there, Nora. That's where we'll stay. Can you walk that far, do you think?"

Halfway up the drive in the yard at the hilltop farm, was a hand water pump. As soon as they saw it, the two of them ran and started pumping. Strong, sulfur-smelling water poured onto their hands and they drank in grateful gulps. Cold water refreshed them, cleaned their faces and hands, and felt like the mercy Ruth remembered from her childhood Sunday school classes. She straightened her dress and Nora's as best she could and knocked on the farmhouse door.

A big woman with black curls secured by bobby pins stood behind the screen door. "Who're you?"

"I'm Ruth and this is my daughter Nora," she began. "We need food and a place to stay. I'll work for you and my daughter can gather eggs or do small chores."

The woman said nothing but stared at the two of them.

"Please." Nora's voice wavered. "We have no place to go."

The woman stepped out the door and motioned for them to follow her. She showed them a vegetable garden full of weeds.

"When I was a girl, I lived on a farm in Michigan."

"The chickens will need feeding and the coop is in need of a good clean, and the beehive will need honey harvested every month," the woman said.

They came to an arrangement. At the end of the summer, after canning season was over, the two of them would have to find another place to stay. In exchange for help, she and Nora could sleep in the barn and have food to eat.

The barn became their home for the summer. They saw the farmer in his work around the yard, yet they rarely had any communication with him beyond a serious nod. Nora helped out with the chickens, gathering eggs, and playing with the goats in the pen. Ruth watched her daughter laugh and run around the yard, but she was terrified. Once canning season was over, they would be back on the road with a crisp Indiana fall and cold winter ahead.

She continued to write Kioshi, now with an address in the care of the farmer's wife, but where were his letters? When he first arrived in California, their flurry of letters would cross in the mail. He had found jobs at the docks and gave speeches there. Although he had lost his grandfather years ago, the community was still there. Kioshi found an elderly man who sold traditional healing herbs and remembered his grandfather. Kioshi mentioned odd jobs and his rallies at the university, promoting workers' rights.

She sensed the impatience, and always the longing to be together. Among the few possessions she brought from the boarding house were his letters. After Nora fell asleep on the old crib quilt the farmer's wife had given her, she read them by candlelight. Every day when the wife checked the mail, she shook her head in response to Ruth's hopeful look.

She learned how to put on the protective white bee suit and harvest honey from the hive boxes. Once the combs were capped with wax, she removed them carefully, but not so much that the bees wouldn't have enough to eat. Behind the hives were two cherry trees that produced an astounding number of cherries. Some they sold at the produce stand by the road, but many were pitted and canned for pies in the winter.

Ruth stood for hours at the sink, cherry juice staining her fingers and Mrs. Simmon's apron. Each week brought her closer to the end of summer and feeling further from Kioshi. How could she tell him about Nora? She dreamed of so many ways, a singing phone call with both of their voices, a photo perhaps? But they had never spoken of children and there was the doubt as strong as the stain on her fingers that he never wanted a child.

On one of their last afternoons in the barn, Ruth was wide awake with worry. If she had earned a teaching or nursing degree, she would have the skill to support the two of them, and maybe Kioshi too. The letters she had sent him were returned, address unknown. Nora with her sweet face lay nearby, quilt corner tucked under her chin, dark, auburn hair like hers fanned out in waves on the straw.

If only her parents had responded to her letters for help. Already the warm summer nights were beginning to cool down. How would she keep Nora warm at night on the side of the road? A goat wandered over from its stall. "We're out of time." she put her arm around the goat and rested her head on its side. "I have to find shelter for Nora."

The goat bleated and blinked.

"She'll need a school, books, and pencils. Whatever it takes to help her, I have to do it."

The afternoon she had confronted Kioshi in the hallway outside the university pool, she did not feel *hazukashii*, but embarrassment. He had underestimated her capabilities. Maybe Japanese women needed help, but American women could fend for themselves. She stared daggers into his eyes as she spoke, but saw no anger in his. He didn't argue back. He merely said "Mmm.." walking close enough for her to see water drops on his body. His arms encircled her as they had deep in the pool and he kissed her behind the ear. "I wanted to do this ever since we were at the bottom of the pool," he said. "It's all I can think of."

Ruth was rattled. He stood back with a suddenly shy grin, then a silly smile. Ruth's gritted teeth relaxed and her lips parted. She found herself smiling back.

She bit her lip and let the memory of Kioshi wash over her. Nora the farmhouse, asking the wife to check in on Nora. She was going to the dance.

At dusk, Mr. Simmons drove his pickup truck down the long country roads and dropped off his nervous passenger at the VFW hall. He gave her a dime for the phone when she was ready to come home.

Lively with fiddle music, the rough-hewn room was filled with smiling locals coupled up around barrels, their faces lit by the kerosine lanterns on the barrel tops. A dance commenced with six circles of four couples in promenade position. Nora walked to a punch bowl in the corner to watch. The next dance consisted of one big circle, and someone grabbed Nora's hand, sweeping her up with the group. After a few reels, she let herself relax into the crowd of local men with shiny Brylcream hair and women whose shoulders were scented with apple blossom cologne.

Back at the punch bowl, she chatted with one of the women who had danced the reel. "Watch this guy," the woman pointed to a man in uniform. "He's been losing dance partners all night."

They watched while the man approached a woman in a pink flowered dress and instead of agreeing to dance, her eyes grew wide. She turned her back on him and hurried away.

"See? That's been happening all evening."

"What do you suppose is wrong?" Ruth asked.

"Whatever it is, I don't want to dance with him," the woman said. "But see Jake in the corner there?" She pointed to a tall, curly-haired man who looked much more comfortable with cows than women. "I'm gonna go ask him."

A fiddle player tapped his foot and changed to a slow dance melody. Ruth turned to the corner of the table. She watched the couples on the dance floor and looked around the room for someone who might know of any place to live or any kind of work. What would such a person look like?

"Will you dance?"

It was the man in uniform. "You don't look scary to me. Why did the other women turn their backs on you?" Ruth said.

He shook his head. "Hard to say. Maybe the uniform scares them off," he said.

Ruth decided one dance couldn't be too dangerous.

The band played "Sunrise Serenade" and Ruth felt swept away. He wasn't a bad dancer and she forgot her reason for being there. "Tell me about yourself, soldier."

"Engineer Combat Battalion, stationed in Belfast, then we were sent to Omaha Beach. That's all I want to say about that." He searched her face with a serious expression. "Say, I got a civilian project in Indianapolis, housing for the returning vets. I start next week. The boss says if I want to move up the ladder, I should find a wife and not a Jewish one. I'm Jewish. You have a problem with that?"

Was this soldier asking for a wife? No wonder women were turning away. But these women weren't in Ruth's situation. A steady job in Indianapolis could mean a home for Ruth and Nora too.

"Do you mean – no, I don't mind that you're Jewish. Are you saying – "

"Yes."

He seemed to be looking at her auburn hair in the kerosine lamplight. She had forgotten what it felt like to have a man look at her. But this was a practical engineer finding a solution to a problem.

"I'm asking you to get married and go with me to Indianapolis. I need a wife now."

Ruth's mind raced. Her decision was not hers; it was Nora who condemned her to accept this proposal. Without a choice, she was forced by blood to do this thing. Whatever she had to do, she wouldn't leave Nora the way her mother had abandoned her and her child. Never would Nora feel the loss of her mother. "Yes, I will marry you." Ruth stretched her arms closer around the man in front of her and her hands shook. "But I have a daughter."

Before the dance tune ended, he took her hand, and together they walked to his car. On the street, Ruth stole a glance and he looked back. His eyes looked kind, she thought. Then she thought of Kioshi's eyes and her heart sank. Kioshi whose eyes that seemed fathoms deep, enticed her in. Kioshi proclaimed he could do more, be more, change his new country into something more, and would she be a part of it all. She looked down at her hand, Kioshi's pearl ring shone in the passing glow of a street lamp. What was this soldier's name? The farther they drove from the dance back to the farm, the more terrified Ruth became.

8

Nora

Michigan, 1948

Buttoned in her winter coat against the constant, cold whoosh from the doors, Nora sits alone and waits at the bus station in Michigan. With her boot, she kicks a piece of gum free from the floor as people come and go. When the station manager asks whom she is supposed to meet, she can't answer with a name. "Grandmother," she says.

Day traffic at the station thins as riders find their way home for supper and she wonders what to do. It's nearly dark and she is dog hungry when a pickup truck pulls up. A farmer in worn overalls and mud-caked boots walks up to stand in front of her. "You Nora?" he asked.

Nora nods. Grandfather rushes her out the door and tosses her small bag in the back. In the cab, the only sound comes from the noisy truck as Grandfather works the gear shift. Nora's stomach growls. Without a word, one hand on the steering wheel, Grandfather picks up a pipe from the ashtray. He opens a pouch and takes out a pinch of tobacco, then sprinkles it in the bottom of the pipe bowl. He tamps it down with his finger and adds another pinch. After the third tamp down, he puffs on it before lighting. Maybe it was a test. She's never seen anyone put tobacco in a pipe before.

It takes two matches traced around the bowl before the tobacco is just the way Grandfather wants it. When he takes a puff and exhales, Nora smells the most comforting aroma, like cherries in a pie her mother baked. Together they drive into the darkness. Outside of Flint, the paved roads turn to dirt with bumps and ruts. After miles of silence, Grandfather speaks around the pipe in his mouth. "How is your mother?"

Nora sighs. "Mama is at home with Asher." Nora tries to say more but doesn't. Her voice warbles.

That morning her mother rushed into her room. "You don't have to go to first grade today. It's a special day."

"But I like school," Nora wiped the sleep from her eyes.

"You're going on a trip all the way to Michigan. You're going to visit Grandmother and Grandfather on the farm."

Nora grew wary. She thought of the argument in the kitchen. "Are you coming too?"

Her mother didn't answer but talked without a space for a question. She talked about the big farmhouse, the chickens, the barn, how Nora could make friends with the goats - until it became a jumble. Nora couldn't listen.

"Are you and Asher coming too?"

Her mother ignored her and whisked a small suitcase onto her bed. She opened drawers and emptied a few hangers, tossed clothes in the suitcase, and closed the latches. "There we go. Brush your teeth and we'll get you to the bus station so you won't be late."

"Is Asher coming?

Nora and Asher sat in the back seat of the car. He still wore his bedroom slippers. She looked at him for a long time and noticed a piece of fluff from his blanket caught in th e wave of his hair. Her

fingers reached to pull it out, and he turned his head to look at her.

At the bus station in Indianapolis, Mama said, "Here's your ticket. Give it to the driver on the bus. When you get to Michigan, Grandmother will meet you at the bus station." Ruth handed her daughter the small suitcase and got back in the driver's seat.

Nora walked away from the car and looked back. Her mother was already driving away and Asher was watching her with his hand spread on the window.

Finally, Nora asks, "What am I doing here?"

Grandfather's eyebrows shoot up but he doesn't answer. Reflected in the truck's headlights she sees a sign. The truck turns a wide corner and she reads the words - Hill Rd. The road becomes more narrow and rutted until Grandfather pulls into the gravel drive. In the darkness, she sees the outline of a rambling farmhouse with a snow-covered roof. Nora has never seen such an old house. Two lamps glow in the windows, and she sees one more window light up as they walk to the back door. Her grandmother is lighting kerosene lamps in the kitchen and says nothing when the two of them walk in. Nora can smell baked food and asks for something to eat.

Grandmother looks her up and down. "You missed dinner. You should have gotten here earlier. Come with me."

She leads the way up the bare wooden stairway in the lantern light and then points to another narrow stair. A third-floor attic room would be Nora's.

"Leave the door open. The room has no heat. Take this lantern, but lamp oil is expensive, I tell you. Put your things away, then blow out the flame real quick." Grandmother bats away a few cobwebs. No one had been to the third floor in some time. "I'll call you down early and be prepared to work. Everybody has chores to do in this house."

The cramped attic room is quiet except for the creaky floor and a small windowpane that rattles when the wind blows. Here is that one moment when her world has been split into a before and an after. Not the long hot walk on graduation day with nothing to eat, not living on tiptoe with her stepfather, but this forced banishment and its inescapable cost.

Nora misses the sound of Asher running down the hall or Asher knocking on her bedroom wall to say goodnight, her bright, warm room at home, now empty. Dust wafts up from the small desk beside the bed as she blows out the lamp flame. She coughs and huddles under the quilt, trying to understand what had happened, trying not to think of Asher's hand on the window and her mother's car driving away.

9

Nora
Michigan, 1948

Nora looked up at the two-story red brick schoolhouse, bigger than her school in Indianapolis. There was a football stadium out in back, and on the sign was the name "Big Reds." The school bus dropped the children off behind the school. Everyone seemed to know each other and where to go. She wandered the hallways festooned with red and green paper decorations, like her school at home. They must have Christmas here too. Suddenly the bell rang and every student disappeared into a room. She walked down the long terrazzo hallway, her steps echoing in the silence. Miss McFarlen, a secretary, found her. "Shouldn't you be in class?"

"Which one?" Nora asked.

Miss McFarlan ushered Nora into the office and sat her down in an uncomfortable wooden chair. Grandmother had called the school and told them Nora was in first grade. Without her records, the school suggested Kindergarten classes, which were only half-day classes. Grandmother wanted Nora in school all day. She told the office that school records were coming from Indianapolis but it may take weeks because you know how those Hoosiers are.

Nora watched Miss McFarlen open drawers in a big wooden desk where she found sheets of paper she was looking for. She waited as Miss McFarlen checked the papers and wrote something that looked important. "Let's get you to your new first-grade class, Nora," she said. Nora wanted to say she was in kindergarten, not first grade, but Miss McFarlen seemed so sure, that she didn't say a word. She handed the office papers to her new teacher, Miss North.

She frowned as she read the papers, and then frowned at Nora. Miss North pursed her lips, but she extended her arm to welcome Nora into the room.

"Children, I'd like you to meet our new student, Nora – Ishiguro." the teacher said.

Her voice sounded squeaky and Nora had to stifle a giggle.

"Nora, you may sit in the third row in the back."

The children stared at her. She remembered what her stepfather had said when she listened through the door. The teacher didn't say her name the right way. Nora wanted to correct her but not on her first day. She wished she could run out the door.

"Nora, do you have a pencil?"

"No."

"Paper?"

"No." She had never needed to bring anything to school before.

"No ma'am," Miss North corrected, and continued the lesson. A girl with a long blonde braid gave her a piece of paper and a pencil.

"Thank you," Nora sank into her seat. The unexpected cold draft from the window next to her made Nora shiver. She longed to hide behind her long auburn hair, but Grandmother had cut it off yesterday. It was too hard to manage, she said, so she grabbed fistfuls of it and cut it within a few inches of her head. The hair that was left circled this way and that, leaving her neck bare. She wished herself invisible.

10

Nora

Michigan, 1951

Each year Nora was given new farm chores added to the old ones. Before school, she gathered eggs and cleaned the coop. Two of the chickens would follow her around until she turned to pet them. When she told them about her day at school they'd cock their heads and look into her face with bright eyes. Before nightfall year-round, she stacked wood for the kitchen stove, and in the fall season, helped with canning fruits and vegetables.

"What's wrong with you?" Grandmother's voice had a sharper edge than usual. "You don't write with that hand!"

Nora looked up from the kitchen counter where she was carefully writing Grandmother's dictated feed list for the chickens and goats before their trip to the Co-op one winter afternoon. She had forgotten Papa's warning about writing with her left hand.

"Don't you let me catch you writing like that again. Here." Grandmother took Grandpa's belt from the nail by the back door and tied Nora's left hand to her back. "You use your right hand and write that list over again. Always use your right hand." She cinched the belt tighter so it pinched Nora's wrist behind her waist. "I catch you using that left hand again and it's no dinner for you. No breakfast either."

Nora grasped the pencil with her right hand, but it was like learning to write all over again. Her teachers didn't mind her using her left hand. Scissors she used to cut construction paper hearts for Ms. Bird's Valentine's Day decorations were hard to use with her left hand, but she managed.

It seemed there was no end to the things about Nora that Grandmother didn't approve of. The more pressure she applied to the pencil, the worse the letters looked. Before Grandmother came to check her letters, she smoothed out a tear she had made in the paper, trying to make letters look like her left-handed ones.

"Look at that. I can't read one word of it. The belt stays on until you write a list I can read," Grandmother said.

When Grandfather had emptied out a feed sack that had flowers printed on it, he gave it to her to make skirts for school. Unlike Grandmother, Papa had encouraging words for her grades and her clever sewing on a treadle machine in the attic. Old clothing patterns were stuffed in the sewing machine drawer, and she made use of one with a simple drawstring tie. Papa slipped her coins when he could and told her to save them for something she wanted.

In school, Nora asked one teacher, "How much does the earth weigh? She asked another, "How do airplanes fly?" The children taunted her and the teachers ignored many of her questions. The only exception was her music teacher. One day when she told Miss Bird that she had tried to make friends at lunch but the girls were mean to her, Miss Bird patted the seat beside her desk. They ate lunch
together each day so Nora could tune out classmates who told her to go home to Japan. Her music teacher would answer any question she asked, and often asked questions back.

Another day, Miss Bird played a recording of Beethoven's *Violin Concerto in D Major*. Beethoven's melody was a map to a place Nora hadn't seen, a place she wanted to find. It was mystifying how the music knew how she felt. The concerto was like a declaration, a screed against the lunch kids. She'd found a safe place. She sat perfectly still to listen to the last chords. Nora looked at Miss Bird and saw on her face the pleasure she felt as they experienced together the roller coaster tumble through the last notes. "Can we listen again tomorrow?" she asked.

Her teacher nodded. "Beethoven wrote his music around a motif, like patterns in a patchwork quilt that use different colorful pieces of favorite dresses and shirts." She lifted the pickup arm and put the record back in its jacket. "You can look at the quilt and see the memories in the patterns. In Beethoven's music, we can feel that emotion in the different patterns he makes."

Nora thought about the quilt on her bed and the faded scraps of fabric. There were patterns, but that didn't fit the way she felt the music. She loved the concerto in a different way. So much of her life felt lonely, but not the time Nora spent during lunch with Miss Bird.

The violinist Jascha Heifetz, Miss Bird explained, was one of the best in the world, and Nora repeated the name to herself. Later that week, Miss Bird brought out a violin during their lunch and played part of the tune from the concerto. Nora was captivated by the rich sound of the bow on the strings, better than the recording because she could see the creation of the music. Her fingers on the strings knew exactly where to touch down.

When Miss Bird finished the passage, Nora waited for the memorable last notes to resonate into silence. "I want to play that, Miss Bird. More than anything, I want to play the violin."

Now Nora had a reason to come to school. The other children's scowls didn't matter because for a half-hour at lunch each day, their disapproval didn't exist. She could forget Grandmother's anger and her attic room, forget how much she missed Asher, and her world became the violin and its music.

At first, when Miss Bird showed her how to hold the instrument, she saw her fingers like the daddy longlegs in her attic room, shifting from left to right, searching for the right place to be. Miss Bird changed the strings so Nora could play left-handed. Later when she held the violin and drew the bow across the strings, the sounds of strength and solace, struggle, and joy took her beyond the fifth grade and she felt something bigger, greater than all this. The anticipation of music came to her as soon as she tucked it under her chin.

11

Nora

Michigan, 1954

Nora stepped off the bus at the end of her road and walked the half-mile skipping over the muddy ruts. Her grip on the violin case was firm. During their lunch together Miss Bird said, "You've been playing a right-handed violin and that wasn't quite right. So I visited an old teacher of mine and told him about you. He said you may have this violin that belongs to him, as long as you practice it faithfully."

Nora shook her head swallowing the last of her peanut butter sandwich. She folded the waxed paper and wiped her hands on the rough cloth napkin, returning everything to the lunch sack for the next day. "I can't. Grandmother would never pay."

"He's giving it to you, Nora. You don't have to pay." Look, at the unusual color, almost black." Miss Bird left her lunch on her desk and turned to the shelf behind her. She unclasped a case and drew out the shining instrument. She turned the instrument onto its strings and the light shone on the wood.

Nora held her breath.

"He calls it his sable violin and he was pleased to think that you might want it. You can play it with your left hand. Try it. I think you'll like the sound."

Nora held the shiny dark instrument, tucked it under her chin, and drew the bow across the strings. What a sound! She placed her left hand in position on the fretboard and in no time her fingers felt at home.

She had no words, playing with a ferocity that wouldn't stop. A thrill went through Nora followed by dread.

"What's wrong?" Ms. Bird saw the conflicted expression cross over her face.

"What if Grandmother won't let me keep it?" Miss Bird wrinkled her forehead. "Nora, sorrow and joy, they come and go." She grabbed her hand and squeezed it. "I'll talk to her. Nothing lasts forever." Grandmother couldn't complain about a free violin. She didn't have to know it was left-handed.

After school, Nora walked in the back door and quietly tucked her muddy shoes in the corner. She left the violin in the egg room and checked to see if she could get upstairs without Grandmother seeing her. In the kitchen where the kettle was boiling for tea, she saw a letter from California on the kitchen table. Her grandparents seldom got letters, just bills, and never one from so far away. She tiptoed back with the case held tight.

"What's that in your hand?"

Nora tensed. "It's a violin, Grandmother. Miss Bird has been giving me lessons at lunch. It doesn't cost anything. I can keep the violin and get the lessons free if I practice."

"Violin! Is that what they teach you at that school? Worthless, that's what! Can't use it for work, can't grow crops with it, can't feed us, can't keep us warm." Grandmother yelled in her face, "It's worthless!"

Nora swallowed hard and backed away toward her attic room, but Grandmother blocked the stairway.

"Worthless, I say, as worthless as you! As worthless as your mother with her throwing away good scholarship money on art classes. She found that Jap, your father, just as worthless and lazy as she is, worthless and lazy like you are! Do you know who your real father is? That worthless Jap out somewhere in California, that's who."

Nora stood frozen in place. Grandfather heard the noise and shuffled into the kitchen between them. "All right, Blanche, all right now."

"You're a bastard child born with no name and a worthless Japanese father. Did your mother tell you that?" Grandmother's face was red and her breathing was labored. "And now there she is, your mother, living with that Jew husband of hers while my sweet Daniel - so brave, he was. He loved his mother. Why couldn't it have been slugabed Ruth? But no. My Daniel is gone."

Her face red, Grandmother stared at Nora with renewed moral outrage, as if she'd awakened from a night terror. "You take that *thing* back to school tomorrow and never bring it home again. If I see it, it's going into the pile for firewood."

"That's enough, Blanche, you'll wear yourself out now," Grandfather said, steering her to the living room with her elbow. "Come sit down and rest awhile. I'll bring your tea."

Nora's heart was pounding. What had been one of the happiest days since she came to live here, was now the most shameful. Grandmother's words stung. She watched Papa guide Grandmother who muttered and breathed raspy sounds. Nora raced up the stairs, her own breath coming in short gasps.

Her room was cold but her face and hands were hot. She crawled under the musty quilt pulling it up to her neck. Imagine how angry she'd be if Grandmother knew it was a left-handed violin. And what did she mean by the bastard and Daniel? Staring at the attic beams, she waited for the shivering to subside. Her eyes looked at the violin that Grandmother had called worthless. Grandmother's anger rang in her ears and she couldn't escape it.

She pulled the quilt back and carefully opened the clasps on the violin case. The wood of the instrument felt smooth on her hand and tucking it under her chin gave her comfort. She plucked the strings to tune them, just as Miss Bird had taught her, and reached for the bow. Her shivering stopped as she drew the bow over the strings and played music from her memory, her agile fingers finding their way, speaking a lonely tremolo when words couldn't be found.

She stood and looked over the stubble in the fields from the dust-caked window, sighed, and played the song again, a strange and ethereal passage. She paused, raising her bow to listen to the echo in
the air, and picked up again in an angry cadenza pushing hard against the strings until the music took her over so completely that it was the only thing that mattered and everything was blocked out.

"Nora?" Papa's voice was just outside the closed door.

She stopped playing. "Was I too loud?"

"Can I come in?"

She opened the door and looked at Papa. She could smell the cherry tobacco from his pipe, although he wasn't smoking it. From his back pocket, he pulled a handkerchief, looked away from her, and touched his eye with it. He was breathing hard probably from the last set of stairs. Rarely did Grandmother or Papa come up here since she'd moved in.

"Nora, your music is beautiful. It makes me cry. Your music isn't worthless and neither are you." He rubbed his arms from the cold. "Forget what your Grandma said. You keep playing that violin." He put his hand gently on her shoulder and held it there."That's a gift you have, the way you play."

"Papa – "

"Just practice a little softer next time," he said. "I'll talk to your grandmother."

After Papa left, she imagined she could still feel his calloused, gentle hand on her shoulder. She closed the door and checked under her mattress for the coins she'd saved there, counting them again, calculating how much more she needed. There would be no dinner for her tonight, so she stayed in her room, thinking about her grandfather's words. One thing her grandmother said must be true.

Her real father lived in California. Reaching down she touched the violin in its case beside her bed.

12

Nora

Michigan, 1954

The next day Nora played in her mind the words she would say to Miss Bird, trying to explain why she didn't dare keep the violin. The night before had been so unsettling that she took the coins from under her mattress, just in case Grandmother searched her room. It was unlikely, but Grandmother had never been that angry and she couldn't trust her. When Nora had met her in the kitchen that morning to toast some bread for breakfast, Grandmother glared and turned away, unable to be in the same room with her.

When she met Miss Bird for lunch, she could tell something had changed. Her teacher's expression was hard to read as if she might be nervous, excited, or both.

Nora sat at the desk and opened her sandwich wrapper, but Miss Bird paced the floor before her. "Nora, this is an anxious day for me."

Nora put her hands in her lap. "What's wrong?"

"It's hard for me to tell you, watching you grow, our lunch talks, seeing your musical talent unfold - " She paused and adjusted a curl in her hair, although it returned just where it had been.

"No. You're not telling me I can't come here for lunch anymore, are you?" Her face grew hot. "If I go back to that lunch room I'll get mad and get sent to the office for sure. The kids are so mean – "

"Oh, Nora, I know kids can be mean." Miss Bird twisted her hands and stood still. "But today is my last day here. I leave tonight for a teaching job in Chicago."

Her voice said Chicago as if it explained everything, but it only added to the confusion. "You see, my fiance lives there and we're getting married in the fall. We're going to live there." She waited for Nora to say something.

"No. No. No..." Nora shook her head.

"This is sudden, but I need time to plan for my wedding. There is so much to do. And the violin is yours to keep." Miss Bird sat down and looked closely at Nora. "You have a talent. You must keep playing."

"You don't understand." Nora looked around the room, unable to look at her teacher. "I won't be able to – everything will be different."

"I'll send you my address and we can write letters."

Miss Bird shifted in her seat, turning the engagement ring on her finger. "This will be a big change for both of us." She reached for her lunch box. "You can tell me what you're playing in your letters, and I can recommend pieces for you." Neither of them could eat. In the time they had left, Miss Bird spoke without stopping about music Nora hadn't heard of, but she couldn't listen to any of it.

When the bell rang, Miss Bird gave Nora a hug and wished her well. Nora couldn't take in what had happened. She walked out of the room and out of the school. She left her school books on a bench by the door but took her notebook and violin with her.

Gripping the handle on the case, she decided to keep her promise to practice. Across from the school was the public bus stop. There she waited for the second bus, which the last driver told her would stop at the station in Flint.

Her coins clinked in the fare box and she maneuvered her way to the back to find a seat for her and her violin. Staring out the window Nora made a decision. She would go to Chicago and find Miss Bird and her fiancé. Somehow they would help her save money to travel to California and find her father. It didn't matter where he was. She would search until she found him.

13

Kioshi
Yokohama, 1935

The twisty alleyway too narrow for a rickshaw led downhill. Past a smoky brazier, shouting men threw *cho-han* dice. His *zori* slapping his feet, Kioshi ran a wide circle around the men at the corner, not wanting to attract the police or anyone who might detain him.

"Get your father now,"

He saw the pained look on his mother's face, the defeated curve of her back. His heart sank. The final eviction notice with bold characters was taped securely to their front door. After months of warnings and years of giving her his earnings, he thought he could put off this day. The pearls in his pocket would save them from the street for a while.

"I know where he is," Kioshi said.

On his way out the door, he saw his aunt. Her expression told him she was there to comfort her sister.

Down the block, someone from above threw what he hoped was rinse water, from a second-story window. He dashed into a narrow gap between walls. Further on, he skirted a vegetable cart with daikon radishes and carrots that blocked his way. The vendor sneered at him and placed carrots in a woman's basket. A neighbor woman cried out when her child dashed in front of a horse. Kioshi halted and gripped the boy's shoulders steering him back to his neighbor.

He crossed a busy street past the Yokohama Silk Conditioning House with its wide sidewalk where men in business suits with purposeful strides walked up the steps. Block after block he kept his pace until he reached the Bund area of the wharf, rebuilt after the earthquake. His pace slowed when he saw the American Consulate Building on the other side of the Bund. It stood next to the ship launch. He checked the pearls in his pocket.

On the other side of the quay stood the Sea and Star with its weathered siding and faded sign, the bar where his father would be. His fingers tightened around the handle and he pulled the door, always sticky from the humid harbor air. The men in the bar turned to look at him, their eyes squinting against the sunlight outside. As soon as they recognized him they turned back to their drinks and the door closed into near darkness.

Kioshi's eyes adjusted to the dark and he walked between the stale-smelling men, the claggy floor clicking on the bottom of his zori. At the back corner table, he found his father. *"Oyaji, Okaa-san* needs you now. The notice is on the door. We have to go." Kioshi grasped the pearls in his pocket and peered down at this man who taught him how to swim, and how to tell stories. The man who gently placed cold cloths on his forehead when he was feverish and sang him to sleep, squinted at him.

"I'm busy," *Oyaji* said. "Let *Okaa-san* handle women's work."

Kioshi understood the need for his father to save face, but this was not the time. "The notice. This is it. They will take our house now."

"Get out of here." *Oyaji* bellowed. "Don't talk to me."

Kioshi softened his voice. "*Okaa-san* said we will be put out in the street."

His father was unsteady, but he stood and tensed his arm with the glass in his hand behind him. "Get out of here before I kill you."

Kioshi backed away toward the door. Everyone in the bar turned to look.

"I never want to see you again." He threw the glass.

Kioshi dodged and the glass hit the door behind him. The men laughed, but his father didn't move. Kioshi pushed his weight against the door and ran down the street past the shops. An oncoming roadster honked and he veered toward a docked boat on the quayside. His foot caught in a fishing net and he fell to the ground as if in slow motion. A dock hand yelled and ran at him, but he untangled his foot and limped away.

Across the street, he leaned against the side of a sail rig shop doubled over and breathing hard. His knee was bloody and any weight on the ankle resulted in an electric jolt. *Oyaji's* words played in his mind in a repeating loop. He had almost given the pearls to his father. Now Kioshi would cross the sea to America.

14

Nora

Chicago, 1954

When the bus stopped In Chicago she guardedly stepped down into a jostle of other travelers. There were so many people and everyone seemed to be in a hurry. Feeling alone and disoriented, she walked a few blocks and found a diner. The waitress suggested a bowl of chicken soup. When the last spoonful was gone, she reached for her coins from the drawstring bag she had sewn, but the bag was gone. She checked a pocket and checked the inside of her violin case. Nothing. Horror-stricken, she waited for the waitress to turn her back and dashed out of the diner.

In a panic, she ran off down the block gasping for breath. She looked behind her expecting the waitress had followed, or maybe the police. Before her stood a powerful architectural icon with golden front doors. A plaque that looked like gold identified the landmark name, Wrigley Building. A busker with a violin played near the front door, his case open for money. His hair was long and ragged for a man and he covered it with a cap like newsboys wore, but he was much older. His gloves had the fingers cut out of them. At least most of his hand was protected from the cold.

She recognized the tune, opened her case, and set it beside his. Taking one big breath, she held her violin and listened carefully, figuring out the key and softly playing a few staccato notes to harmonize. Tapping her foot to the beat, she played more notes until the end of the song where she played alone, adding a twisting scale and two ending bump notes. A small group gathered to listen, and at the end of the song, people dropped a few coins in both violin cases.

"Do you know this one?" the man said.

She looked puzzled. He played a few bars and she recognized the tune, "Mr. Sandman," making up a part that played over and under his melody. A few more passers-by dropped coins for them. After a time, she came to wrap herself in the busker's songs to the point that she nearly forgot about her stolen change.

Day turned to dusk and more wind as she made a fist with one hand to warm her fingers. The violin player put away his instrument. "Hey, kid, you're pretty good, but this is my corner, understand? I don't want to see you here again, get it?"

His voice was gruff, so different from his playful, spirited violin voice. She nodded before he disappeared into the pedestrians and she was alone on the sidewalk.

Straight away the wind felt colder. With care, she placed her violin in the case and double-checked the latches. A group of women deep in conversation opened the doors of the Wrigley Building behind her and headed in opposite directions. Nora watched one woman pause, turn and come back to her.

"What are you doing out here at night in the cold?" The woman bundled in a coat and scarf watched Nora, looking at coins in her hand. The woman waited, unlike other people rushing by. She expected an answer.

"I just got here and someone stole all my money and I tried to earn money playing violin but it's getting dark and I don't know where to go." Nora's words were rushed, her voice seeming to trail away in the wind.

Instead of the usual scowl that she saw from almost everyone, this woman looked puzzled. "You're in downtown Chicago with no money and nowhere to stay. Your parents must be worried. Let's find a phone."

"No. I don't live with my parents. There is no one."

The woman looked down the sidewalk and tightened her coat around her. "I'm Mrs. Johnson. I have a daughter just about your age."

Nora's gathered the remaining coins and gripped her violin.

"I live nearby. Why don't you join us for dinner? You need to eat, right?"

Nora nodded.

"We'll talk it over with Mr. Johnson. We'll figure out what you can do."

A sigh escaped her and she introduced herself. On their way to the train, they passed the diner. "Can we stop? I have to pay the waitress for my soup."

Mrs. Johnson waited outside and watched Nora through the window as she found a waitress and dropped coins in her hand. It was one act that she would remind Nora of for years to come.

Once they found their seats on the elevated train, Mrs. Johnson asked about the violin. She explained that hers was a musical family. "No one in the family gets away without singing or playing an instrument."

Nora couldn't stop looking at the sights from this train that ran above the city. From the window she watched, marveling at block after block of tall buildings crammed together. Streets with lines of cars, their headlights shining, looked so small. That's why they called it the Elevated, or L, Mrs. Johnson said.

At the next stop, they stood to leave. Nora carried her violin and notebook for two blocks, then up three flights of stairs to the Johnson's cozy apartment. Mrs. Johnson left her shoes inside the door with pairs of others, and Nora took hers off as well. She met the Johnson's four children and found Mr. Johnson in the kitchen, frying something on the stove. The smell made her hungry. Nora tucked her violin and notebook by the door and tried to take it all in - the noisy banter of the children, the bright electric warmth of the room. How different from the cold, kerosine lamp-lit farmhouse. There, she was the unwelcome, tolerated visitor. Here, she was far from anyone she knew, with a big noisy family.

"Shayla's turn to set the table," one child yelled.

"I set it yesterday," Shayla said.

The Johnsons knew what it would be like when they returned home at the end of a day. They didn't have to worry about being put on a bus and sent away so they'd never see their brothers and sisters again.

"I'll help," Nora said picking up the silverware from Shayla. This must be the daughter who was about her age. The squabble ended and the two girls began to talk.

Squeezed around the kitchen table, the family talked with as much appetite as they ate. All of these brown faces around the table hadn't yet made one rude comment like the kind she always braced herself to hear. About her, bowls of fluffy potatoes and buttery vegetables passed between them, as well as a plate heaped with chicken. Nora was never allowed a big portion of food at Grandmother's table, and she ate with gusto until she was full. Mrs. Johnson said, "You look fit to burst, honey!" Everyone laughed.

"Get that fiddle out and let's have some music." Mr. Johnson said. Nora heard the children yelling in the kitchen about who should clear the table and who should wash tonight. She braced herself for remarks she was so used to with her grandmother, but the parents let the children settle their squabble.

As their chores ended, the children wandered in from the kitchen. From bedrooms, they pulled out a clarinet and a guitar. Mr. Johnson began to play some easy folk tunes like "Wabash Cannonball" and everyone joined in. No music changed hands, and for "Crossroads Blues" Mrs. Johnson sang with a throaty soulful sound that wove between the instruments. Nora knew the tunes picking out melodies and refrains along with them. When Mr. Johnson announced it was time for bed, Nora asked, "Can I play my favorite song?"

Mrs. Johnson nodded. Nora began to play the first movement from the familiar violin concerto, feeling the music in her heart, filling the room with melody. The Johnsons stopped moving to listen. Mrs. Johnson shook her head. "Honey, where did you learn to play like that?"

Nora relaxed the violin at her side. "My teacher Miss Bird taught me. I came here to find her. I hope she can help me. And when I save enough money I'm going to California to find my father."

"California! All that way at your age," Mr. Johnson said. "Where in California is your father?"

"I don't know," Nora said. "All I know is he's a Japanese American."

"Flo, call Theresa," Mr. Johnson said. "Let's see if we can find this Miss Bird."

"Right now, it's time for bed. Tomorrow's a school day." Flo said, ushering the children to their rooms. Instruments were packed away. Mr. Johnson played a last jazz riff on the piano and said goodnight to his family. "G'night Nora," he said. He picked up his lunch pail from the kitchen and grabbed his jacket for the night shift at the fire station.

Mrs. Johnson brought out a blanket and pillow. "I'm afraid we don't have an extra bed, but the sofa should be comfortable," she said.

Flo handed Nora a fluffy comforter and pillow that smelled like lavender. "I want to say more than thank you," Nora said. "You have a good heart."

Together they arranged the blanket on the sofa and Nora slipped her feet under it. Mrs. Johnson turned on the lights except for one and sat down on the end of the sofa. Nora gathered the blanket up around until only her face was above it.

"Do you have grandparents?"

"No, Mrs. Johnson." She sat up. "Please don't send me back."

Flo reached for her hand and patted it. "Nobody's gonna send you someplace you don't want to go, but we need a plan." She paused in thought. "I know some people from work.

"First things first like Mr. Johnson said, we'll try to find Miss Bird." She looked at Nora. "But we sure don't have much to go on."

15

Nora

California, 1955

On the train to California, Nora felt the ache in the pit of her stomach as each mile of prairie lands and phone poles took her farther away from the Johnsons. Even though Mrs. Johnson soon found Nora a home just outside of Chicago in Mooseheart City for Children, she didn't forget Nora. Mr. Johnson drove out every few weeks to pick her up for Sunday dinner and they continued to look for Miss Bird.

Nora's roommate at Mooseheart was a quiet girl who lost both parents, medics in Europe during WWII. When she confided to Evie that she was saving up her money working in the dormitory kitchen, for a ticket to California, Evie barely looked up. She turned the pages of a history textbook that Nora knew she was not reading.

Evie wanted to be a secretary in one of Chicago's tall buildings, and couldn't understand Nora's hours in the downstairs study room practicing her violin. Each Thursday afternoon Nora took the bus to the city where she had a music lesson and her weekly practice with the Preparatory Orchestra. Sometimes they played with the Young People's Song Festival, but the most memorable concert in Nora's mind was due to a special guest conductor.

The young orchestra members were electrified about the concert and James, the boy who sat next to her in the second violin position, even more so. Before that day, she had ignored the tall, serious boy with hair slicked back over his ears and a pile of curls over his deep-set eyes.

Their guest conductor, Joe Freyre who came all the way from Cuba, paused their rehearsal and they knew he was going to tell another story. They had to listen carefully to understand his accent, something about picking up jazz musicians in an old Chevrolet and driving to a barn on the outskirts of Havana. There would be musicians from New Orleans, a few local women from Havana who sang, and a few from Latin countries and islands between, all mixing their musical styles. They played for hours and people nearby would come to dance the mambo. Here Joe paused and demonstrated another dance to the snickers and laughter of the orchestra.

"And they danced the cha cha cha." When Joe bent his knees and swayed his hips with his invisible dance partner, they could almost hear the Cuban band playing. "Did I tell you the story about the woman with the big hat in the conga line?" They shook their heads. Joe paused. "I think you're too young for that story anyway."

Now he had their attention and the ever-rowdy percussion section called out, "What's the conga?"

Joe paused again. "Maybe in a few years, you can hear the conga story." He changed the subject and told the students how Cuban musicians listened and built on the ideas of other musicians, living the music. His conductor's arms flew around, his dark, mane of hair making a dancing frame around his face. Freyre said musicians like him from all over the Caribbean would listen to music in bars and follow local musicians home to trade musical stories into the morning.

"Now," he stomped his foot. "We tell our own musical story." He talked about the piece they would play and the style he was looking for. As he brought up his arms, the young musicians brought up their instruments as if pulled by invisible strings. "Okay you Kats and you Kittens," he said, "Let's get in the groove."

They froze at his words. Then the room broke out in cacophonous laughter, the musical moment smashed, shattered, and crushed. Joe raised his eyebrow. The young musicians couldn't stop, but picked up their instruments and played all manner of cat scratch sounds. "It's what you said," James told him. "Nobody ever told us to get in the groove before."

"What?" Joe Freyre shouted. "You squares do this all the time."

They put down their instruments.

"That's why you're here." He turned around on the podium with his hands in the air. "You get it. Because the music is in you, and you're gonna make it *sound* like that when it comes out of you." He looked around at the music squares side-eying each other, trying to grasp the feel of this groove.

"Like this, yes?" He danced sliding and rocking to the music in his head. The students sighed and readied their instruments. "Your fingers dance on the keys – or strings. You play your instrument; you don't work at it. Play is fun, no?" The rehearsal proceeded with precision and efficiency. From that point, Joe Freyre got every ounce of practice time from the students, but he stopped short of the end of class.

"Now I hear we gotta challenge for this TV gig."

"Yes, sir," James piped up. The student musicians focused their attention. The excitement over their first-ever performance on a local Chicago television station delighted and terrified them. "I challenge Nora."

"Okay, so I don't know how your regular conductor does this, but here's how we'll do it." Joe told them they would each play a passage, and the player with the most votes would play the solo on television. Freyre left the podium for a moment and walked to the back for a talk with the percussion section to demonstrate how he wanted the marimba to sound.

While the students tuned their strings, James turned to Nora's glare. "I gotta basketball game this Thursday. You should come to see me play."

Nora looked him in the eye. Basketball was the furthest thing from her mind. She had practiced her solo and it was hers! She wasn't giving it up to anyone. She turned back to her music and warmed up with a few quiet scales.

"Coach says if I keep up my jump shots, I can get a scholarship." He drew closer. "To a big university."

At this point, Nora figured she was supposed to say something. "You have one eye that's a different color. Instead of blue, it has some - amber color in it." Although she found James' eyes penetrating and had sneaked glances at them before, she was trying to throw him off balance.

"And then I can take photography classes and learn how to make movies and go to Hollywood and work for my uncle out there." James' voice jumped with excitement. "He's worked the movie cameras for Lana Turner and Grace Kelly, and once even for John Wayne."

He didn't listen to her. She was prepared for a snappy comeback about her own appearance, but it never came. He wouldn't quit talking no matter how she tried to throw him off. "Don't talk to me. Just don't!" Nora yelled. Everyone stopped tuning to hear.

"*Ay ay ay Venga....*" Joe returned to the podium and shook his head. "The challenge is now! We have to finish this."

To her surprise, Nora won the student vote. Despite her pique, she kept her first chair and her solo. James said he needed a drink of water and asked to be excused. Nora gave him a look, but he wouldn't meet her gaze. At the end of practice, Freyre took Nora aside. "You know, you play your violin like you're uncovering your story." He pushed his chaotic hair back from his forehead. "But try it with more groove and less *enojo* for the concert."

A herd of cattle drew Nora's attention from the window. Time crawled by as the train carried her away from everything she knew. Last summer Nora invited Evie to Humboldt Park for an outdoor youth concert. The day was warm, and the breeze was a welcome one. The orchestra members and conductor had to keep moving

clothespins to keep their music from blowing away. The Johnsons
brought their lawn chairs and invited Evie to get her nose out of her books to join them. Nora caught up with the Johnsons on the lawn afterward as they were folding up their chairs.

"Let's get some ice cream," Mr. Johnson said. Evie, Nora, and Shayla each chose butter pecan and sat at their own picnic table at the ice cream stand trying to lick the cones before they dripped in the heat. "I saw the way that guy next to you kept looking at you," Shayla told Nora in a sing-songy voice. "Yeah," Evie teased. "He is so cool. I bet he'd be ready for a little backseat bingo!" Nora said she didn't know what they were talking about, but still, their comments about James triggered a smile. As they said their goodbyes, Nora told the Johnsons that the ice cream was about the best she'd ever tasted. Back in their room that evening, Evie said she admired the Johnsons. Evie had aunts and uncles who visited now and then, but the Johnsons felt like a real family. "They are why the butter pecan cone tasted so good to you," she said.

The following Sunday Mrs, Johnson gave Nora a letter from the Red Cross. "I wrote to them in California to see if they could find your father," she said. Nora's hands shook as she opened the letter. "Kioshi Iguro is an American citizen who was living in California during the time of Japanese Internment..." Nora's throat tightened. "...record of transfer to Camp Tule Lake, California, July 27, 1943... Nora read quickly through the location of the camp waiting to see the words she longed for. "Iguro was released from camp.... No current address is available." Nora dropped the letter and Flo gave her a fierce hug.

"That's okay, honey," she patted her back. "I've got other letters out there. We'll hear something."

The rhythmic clack-clack of the train tracks sounded lonely. Nora thought of all Mrs. Johnson had done for her. She pulled out a notepad and pencil to write to her and stared out the window at the flat Kansas farmland as if it would help her decide what to say.

After her last concert with the Chicago Preparatory Orchestra, Nora turned to see a familiar face at the curtain. "Miss Bird," Nora said, running to embrace her in a way that nearly knocked them both off their feet. "I think of you every day. And here you are." Nora bounced with excitement. She hastily grabbed her violin and led Miss Bird out to meet the Johnsons. "I was so surprised to see Nora's name in the concert program, I had to try and find her," Miss Bird explained.

The Johnsons waited patiently as Nora told Miss Bird about their weekly dinners and family music after. She told her about trying to find her father in California.

"I have a friend who works for Orange County State College, Nora. He may be able to help you."

"See ya, Nora," James cut in and stood in front of her, intent and direct. "Have a good summer."

Nora couldn't hide the annoyance in her voice. James had a knack for poor timing. "Sure, you too."

Miss Bird moved around him and he walked away. "My friend lives in a Japanese community in Fountain Valley. Maybe he would have records of your father?"

Nora saw a fleeting look of distrust from Flo. "Mrs. Johnson has been like my mom this year." Nora moved close and put an arm around her. "It's cool to be here with you both at the same time."

16

Kioshi
California, 1944

Late at night after others were sleeping, Kioshi and a few men in his internment camp barracks met in a corner. They spoke to each other in whispers. "We have the Fifth Amendment right to life and liberty, the same as any American," Kioshi told them. "Look at us. We are few in this barracks but tomorrow we will spread out and find others."

"The more of us there are, the stronger we are," another man whispered. "We have committed no crimes, but they claim we are not loyal. No other Americans have to pledge loyalty."

Kioshi and the men devised a plan over the coming days to find at least eighty men who would stand up together in protest of their internment. That many men might bring journalists to Camp Topaz.

The next morning, Kioshi was walking back from the fields with his friend when a photographer arrived, breaking the dull monotony of the day. A small group had gathered and they whispered the photographer's name, Ansel Adams. Maybe photographs would bring journalists. They watched Adams gather a family in front of their barracks. From a box with props for photographs, he pulled a basket and woolens, handing it to the wife.

The son was handed a soccer ball and he start to run, so the assistant whisked the ball away and reprimanded him. Adams posed the three of them outside the rough-hewn barracks door and returned the ball to the boy, backing away with words of warning not to move. In synchronous motion, the crew moved in Adam's direction, angling the tripod for the best view of the family and the mountains beyond.

Kioshi and the others watched Adams snap photographs, repositioning the family in different poses after a few clicks of the shutter.

When the crew moved to other barracks and the mess hall, Kioshi and his friend followed from a distance. Adams seemed careful to show the tidy side of camp life, not its barbed wire, machine guns, or desolation, The beautiful mountain backdrops and the sign over the tiny camp newspaper office *Topaz Free Press* seemed to be the photographer's focus. Adams grabbed two men by the arm and posed them with newspapers, instructing them to read.

They followed the photographer to the hospital, woefully understaffed and ill-equipped, but it seemed to be cleaned up for the guest and his crew. Prohibited from following the crew inside, they could only guess that the wards crowded with patients had been thinned as well.

"I bet he takes no pictures of Japanese traditions or crafts. Americans will be able to feel good when they see our spirit and hard work to assimilate," Kioshi told his friend. "Everything is hunky dory, right?

He looked from the side of his eye, "Hunky dory."

Kioshi was called to the commissioner's office the following day. The commissioner ordered his immediate transfer to Camp Tule.

17

Nora
California, 1955

After two days on the train through Omaha, Denver, Salt Lake City, and Pleasanton, Nora arrived in Oakland, California. From there, she found a bus to Fountain Valley, where she was sure each mile brought her closer to her father. As soon as she stepped off the bus, she had that panicked feeling from her first day in Chicago. Her first impulse was to hold tight to her belongings and look for anyone who might appear suspicious.

Once it appeared that everyone around paid her no attention, she spied a bulletin board with notices on the bus station wall. Among notices for lost dogs and bicycles for sale, was a smaller notice in the bottom corner for a babysitter. She removed the slip of paper with the phone number of Miss Bird's friend and copied another important phone number for the babysitter job on it.

Nora used her most polite voice on the phone and was surprised that they asked her to come that day for an interview. They offered to pick her up from the bus station, but after the train and the bus, she preferred to walk. It would give her a chance to see her new home and think of a plan to find her father.

She passed Winchell's market and a billboard for the Fountain Valley drive-in. Clint Eastwood's *Revenge of the Creature* was playing. Everything was lower to the ground and less crowded than in Chicago. Beside Irvine Park Lake, a family picnicked on a grassy hill. A rowboat crisscrossed from behind a weeping willow where boaters ducked under its arched branches, to dock on the other side. Nora admired this lake and its calm, unlike the waves of Lake Michigan crashing on the windy shores of Chicago. Maybe she could ride in a rowboat too. By the time she passed the Mulholland Fountain, she tired of walking and felt maybe she should have gotten a ride after all.

She checked the address and looked up at a modest two-story home. The tidy front porch had one flowerpot by the door. The whole Anderson family met her at the door before she knocked and Mrs. Anderson led the way into the living room, picking up comic books and a baseball glove along the way. Mr. and Mrs. Anderson's words tumbled over each other as they asked how old she was and explained their expectations. Nora would prepare meals for the two boys. Evan, the eight-year-old, was the quiet one. When Edward, the nine-year-old, asked what was in the case with the funny sticker, Nora felt embarrassed. "The sticker is from my school orchestra, the Chicago Preparatory Orchestra." She smoothed her fingers over the tattered sticker.

Mrs. Anderson bristled when Nora spoke of the children's home, Mooseheart. She asked pointed questions about delinquents and bad influences Nora may bring into the house.

"It takes all kinds," Nora said. She thought about the less upstanding residents of Mooseheart, those who stole, threatened other students with knives and violence or generally made the campus atmosphere one of watchfulness. "My roommate Evie and I looked out for one another."

When Mrs. Anderson suddenly stood and paced the floor, Nora feared they would tell her to leave.

"Can you play Go Fish with me?" Edward asked.

"I love Go Fish." Nora clapped her hands, relieved at the change in the conversation. "I used to play it with - my mother."

Mr. Anderson found a deck of cards. "It's settled then. Why don't you two play while dinner is cooking?" He turned to his wife. "And maybe Nora can give Edward some violin lessons too?"

Mrs. Anderson looked seriously at her husband and walked to the kitchen without a word.

That night, slipping under strange bed covers, Nora turned her head on the pillow and felt a small quake of memory. The floral scent of the clean pillowcase brought with it her childhood bed and Asher's voice saying goodnight from his room next door. The fizzy sound of car tires after an evening rain interrupted her thoughts, so different from the clattering sounds outside her dorm room at Mooseheart. In the distance, she heard the short bursts of a train's whistle, reminding her of a snowy night in Michigan. Tears from her closed eyes dampened the pillow and she sat up to brush them away, refusing any evidence of unhappiness.

When she woke, it was early and the children weren't up yet. The Andersons called her room the spare room, yet it was anything but spare. Knick-knacks in front of rows of books lined a floor-to-ceiling bookshelf. The room was cozy, holding so many treasures the Andersons probably seldom used but weren't ready to part with - extra quilts on a shelf, a plant stand with a homemade clay bowl glazed in polka dots, and a stack of board games she'd played at Mooseheart from *Monopoly* to *Clue*.

As carefully as she had spoken to them the day before, she felt relief. They never asked about her parents, probably assuming she was an orphan from Mooseheart. She didn't have to lie to them. The Andersons seemed so normal, she told herself to be extra careful not to stir up trouble.

Months later, Nora came home from junior high school and saw a letter from the Japanese Heritage Foundation addressed to her, by the telephone. The phone conversation with Miss Bird's friend and the long wait for a reply gave her hope that she might find news of her

father. She dropped her books and tore open the letter. At least the foundation said they would continue the search. Her steps were slow as she took the letter and the books to her room to work on a history assignment before the children returned from school. There had to be something else she could do.

That evening the Andersons had a guest for dinner. Since Mr, Wakefield enjoyed music, Nora was asked to arrange a concert with the children after dinner. The boys had learned the melody of a funny song she taught them called "Chickory Chick." Quiet Evan sang the song with joy and confidence, if not in tune. Edward was proud he had learned some primary notes and bowing on a half-size student violin that Mrs. Anderson had rented. The song put everyone in a good mood, and Mrs. Anderson even smiled at Nora.

"May I play a song?" Nora asked. She chose a song she played in her farmhouse attic room, with sonorous tones. Mr. Wakefield was clearly moved by the interpretation. He was deep in conversation with the Andersons when Nora took the boys upstairs to brush their teeth for bed.

Nora returned to say goodnight to Mr. Wakefield before finishing her homework.

"Music seems to be pretty important to you, Nora," Mr. Wakefield said. "I'm going to get tickets for you and the boys to the San Francisco Youth Orchestra concert," he said.

Nora looked at Mrs. Anderson. "Would you mind if we went?"

That night, Nora thought about what it might be like to play with a youth orchestra again. As soon as Mrs. Anderson approved, the concert was all she could think of. Her school orchestra was small and some instruments were missing. The director was patient, but students didn't practice and they spent each day going over the same boring passages. She dared to think about playing with the San Francisco Youth Orchestra, and it became almost as much of a dream as finding her father.

18

Nora
1968

James spread the black and white photos on the kitchen table. "Okay, here. This one. This will be the beginning of the first movement." Photos of abstract art by local artists would be screened behind the orchestra as it played James's and Nora's composition. "What kind of feel do you get from this?"

"No good. This one's too edgy for the viola melody. All these decisions. I need time." It was a struggle. She had never written down music before except for university assignments, just played tunes in her head. Her music had to tell a story her way, feel it before an audience ever could.

James flipped through their albums and put *The Complete Billie Holiday* on the stereo for inspiration. "Time we don't have." He waited after the needle touched the vinyl to hear the crackling sound before the song. "They have to accept our presentation by

Friday or we lose the grant. Just because the grant is for first-time composers doesn't mean they'll expect something dull."

"Or worse, uninspired."

"Or monotonous or repetitious."

"I'm thinking something loud and then slow and mysterious. Think of last year when Julio Martinez directed us in – "

Nora couldn't listen to him and look at the photos. James would do this, tell these long stories and then switch course to something new. By the time he was finished, she forgot what her question was. The stories were countless, unlike the story of their finding each other.

That concert with the Anderson boys and Mr. Wakefield astonished her. Not because of the caliber of the youth symphony and the way they played one of her favorites, Tchaikovsky's *Romeo and Juliet Fantasy Overture,* but because of who she saw on the stage. Only one Black student, one Asian student, and sitting in the first chair violin position, James. She wondered how he had come all the way from Chicago, but no matter. She spent the next two years and three auditions trying for admission, and after the third try, she succeeded. She would never forget that first practice, looking to her right and finding him there. After university, James claimed a chair in the Los Angeles Symphony. Three years and four auditions later, she was now one of the newest members.

"Have you been listening at all?"

She ignored him. The Billie Holiday song "Strange Fruit" ended and "God Bless the Child" began. "I think these two go together." She juxtaposed two photos and pointed to parts of them that seemed to beg for interpretation. "I could do a solo for the first movement just with these two. See these parts? I'm thinking a contrast - hollow and soulful like when I think about my father and I wonder if – " Nora penciled in some notes on the accordion of staff paper.

"Okay let it out, then build it here."

They moved and switched the artwork and photos, agreeing, changing, and deciding on a final order. Nora brought out more staff paper and mapped outlines of the last movement with a melody's final capitulation.

"The flutes will need some woodshedding on this," James pointed to a complex 16th note run riddled with accidentals.

"How do we write this so the tympani will alternate with tubular bells?" She pointed to a rhythmic pattern. "Or the french horns to soar over them here?" Her hand waved over the ending capitulation again. "It has to be a reverie of french horn."

"I watch you work during rehearsal," James looked at her. "Why did it take the Symphony so long to hire you?"

Nora was caught up in the end of their music, her fractured mind splintering into the writing, imagining different dimensions, loud thunders, and sonorous silklike movements. It would be recognizable and memorable, so the audience would leave the auditorium humming it. Yet each movement would send the little melody in very different directions. From this, their orchestrator could make a transcription of parts for every instrument. "Remember when Joe Freyre taught us about capitulation?" She was charmed that James didn't march through her ideas but instead camped out, listening to her general orders.

"I'd like to capitulate you," James winked at her. What started out as wrangling had shifted. Nora swayed to imaginary Cuban music and James slipped into her arms.

I'm thinking of Joe Freyre and his trading Caribbean music styles, Cuban or Arubian, New Orleans jazz or New York jazz." James spun her around and dipped her back. "They traded licks and didn't think it was stealing. They kept creating something new from what came before, carrying a tradition forward so it wouldn't be forgotten, celebrating, and adding new fingerprints to the mix."

"Okay, Kitten," he said whispering into her ear. "Let's get in the groove."

They laughed. No one could make those words sound cool but the Cuban himself, Joe Freyre.

With some reluctance, James and Nora returned to the music. After battling between attitude and inspiration, they reached their ultimate point - common ground. "Let's celebrate," James stretched his arms up nearly to the ceiling fan.

"Who do we think we are, doing this?" Nora looked from the kitchen table with its arms and legs of music and photos to James. What if it's not good enough and doesn't sound the way we think it will?" She looked back at the black and white photos and the big contrasts in their music. "Let's call it Black and White." Nora knew James would argue with her idea.

Instead, he agreed. "You are your truest self when you make your music." He looked at her and held up one finger. "Don't move."

He ruffled through the albums and pulled out the Beach Boy's *Pet Sounds*. Flipping the album to the second side, he placed the pickup arm just so. The song began to play, and they fell into a slow dance to the tune, "God Only Knows." For once, neither spoke, just let the song work its magic.

In the end, Nora couldn't help but smile. "*Black and White* is *our* music, not mine," she reminded him. "It's two in the morning. Aren't you exhausted?" Nora fell back on the couch.

"No way. And neither are you." There are people you need to know better, and this is the best time for it." James grabbed the car keys and they headed for the heart of Japantown.

Nora had to admit, she was more energized than tired. James opened the door to the ranch-style home without knocking first.

"A party?" Nora looked at a dozen people, heads together in conversation and others heading back from the kitchen with drinks and chips.

"*Konbanwa*," Saiko Mori made her way to them, her dark eyes shining. "Nora, isn't it?"

"And you are – a cellist?" Nora tried to place the familiar face with her instrument. After her first year in the orchestra, she was still matching names and faces.

"Principal, yes," Saiko said, more as a clarification than a point of pride. "I told James he should bring you here last week."

Saiko took Nora's arm and walked her around the room. "My name is easy to remember because it's pronounced like *psycho*. It's a tired old joke, but I still hear it." She introduced the other cellists, bassists, and a few violins in Nora's section, connecting names to the faces. "We were talking about our auditions. So what was your audition like?"

"Petrifying. Yours?"

Saiko sat down with her. "That morning, I couldn't decide what shoes to wear so when I walked to the music stand I didn't sound like a man or woman to the judges behind the curtain. No stiletto heel taps, no leather loafer clicks. I got to the car with my cello and music, Dvořák's *Songs My Mother Taught Me*, started the car, and noticed I was in stocking feet."

"The audition room was so incredibly quiet for me; damn those acoustics," Nora said. "I turned my music to the page, and I wanted to take a big breath to clear my head. But I was terrified to take a breath that might make me sound like a woman."

"The men outnumber us. You can bet they don't suffer the way we do. They probably clear their throats and scuff their shoes with abandon," Saiko sipped her wine.

"One of the passages they requested sounded like the fourth instead of the fifth movement. Rather than ask and reveal my voice, I played the wrong one," Nora said.

"What happened?"

"The judge was a woman. She called out my mistake and repeated the fifth movement very clearly. I ended up playing ten minutes past the audition time. I was already exhausted after the first ten minutes!"

"That was a good sign. If they weren't considering you, they never would have asked you to play beyond the allotted time."

Nora laughed. "Now you tell me! It was a week of waiting with my heart in my throat each time the phone rang."

"No, really - I heard you in rehearsal the other day and you play with your heart. The impressions of your life sound right through the strings. The audience will sense that."

"Hadn't thought of that." She shook the ice in her glass and took a drink. "When I play, sometimes my head is someplace else."

"Just don't lose your ability to play like that or they'll toss you out on your ear. Just kidding," Saiko laughed. "Well maybe."

"Only for solos. In ensemble pieces, we're the Pips, not Gladys Knight. Since I'm seated right up front, I got the stink eye from our last guest soloist. I guess he thought I was somehow stealing notes from him by playing back up."

Now Saiko rolled her eyes. "Anytime someone asks what it's like playing in the symphony, I tell them it's the best job in the world."

Nora wasn't sure if she agreed yet.

"Don't mind the wall," Saiko said when she noticed Nora's distraction with the back wall of the living room behind her. Splashes of reddish copper, deep red, and sea green paint in various places, surrounded paintings and dipped under a mirror. Roller marks contrasted against the beige wall. "I'm trying to decide, but nothing is screaming pick me."

Saiko left Nora in a conversation that was at one minute pedantic and the next, silly and familiar. "What's the difference between a viola and an onion?" A man in a bulky sweater asked. She shrugged. "No one cries when you cut up an onion." He paused and listened, but when no one responded, he chuckled at his own joke.

Nora looked over at James and saw him watching her from the other side of the room. She joined a group of violinists who talked about a new movie, *2001 A Space Odyssey*. "Colossal tympani part." The man tapped the rhythm on the table as he spoke.

"I saw people walk out in the middle. It was so puzzling," said a woman with a slender neck and upswept hair like Audrey Hepburn in *Breakfast at Tiffany's*.

"I have so many questions. I think I'll go see it again," said Ruby.

Nora nodded and told Ruby, the violinist whose orchestra seat was between them, that they could both convince him to see it.

"Some of us have to work tomorrow. During the *day*," Les Harding, the lone euphonium player made his way to the door.

Nora saw James pick up his drink and a plate to take to the kitchen.

"Stop by tomorrow afternoon, Nora." Saiko tugged at her hand. "I have some friends I'd like you to meet."

Too wired to sleep, Nora rose unusually early to arrange the scattered mess of music outlines and photographs. She paperclipped the photos to their musical movements. It was too early to call the orchestrator. She imagined James pitching the plan to him, arranging their photos and her outlines with push pins while Nora picked up her instrument and practiced the three styles of the piece, adding bold plucks of the strings and whispers of notes. Finally, she fine-tuned her changes enough to include them in her outline. With a few erasures and more notes, the anticipation grew like tendrils on the sweet peas at her grandparents' farm.

She looked over the table with the accordion of paper and photos strategically placed and her heart swelled with the beauty of it.
The fragments of note melodies, the sandwiched additions of percussion and trumpet cues, every scrap and piece. The anticipation of hearing their composition in concert felt like the time James explained to her what it was like for him as a child waiting for Christmas morning.

James had already left for a high school in Newport Beach to conduct a lecture and orchestra master class. She poured coffee and relived the feeling of creating something new together. When they composed music, James' competitive spirit vexed her, possibly because it was a quality she disliked in herself. But together they were making something never seen or heard before, and few experiences made her this happy.

By afternoon, Nora found herself eager to return to Saiko's house. She wanted to ask if there could be any Japanese community connection to her father. Over the years she collected polite letters from Japanese organizations between San Francisco and Los Angeles, responding to her many requests for information. Now consumed with the composition, rehearsals, and the upcoming symphony concert, she had spent little time researching her father's whereabouts. Saiko's friends might have just the clues she needed.

19

Nora
1968

Nora arrived in mid-afternoon and almost didn't recognize the house in daylight. There was little lawn in the front, but plants grew large, vines trailed over rocks, and a winding path to the front door encouraged meandering. Nora caught a whiff of gardenia and breathed its scent. Wind chimes on the porch crafted relaxing tones and a fence lizard skittered across a rattan chair to disappear into the foliage.

The front screen door swung open. "Come in come in." Saiko motioned. "We're all out in back."

She led Nora through the house, still littered with last night's party detritus, plastic cups, bowls of peanuts, and an orange scarf. Once she stepped to the back porch, Nora looked past the three women seated around a table. Her eyes rested on a bamboo chicken coop and several chickens of multiple colors, chasing each other around the yard. Upon seeing her, they changed direction, one making a soft growling sound, another, a deep rhythmic clucking, and still others, warbling trills.

Nora ignored the women and walked out among the chickens. She talked to them and one walked up, pecking at her feet. She picked it up and laughed as it warbled in conversation with her. She turned to the women who were watching. "I used to care for chickens and collect eggs when I was small. I haven't picked one up in such a long time."

"That's Hen Solo, in your arms," Saiko told her. "Bring her over. She'll sit on your lap."

Nora carried her to the table and the chicken sat comfortably as if it was the most natural place to be.

Introductions were made and Nora poured herself a drink from the big pitcher of tea. After a few thirsty gulps, she stopped.

"You like? It's sweetened with melon, tequila, and rum." Maki offered to share her recipe.

"Now you know - go slow with Maki's tea," Jae Kane laughed. She introduced herself by explaining her work. "I glean scraps from auto salvage yards, and *dekiagari*, it becomes sculpture. So if you know anyone in the orchestra who wants to give up their old brass instruments – "

"Jae Kane's always looking for heavy metal and quirky titles,' said Dorothy, a square-shouldered woman whose father was a GI in the war. He worked with his Japanese buddy in the Navy yards after the surrender. His buddy's son Li, who fought in Vietnam, later became her husband. "Have you tried a tea ceremony?" Dorothy asked. "A *sento* hot spring bath? A mochi pounding ceremony?" Dorothy expressed her Japanese bona fides before Nora could say anything.

Saiko ignored her irritation at Dorothy's questions and her face expressed concern. "I brought my friends here Nora, to let you know that we support one another." Their lively conversation turned quiet. "Nora, sometimes these days we are not safe, even in Fountain Valley. You have to be careful where you go."

"Yeah and sometimes I can help keep troublemakers in their places," Dorothy said. Nora thought Dorothy reminded her of the sinewy woman in the red bandana, the one on the "We Can Do It" poster.

Jae Kane said, "We know how hard it is to fit in and make friendships," she said. "And sometimes it's safer if you don't go alone. Just call us and we'll come with. We're better off with two or three of us."

"People stare at me, that's all." Nora looked at their faces, not sure if they were as serious as they sounded.

"Just trust us – we welcome you, but not everyone is so welcoming."

"And some of them can be dangerous. If you're not sure, call us." Dorothy said. "Sometimes just being with us keeps you safe."

That evening Nora unlocked the door to find James already home. "How was your visit with Saiko?" He asked.

"What are you doing in the kitchen?" Nora dropped her keys and headed to the refrigerator with the fresh eggs Saiko had given her.

"I figured it was time I make my croissants for you," James said. "You've never had them."

Nora pulled up the counter stool and watched as his hands folded the laminated dough with a confident rhythm. "Where did you learn this?"

"Remember my uncle? He never got me that job in Hollywood, but he could bake all sorts of pastry. He let me practice in his kitchen, and I picked it up. You start with pastry flour. That's the best. The butter block is entered into the first layer, then as you roll it out and fold it –" He made another fold with a perfect corner. "You get flakey, buttery layers." He folded again. "By the time I'm done, I'll have 55 layers."

Nora couldn't take her eyes off his hands. "What happens if you make too many layers?"

"The butter gets too thin and melts into the dough. It's more like bread."

She watched as he cut the dough and before rolling, added thin sticks of dark chocolate and a sprinkle of chopped, dried cherries to each croissant.

She read the package. "Michigan tart cherries – my favorite!" Nora beamed. She watched his face, all concentration on the precision of cutting and rolling, the set of his mouth when one dough curve was just right or just off, his hands rolling the pastry dough with a kind of reverence. He raised one spiky eyebrow and caught her watching him. How wondrous was a man baking in the kitchen.

The pan was filled with plump croissants and James put it in the oven as if he was laying a baby in a crib. *"Tu eres mi azúcar."*

"I love it when you speak Spanish. How many minutes?" Nora asked.

"About 16 give or take – "

"Come with me." Nora squeezed his hand and led him to their bedroom.

Later when the baked croissants lured them with the smell of butter, chocolate, and tart cherries, they left their tousled bed. "How about croissants for dinner?" Nora said. Along with a glass of white Zinfandel, the two of them ate and rambled. James watched and counted as Nora tucked away one croissant after another. She told James about the exceptional tea and the casual camaraderie of her new friends. "The conversation moved too fast. There were things I wanted to ask about my father, advice about where to look for him. It's just that I wanted to say things and the talk drifted away. The moment was gone." Then she mentioned the warning about being careful where she walked.

James laughed. "They're paranoid." He shook his head. "You don't have to worry about that. This is 1968, not 1945!" Anyway, I knew you'd like Saiko. And no, I've never made fun of her name. Never would. Too bad, though, she gets a lot of that."

"But they were so serious," Too full for the last bite, Nora returned it to the plate. "I really like them, especially Saiko. I hope they like me." She added a splash to her wine glass. "I'll send Saiko a thank you note. I don't always seem like a friendly person when people meet me, but maybe I'll sound more like myself in writing." Sheepishly, she told James about her rush to hold the chicken before she even said hello to the women. She leafed through the drawer for paper. "I can ask her about my dad in the note." James was watching her with a puzzled expression. "You laughed, but you didn't see the looks on their faces," she said. "Maybe you don't know Fountain Valley like you think you do."

20

Nora

1968

James and Nora created, argued, fought, and made up over their composition. The first deadline was not met. The music arranger needed more time. The orchestra members didn't get their parts until a week before the performance and they openly grumbled and blamed. Each rehearsal that followed brought new last-minute changes from the arrangers and more condemnation of both of them.

At the end of their orchestra dress rehearsal, Nora left her chair when an anxious cellist called her name. She wasn't sure if the debut of *Black and White* would be worth the anxiety over the performance. After a long explanation, she threaded her way back through music stands to gather her things. "Where's my violin?" she said. It wasn't on her chair where she'd left it. The case was gone too. Nora's eyes darted everywhere on the stage, her heart pounding. "Have you seen my violin? Did someone move it?" She asked a violinist who was marking her music.

"Nora, it's time to get a new violin anyway. You're a professional. That old thing had a school sticker on the case."

"I'd get that violin rebuilt and restrung a million times before I'd part with it," Nora told her.

She asked the stagehand who knew every backstage rope and lever, the grandfather of the orchestra. "Burt, did you see anything?" She asked.

"Nora, I didn't see a thing." He noted her frantic expression and touched her shoulder. "Looks like you'd better call security."

It was one more day until the concert and she had a solo to play.

"Do we all have to go?" Dorothy said.

"Dorothy, with this trade war and all the blame, I'm not driving there alone." Saiko gripped the steering wheel and waited while a woman with a stroller crossed the street and maneuvered up the curb on the other side.

"It's so bad," said Maki. "Just the other day I got the stink-eye a couple of times, in produce at the Alpha Beta."

"So, Nora, you've looked all this time and you haven't found out anything about your dad. He's probably dead. It's time to move on, don't you think?"

"Look, I don't want to hear it. That violin is my job. Without it, I can't pay for food or housing. Do you have to talk about my dad right now Dorothy?" Nora tugged her earlobe.

"There you go with the earlobe again. It's so annoying!" Dorothy pushed Nora's arm.

"Dorothy, now is not the time," said Saiko

"It's a perfect time. What if your dad's family had some inherited disease and you don't know about it, like a rare cancer? What if he was rich and the family kept all the moolah from you - enough so you wouldn't have to worry about a stupid violin?"

"Dorothy, tone it down," said Jae Kane.

"Oh, you're all on her side, are you? Is that the way it is? You know I'm right. It's always, poor Nora! We have to be kind to Nora! What about me? I'm the different one here. Why doesn't anyone agree with me for a change?"

"Fuck you, Dorothy. The whole state of California understands things from your side," Maki said. The women were shocked into silence. Maki was the quiet one. "That's nothing. If Mr. C heard you, he'd really read you the riot act." Maki referred to her husband as if he was a character in a Marcel Proust novel. She was a fan. "You know, the riot act was a real thing. In 1714 the Riot Act was passed by the British Parliament. It was to speed up consequences for citizens causing civil unrest."

"Who needs a history lesson with you around, Maki." Dorothy glared at her.

The farther Saiko drove, the dicier the area looked. Much of it was abandoned with streets rutted and narrow. "Let's get this violin and scram," Dorothy said. "This place gives me the creeps."

"I need to find another storage unit," Saiko said. "I've stored my violin here for years without a problem, but the area wasn't this - dismal then." She turned the last corner. "It's moisture and temperature regulated, and those places are hard to find at a good price," she said, pulling into a parking spot. My violin is a Maggini – slow growth spruce, beautiful tone. Nora, you should have a great concert on this instrument tonight. Just take good care of it."

The women's footsteps echoed down a long hall lined with numbered, locked doors. Saiko got out her keys and unlocked # 1376. The unit was sparse, only a hand-turned wooden rocking chair, a few boxes, and the violin. "Here you are," Saiko handed the case to Nora.

Saiko clicked the door lock when three men in sweatshirts appeared from around the corner beside the unit. Nora first saw a hand with a tiger tattoo, then the gleam of a knife; another man, a curly-haired *Steve McQueen* type, pulled a gun from a jacket pocket.

Dorothy rushed forward, chopped at his neck with both hands, and everything happened in flashes. She forced the gun from his grasp. It spun away and Dorothy fell back. One of the men shifted in front of Nora and her knee shot up. He growled and shoved her aside, losing his balance. He fell against the man with the knife and it cut into his side. Amid yells and threats, the third man fled.

"I've got a belt. I'll tie his hands." Nora placed the violin case by the wall and loosened her belt. Maki knelt with her weight on the man's knees while Nora looped the leather around his wrists and pulled to tighten it.

The man with the knife checked his bleeding and tried to stand, but Jae Kane gave her purse a mighty swing and knocked him back to the floor.

Speechless, Dorothy and Nora looked at each other. "Hurry," Saiko removed her scarf. Jae Kane kept pounding his hand with her purse until he released the knife.

"I love this scarf. You don't deserve it," Saiko told the gunman as she tied his hands, wrapping the long scarf multiple times and tying a tight knot.

"I think I broke my little finger," Dorothy said. She found an emergency box on the wall and they huddled a distance away, waiting for the police to arrive.

The ride home was noisier than the ride to the storage unit. "Where did you learn to fight like that?" Saiko said

"Years ago my husband's friend started a martial arts class that meets right after my yoga class," Dorothy checked the movement in her sore shoulder." He wanted me to join to help out his friend, and I kind of liked it so I kept at it. It's so focused, you know? It helps me forget the stuff that bothers me. I can put it on the back burner."

"You reacted so fast." Jae Kane shook her head. "I don't think I could ever have done that. When I think of what could have happened – "

"Jae Kane, what the hell is in that purse of yours?" Dorothy asked.

She unzipped her purse to reveal a tractor gear and a meat cleaver. "I bought these this morning for my new sculpture. I almost took them out of my purse before we came, but I ran out of time."

"I thought the police would never quit with their questions. Did they tell you that you're safe now?"

"Maki, I think the short one must've said it at least three times. Then he asked me to tell the whole story, even things that weren't important at all," Jae Kane said.

"They sure weren't in any hurry," Saiko said. "I just wanted to get out of there."

"At least he had a glove to take the gun from my purse, with fingerprints and all," Nora said.

"I thought they might thank us for the way we restrained them," Dorothy said. "It's not like anybody could have done what we did."

"See?" Saiko said to Nora. "See now why we do things together?"

"Most important," Nora said, "I've got a violin to play tonight."

Saiko groaned and Dorothy punched her in the arm with what felt like explosive power. Nora figured it would be black and blue the next day. It was worth it.

After Saiko dropped off Jae Kane, she pushed open the garage door and got to work. She unzipped her purse and pulled out the meat cleaver, dropping it on the garage floor with a clunk. With both hands, she pulled out the weighty tractor gear. The gear teeth bit into her hands but she held on tighter. Reo opened the door from the kitchen to ask her what was going on.

"I just can't say right now." Jae Kane shook her head to clear her mind of what almost happened. "I'll tell you later." She waved Reo off. The sound of the gear she dropped on the garage floor rang in her ears. She arranged the torch in its holder. After a few tastes of gas and a push on the lever, the flames leaped high. What to create that expressed wild agitation? The foreboding? She walked around the garage scouring the walls with her eyes, grabbing a windmill gear here and a pitchfork tine, dropping them to the cement floor in a jangled heap. To the pile, she dragged a copper spiral of tubing off the back wall and a line of connected brass plates that resembled a spiky spine. From a tall storage bin, she pulled a couple of dozen steel rods of different thicknesses that she thought could splay out in all directions, angry as a raging fire.

Oblivious to the time and the heat of her torch, Jae Kane worked. The angled pieces drove her to craft a sculpture in a style she couldn't yet name. The flame came dangerously close to her and only her experience saved her from burning herself. The metal twisted and turned under her welding gloved hand, angular, forceful juts from every side. Finally, she was at a point where she could stop for the night. Details could be left for the next day.

Reo heard the slowing of her tools and figured it would be safe to open the door a sliver. "I saved some dinner for you."

"Yes. Dinner. That would be good," Jae Kane was exhausted. She stilled the flame and secured her tools. Every muscle ached. Following Reo, she turned her back on the monstrosity she'd created, unable to look at it.

Maki returned to the greenhouse, although she had closed for the day. She grabbed a broom and swept the potting areas that had just been cleaned. With clippers, she slashed away at the overgrown wisteria where it had shaded the fuchsia and prevented the buds from forming. Without plan or purpose, she walked the aisles, snipping a spent flower here and moving a roaming vine, still young enough to bend without breaking, to its rightful place.

Not ready to go home, she had the idea of rearranging the pallets behind the greenhouse. If she could stack them better, they'd have room for an extra car in the back lot. Except for their usefulness during spring, the pallets were always an eyesore. She placed two pallets side by side and started stacking. When they reached her height, she started climbing on the bottom pallets, stacking them twice her height. The pallets began to sway and she heard something break. She scrambled down in time, but the pallets tipped and the stack tumbled to the ground, a heavy weight on Maki's foot. A zing of pain made her curse and draw back her right foot, useless and misshapen.

Hopping and dragging her foot, she made her way to the car. Lightheaded, she used her left foot on the gas pedal and brake, to drive to the emergency. She parked in front of the hospital door and didn't remember anything else.

The fast walk home from Saiko's left Dorothy out of breath. Her car keys weren't in their usual place, but after yelling at herself, she grabbed them and headed for the market. Her thoughts were elsewhere when she returned with bags of produce, napa cabbage, garlic, ginger, green onions, and gochugaru chili powder. Usually, she would make a small amount of kimchi for Li and herself, but she had purchased ten cabbages. She washed and trimmed them, put them on the butcher block at the center of the kitchen, and grabbed her biggest meat cleaver. Taking the cleaver in both hands, she bore down on the cabbages with a resounding whack. Her shoulder throbbed where she'd hit the floor, but her finger still bent. It wasn't broken.

Over and over again she chopped the cabbage past the usual small pieces, into a macerated mess. Sprinkling the cabbage with salt, she scooped the cabbage into the kimchi crock, covered it with water, and sealed the top for its overnight stay in the refrigerator. Tomorrow the other ingredients would be worked through the washed and drained cabbage. For now, she looked back to make sure the kitchen was scrubbed spotless.

Just as Li walked in the door from work, Maki called. "I'm at the hospital. My foot is a mess. I'm on pain pills and I can't drive. I tried everyone else, but no one is picking up. Will you come and take me and my car home?"

"So I was your last choice." Dorothy knew why. "Li and I will be right there."

Back at her apartment, Nora called for James before she remembered he was out with friends. She rested the violin in the place where hers used to be. The violin was a right-handed one, but she'd make it work, grateful that Saiko had saved their premiere of *Black and White*. First of all, she had to wash her hands. A new bar of soap waited by the sink, and once the water was warm, she stood, lathering and rinsing her hands repeatedly. An image of the three men overwhelmed her, the tension still vibrating to the ends of her soapy fingers that wouldn't come clean.

Christmas vacation in her Michigan childhood had just begun, and a blizzard struck. Snow drifts blanketed the house and barn. Papa, Grandmother, and Nora had checked and secured the animals, and there was nothing to be done but wait. Papa and Grandmother read the paper around the stove in the parlor. The kitchen was warmer, and Nora preferred the table next to the cookstove.

Grandmother had a new bar of soap at the kitchen sink. The farmhouse had no toys other than a box of empty, wooden thread spools to stack. She was seven now, too grown up for those. Nora saw a new bar of soap by the sink and took it to the kitchen table. She talked to it like her dolls on the shelf in her old room next to Asher's. She pictured the dolls in their colorful dresses and bright eyes and had an idea. Papa's toothpicks stood in a ceramic barrel holder next to the salt and pepper. She took one each for the doll's arms and legs. Now the soap doll could walk across the table. She needed a face. In the icebox, she spied the bowl of cranberries Grandmother was saving for Christmas relish. Choosing one, she quietly closed the icebox door. On the end of a toothpick, the cranberry improved the look considerably. She thought of a name. *Dance Penelope!* Nora spun the doll on her toothpick leg. Juice from the cranberry dripped red down the toothpick to the soap bar, but no matter. She sang and laughed, forgetting herself, with made-up songs.

Grandmother heard the noise and rushed in. "You wasteful child. Give me that!" Without waiting, she snatched the doll from Nora's hand and slapped her face. "Stop this racket. Out of my sight now!"

Speechless, Nora glared at her grandmother's steel-gray braid swirled around her head with two sprigs of stubborn hair that refused the braid, like demon horns. Grandmother glared back, her brow furrowed in a continual outrage.

Nora's cheek stung and she felt like jumping out of her skin. She ran to the back door for her winter coat before she climbed the attic stairs. She left her door open in case some of the heat from the kitchen would make its way to the third-floor attic. In her room, she buttoned her coat. Grandmother's angry contempt hurt worse than her cheek. She pulled on a pair of jeans she wore to clean out the chicken coup.

This wasn't the first time she handily opened the window and reached for the narrow ledge outside. Without a sound, she lowered herself onto the top of the second-story shutter and side-stepped onto the first-floor trellis beside it. One rung was broken, but she
learned to keep her feet close to the crossbar nails and jump off before she hit the picker bush. The wind gusts made it hard to hang on, but once on the ground, she took off at a run beyond the chicken coop over the snow-covered corn husks in the east field by the railroad tracks.

She arrived in time to see the white light of the 4:40 with its puffs of smoke just breaking through a stand of trees. Nora didn't feel the cold and scooped up a mitten full of snow to hold to her cheek. The train drew closer, and she listened for the somber whistle that meant it was nearing the station in town. Standing as close to the tracks as she dared, she felt the familiar rhythmic rumbling from her shoes to her core. The steel wheels screeched against the track and she looked up at the blur of grimy red and gray cars speeding by, the rhythm of the wheels thumping like a heartbeat. If just one of those freight doors was open – if the train would slow down just a bit, she could jump in. It didn't matter where the train was headed, she would never come back.

The last car passed down the track and the rumbling quieted. No open doors. Soon the train disappeared into the blizzard as if it had never been there. Her breath turned to a misty cloud around her.

A strong gust of wind and snow made the sweat beads on her neck and face feel cold on her slow walk back to the farmhouse.

How long had she been washing her hands at the sink? It wasn't enough. Too much in her life was unthinkable right now. Sorting through albums she found Beethoven's concerto, *Musica Clasica Relajante.* With its calming melodies on high volume, she ran a hot bath and sank into the tub.

21

Nora
1968

James found a new walking path that the two of them hadn't taken before. He was going to suggest it, but grew angry about the events at the storage unit. "You put yourself in danger, and Saiko's just as bad," he yelled.

"You're blaming me. It wasn't my fault," Nora said.

The angst over the upcoming concert made them wary around each other. After the successful performance of *Black and White,* they felt like themselves again. She told James, "I would have enjoyed the concert more if I'd written the cello part in the second movement more - hungrily. Maybe with a rainstick behind it. That's all I could think of as we played the rest of it."

"I wouldn't change anything," James said,

In the days that followed, they found it easier to speak in normal voices. By Saturday, James figured they would be able to enjoy a hike.

The trail was partially paved with some offshoots of mulch or gravel. Within a mile of the trailhead, roller skaters zoomed past walkers. Nora noticed James slow his pace when parents with strollers passed by. Further on, they found a curving path that seemed to disappear. Birds from competing territories trilled and whistled. Wooden stairs led down and around to a landing in front of a ramshackle hut.

"Welcome to Huntes Gardens." A caretaker smiled and handed them a pamphlet with dozens of flowers and birds pictured and named. A map of looped trails connected to this point.

"Is this your first visit?" Leo the caretaker asked. When James and Nora nodded, Leo explained that the botanical garden was created by a former gold miner in the mid-1800s. "This was a giant sinkhole, a collapsed cave, so the property was worthless. No one knew what to do with it. So Mr. Huntes made a garden out of it. Take a look around!"

"Oh, James, Maki has to see this," Nora said, leading the way through the jungle-like foliage. She stopped short when a rock-colored lizard wiggled across the path in front of her. "I recognize some of the tropical flowers from Maki's greenhouse. Look, it's a bromeliad." She showed James the spiky purple and pink blooms.

"There's a begonia." James paused by a hanging basket. "My grandmother used to grow them," he said. He stopped to pull the inhaler from his pocket. The heavy scents around them irritated his breathing.

"I'm so glad you suggested this place," Nora smiled. They stood on a bright red oriental bridge over a creek at the base of the garden. "It's like a tropical island."

Their eyes followed the vines and greenery up the tall sides of the two-acre park. "Let's try this one." Nora took James' hand and together they followed the curved path up several stone steps. Past arching elephant ear-sized leaves and tiny striped leaves below, they found a garden seat. In the middle was a tabby cat stretching in a patch of sun. Nora wanted to scratch his ears but drew back when he meowed. "I'd like to sit down but I can't disturb him. He's too comfortable."

James looked at her, relaxed for the first time since the storage unit spree. He pulled her close.

"Look." Her arm shot out at a striking orange bloom and hit his cheek. "I was going to say it looked like a lobster claw." She dropped her arm and kissed the spot, oblivious to his morning stubble.

They talked about their composition and its promising review in the *Fountain Valley News*. The orchestra director pointed out a small mention in the *Los Angeles Times*. Already the two of them were planning a new musical work, to follow other obligations from the orchestra.

Saiko was asking about her violin and Nora had to make a decision. Calls to the police had produced no leads. She told Saiko that it was time to buy a new left-handed instrument.

Nora missed the sound of her sable violin. Was it being cared for or left somewhere forgotten? She refused to imagine it damaged or worse. Although Seiko offered her violin for as long as Nora needed it, she wanted her own. 'You know choosing a violin will be worse than choosing a mate," Seiko told her.

Seiko knew a friend who had a more affordable Hill & Sons left-handed violin. At the door of an old violin shop on Cahuenga Boulevard, Nora felt hopeful. The wood floors creaked and the closer she came to the counter, the strong smell of rosin hailed her. The place was quiet except for a young woman in the back organizing pages of music. She stood before the man behind the counter, his fuzzy, gray hair covering a face bent over a box of coiled strings, his fingers searching for a particular one. "Ah!" he said holding up the coil in its paper folder. "I knew it. One moment please," he said, dashing to a phone receiver near the wall.

While she waited, half-listening to the man's animated conversation, she looked at the gleaming instruments displayed in glass cases. The occasional repairs on her missing violin had been expensive enough. She had never priced out a new instrument, and the prices were shocking.

"How may I help you, Madam?" The fuzzy gray-haired man now stood before her.

As soon as she mentioned Saiko, the man sprang into action. "Yes yes, the Hill & Sons." He disappeared into the curtained back room and returned with a violin case that had a few scratches but was actually better looking than her case with the Chicago Preparatory Orchestra sticker on it. "Practice rooms are around that corner," he pointed. "I will take it from the case and bring it to you to try. Ask

Julia there for a piece of music to sample." Julia looked up, music folders in hand.

"Thank you. I won't need music," Nora said. The room was only big enough for two chairs and a music stand, but acoustic panels on the walls assured her she would be able to hear the tone and timbre of the sound.

Fuzzy presented the instrument with two hands. "Take your time. Get to know the feel of it. If you want to try again another day before you decide, I can hold it for you." He nodded and closed the door.

Before she played a note, she looked at the price tag. It was nearly as shocking as the new instruments in the glass cases outside, but this instrument would be her livelihood. She took a breath and plucked a few strings, warmed up her fingers with scales, and tried a few emotionless arpeggios. It wasn't as bold sounding and its deep red wood took some getting used to compared to her beloved sable violin, but she could adapt to the fretboard and bridge placement,
a feel familiar for her left hand. Over the next few hours, she tried two comparable violins and decided on the Hill & Sons after all. It was the practical thing to do, she told herself. Within a few years, it would be paid off. Maybe that was more important than the way she felt when she played it.

22

Nora

1970

"What's the champagne for?"

"New job." James launched into the apartment and wedged the bottle in the freezer for a quick chill. He brought two glasses to the counter.

James kissed her neck and she could tell he'd stopped for a pick-up basketball game on the way home. She finished the garlic and jalapeno mince, using the knife to guide the small bits from the cutting board into the skillet for a buttery sauté. The aroma of fish and baking tomatoes wafted from the oven. "So tell me."

"The thing is, I never thought they'd choose me. There must have been 100 applicants. It's the fine arts coordinator job for the Brooklyn Philharmonic, Hon. I've got it."

Nora remembered when he applied for the position, but it was such a long shot. "It's Brooklyn. What about Los Angeles?" Nora stirred the squash soup aggressively and watched it bubble and steam.

He peered in. "It looks like Yellowstone mud pots."

Nora glared at him.

"C'mon Nora. It's twice what I make here. The music scene there would be all new. New connections, new opportunities, ideas – we'd expand our circle." He reached out to hug her but dropped his arm. "We could get married. Marry me and we'll go to New York."

"What's wrong with what we have?" She flipped the saute and turned up the stove. "You want to tear me away from my home?" The idea pierced and pricked at her. "Like when I was a kid and my mother put me on a bus to somewhere I'd never been, to people I'd never met?"

"We'd have each other." He lowered his voice. "It wouldn't be like that."

"What about my dad?" Her fists clenched. "I'd never be able to find him from so far away."

"You haven't been able to find him here."

"I'm trying, James. All I've found are dead ends. I know where he used to be, but not where he is now. If he's alive, I'm going to find him. I'm not going to be pushed out or taken away from my home. He could be nearby and I don't even know it."

"I'm not telling you to give up. Look at it this way. We could afford a family. We could have kids."

"Not kids. Those times on our walks when you pointed out the babies and stopped to ask the parents about them?"

"I've always wanted kids."

"What if I don't? How could we make music and babies too?"

"I'll help take care of them." James seemed not to understand what she was saying.

"One of us will have to drop out of work to stay home. Are you planning on doing that?"

"The mom usually does that. But it would only be for a while."

Nora could smell the sauté burning, but she ignored it. "You know what it was like for me as a kid, people spitting, people telling me to go back to Japan? You know how terrifying it is to think of parenting a child when I didn't have a family to show me how it worked? What if I messed up as bad as they did? I'm not having a baby, a new messed up me."

"Hey, my folks in Chicago pretty much ignored me, even my asthma, and I turned out okay. Don't think about that. Maybe they neglected you, but you could make that up to our kid. We could teach him violin. Or her – "

"Make it up?"

"Most people our age have started families."

"You're thinking of people who look like you – who wouldn't have to explain to their kids why people yell slurs and call them un-

American." The burning jalapenos stung her eyes. She turned off the stove and pushed the pan in a clatter. "Just stop all this talk of New York. I can't listen anymore."

"Whose skin are you in? Who are you?"

"It's exhausting. You don't know. Every comment, every slight takes a little more of me and there's always a next time. That feeling that I have to be twice as good as the next musician just to get what I've earned. It never stops. Forcing that on a kid would be cruel."

He headed for the door and turned back. "Exhausting, I get it." He pointed his finger. "You messed this up. I thought we'd celebrate tonight, but instead, you gut-punched me."

She folded her arms and stood back. "You don't get it. Stop talking about it."

"This was gonna be the best night ever." James looked at her one last time. "I gotta get the hell outta here." He slammed the door behind him.

Nora took a long breath, the only sound in the sudden silence. At length, she relaxed her shoulders and fists. Her hand shook as she took the cold champagne from the freezer. One of the two glasses from the counter she poured to the top. The chair scraped on the floor as she moved it to the window and fell into it, tugging her earlobe and staring out at the clouds. There must be a name, a word for this shook-up feeling, but she couldn't come up with it. She turned off the oven and the soup, muddy, cracked, and unfit to eat. When the glass was empty, she grabbed the bottle by the neck and started walking.

Saiko looked at her with a raised eyebrow, "He's mercurial, that one." They sipped the champagne and watched the chickens scratch, taking dirt baths under the ginkgo tree. Branches seemed to reach away from the porch, their long stretch underappreciated from every angle but the chicken coop. "You're not one to like being alone, are you?" It was more of a statement than a question.

Nora wondered how much she could tell Saiko about James. She was his friend too. "I met him when I was fourteen. He was the only boy in the orchestra who talked to me and even then it was a push-me-pull-you feel, but he never made me feel like there was something wrong with me until today. It was years later when we found each other here, it felt like we had found a part of our Chicago past."

When she heard her own voice, it was almost like Nora was talking about someone from the past. "He was warm, familiar. I lost my mother and brother and I needed to hang on to this." The chickens squawked and chased, Hen Solo the Easter Egger, and a Bantam Blue, Princess Laya. "We've been together three years, Saiko. When I think of him going to New York without me it seems like a colossal waste."

Big Bird wiggled her fluffy brown beard and Saiko removed the hen from her lap. "Nora, I'm going to tell you something I've never told anyone."

Nora knew Saiko too well, to believe this was true. She knew more than a few people who believed they were Saiko's dearest friends. Now it was Nora's turn. She would suspend disbelief and let herself shelter under Saiko's trusted wing.

"Back when Daichi and I had first come here from Kyoto, everything was so strange." Saiko sipped her champagne and looked out past the ginkgo to the wisteria vines on their trellis, crazy with blooms. We would get overwhelmed by our long hours at work. At night we would share memories of Kyoto – our walks holding hands on the *Tsuten-kyo* covered bridge and hopping from stone to stone in the *Hojo* garden." Saiko smiled at the thought.

"There was nothing back here then." She motioned to the backyard. "Year by year we tried to add to the garden to make it feel like home." She patted Nora's hand. "See that purple jacaranda from the neighbor's yard?" A breeze, like a sigh, shimmied through the tree. "So hard to take care of! Every year we hack it back. It's poisonous to the chickens. But it's like a wild thing, stronger than we are. It is beautiful, though. Smell the honey scent?"

Nora was distracted. The neighbor woman with the jacaranda was in the yard next door. She played "Close to You" on her cassette player, and the occasional breeze carried the drifty mix of Coppertone and weed in their direction. Nora tried to locate the sweet, earthy scent Saiko was talking about.

"I keep trimming. So many memories." Saiko took a sip of champagne. "Daichi was older. He grew to be a tough old bird." Saiko's laugh crackled. We tried to create an idea, something in the yard back here that never existed, never could, except in our minds. Her eyes rested on the overgrown rock garden. All that effort for what?" Saiko urged Nora to understand. "I miss Daichi, that's true," she shook her head. "But when he died, I quit trying so hard, to make a new place as I remembered. It was like a weight had been lifted."

Nora wasn't ready to think about a new life, but she understood where Saiko was going. Saiko had her own struggles. "I wish I could have known Daichi. I would have liked him," Nora said.

"He didn't warm up to people easily," Saiko said. "But I think he would've liked you too." Her elbow touched Nora's arm. "He would've hated the chickens." Saiko's own laugh tickled her so that she slapped her knees, and Nora couldn't help but laugh too.

Before the champagne was gone, Jae called and told them to meet her in her garage right away. Saiko grabbed a sweater and paused by the wall. "What do you think of this color?" She waited next to a few roller widths of avocado green.

Nora looked at the new color on the wall and nodded. "Maybe," she said.

Saiko rolled her eyes and they left the house, latching the bamboo security gate. Walking the few blocks to Jae's house, they hoped she wasn't ill. At the crosswalk, they ignored the young man who yelled at them.

When they arrived at Jae's garage, a fire truck was leaving. Black soot dusted Jae's projects and the back wall of the garage was black with soot over the waste bin that caught fire in a flash. Saiko asked if Jae was hurt, but she waved her away and shook her head.

"I told her that torch was risky," Reo said, with his hands in the air. "She could've been killed. Maybe now she'll listen." He slammed the door to the house.

Jae Kane blinked at Saiko and Nora. "Good. You're here. I've got a show this weekend and I almost lost my newest pieces." She turned a piece the size of a small child – a frog jumping a boy made of bolts, gears, and tractor engine parts. "Help me polish, will you? I'm happy to put you to good use." She gave them both soft, red rags. The one in her hand was wet and black with spray and soot, so she dropped it in a pile and grabbed another. They each chose a metalwork and began to clean. Nora's was a poodle with chainmail fur named *Grand Poobah*.

"Reo is right. I didn't want to take the time to find a new torch, you know. You get used to a torch, you know just how it will perform, and it's hard to part with it. Then something like this happens."

"Look at this bird." Nora left Poobah and started polishing the wing of a piece twice the size of a violin. "I think he's glaring at me." The curved wing swooped around, covering the front of the bird and one eye looked back at her with a raised metal brow. The entire wing was covered in spoons, from tiny salt spoons at the tip, graduating to serving spoons at the top. "I bet this is beautiful shined up." It was a slow task, one spoon at a time.

"That's Screech." She checked the welds to see if any parts were melted or weakened. "That wing was a bugger. Might have been the end of my torch."

Nora looked at the sidewall, dusted with soot, but unharmed by the fire. Half of it was covered in spoons, hung, and organized from small to large.

"The scrapyard got three hundred pounds last year. They always give me a call first thing when they get a haul like this."

Nora's eyes traveled around the garage, filled with organized metal pieces, a collection of silver and brass saxophone and trumpet bells near the ceiling followed by steel and bronze gears organized in threes by their size. At a glance, it appeared the walls were thick with junk, but in reality, every metal piece had a place.

Then she found the tractor gear and the meat cleaver. Staring at the metal pieces buried deep in the belly of a dragon-like creature, Nora couldn't help but picture the afternoon at the storage unit, and she swallowed hard, unable to touch the thing.

"You found it," Jae said. "It was my way of letting go of some of that – well, you know."

Nora looked at her. "This spiky, undulating spine. It unsettles me."

"I know. I can't name it. It's just untitled."

Nora approached it with her cloth, half expecting it to paralyze her with a touch. Beneath the soot was shiny brass.

"The fire must've scared your husband." Nora stopped polishing to check for any spots she missed.

"Oh no! We were both married before and that was scary. Disentangling ourselves from divorce – oh – *Kazoku no kon'nan* – it was so difficult. When I moved in with Reo we told our families we were afraid to marry because divorce was such a nightmare. They would not accept us. All through our first ten years together our families pushed. When will you marry? Reo turned to me and said, 'I'll make a promise to you. I'll never divorce you.'

"That's when I knew. He understood how I felt. "I promise I'll never divorce you too," I said. And here we are together unmarried to this day."

"C'mon you two," Seiko said as she shined a loop of metal wire at the bottom of the Poobah, the "J" of Jae's signature. "It's getting dark and I have to put the chickens back in the coop."

"So, Nora, will you do me another favor?" Jae didn't wait for an answer. "I need some musical accompaniment for my show this weekend. Do you think you could play for me for an hour?"

Nora instantly thought of James, but without him, she had no plans. "I'll be glad to help out. Just tell me where and when."

That night, Nora walked around the bare apartment, opened James's side of the empty closet, and stood over the carpet where his chair once lived. She opened the nightstand drawer and even his extra inhaler was gone. The cassette she played to drown out the quiet reminded her of James, so she turned it off. Dinner wasn't possible because she wasn't hungry. So she took her violin and began to play. Sifting through sheets of music, she selected pieces for Jae's art show and kept playing until her fingers were sore.

When she finally looked at the time, it was 2:00, and she thought she might be able to sleep. With all the extra room, the bed should have felt liberating. There was the sound of a car, then a passing ambulance, familiar sounds that failed to fill the unease in her.

Then came the memory, pinpoint clear, of James bursting into her apartment with the idea to coordinate a music composition. Their mutual enthusiasm rushed at them, the energy, a waterfall of ideas. She stared at the dark sky outside the window, willing herself to sleep, yet unable to banish the memory any more than the one of Miss Bird the day she left for Chicago.

23

Nora

1970

"You take your personal misery and turn it into stunner music." Dorothy was one of the first visitors to Jae's art show. Nora kept playing and figured that for Dorothy, that was a compliment.

The art show was at one of the larger contemporary craft galleries in Fountain Valley. Three artists were featured, but from her corner, Nora noticed more people wandering in and staying to look at Jae Kane's pieces. Peeking over her music, she was tickled by the facial expressions. Fingers pointed at the soaring metal wings and more so at the tongue-in-cheek sculpture names. The intimidating dragon creature remained untitled and those who didn't know its history weren't ruffled by it. Visitors crouched down or stood away to get a different view.

As the show wound down, Nora finished her last piece, a toccata. Only one visitor remained, so she felt comfortable putting her violin away. Turning to go, the visitor stood before her. "I enjoyed your music," he said, holding out his hand. "I'm Takami Iguro."

Nora's breath caught. She swallowed hard. "Iguro did you say?"

The tall, Japanese man looked awkward and dropped his hand. Instead, he tried a smile and neither could speak for a moment. She saw him examining her features and found herself doing the same with him. He sighed. "Yes, that was my father's name, and I believe it was your father's name too."

Nora's mind raced. The age was about right, she thought. "Are you – "

"A friend of Jae Kane's told me you'd be playing here and when I heard your last name, I was curious." Nora reached for his hand and gave it a tense grip.

"I can see my father's face in your face, your eyes." He paused. "You have auburn hair, though, and a woman's chin." He chuckled and shifted his weight from one side to the other.

"So you might be my half-brother?" The words were a tectonic plate shift for her.

"Listen." Takami looked around and tugged his earlobe. "I have to get home to my wife and kids now. I want to talk more. Can we meet for coffee or something?"

Nora grabbed Jae Kane's shoulders after the show, her words rushed and loud. "If it hadn't been for you asking me to play, I never would have met my brother. I have a brother, Jae Kane."

"Okay, okay – " Jae backed away from the weight of Nora's hands. "But my show had a good turnout, you think? I sold a few pieces, thanks for asking."

"His name is Takami and he has a letter and it might have been one my father wrote."

Jae gave up talking since Nora was beyond listening to any conversation about the show.

Reo approached them. "I'm tired. Let's go home and pop open a beer."

24

Nora

1970

Takami and Nora arranged to meet at a coffee shop not far from the Navy docks. Nora's face lit up when Takami walked over and sat across from her with his coffee. "I want to see him."

Takami looked irritated at the way Nora jumped in without even a hello, but he shrugged. "My father never mentioned another woman before he met my mother, but I'm sure she was – striking if she looked like you."

"I often asked what my father was like, but Mother rarely spoke of him and I was so young. When she did, I would hang on to every hint. I know they met in Michigan at a university there. She heard him speak once at a political rally."

Takami laughed. "That sounds like my dad." He opened two packets of sugar at the same time. Not quite all of it made the coffee cup.

"He was a lifeguard at the university pool. She went there when he was on duty."

"Oh, god, the man could swim." He stirred the coffee. "I can think of a few stories. There was this one from before I was born. He told it to so many people who came by the house, that it's easy to remember. It starts out after he was freed, after the war when he came here to work on the railroad like his grandfather. When they refused him for being Japanese, he tried the Navy docks. They would have refused him too, but before they said no, he dove in with his clothes on and showed them how long he could stay underwater. They had never seen anything like it, so they hired him.

"That didn't keep the other guys from giving him hell. He put up with a lot back then. At the ILWU, the Longshoreman's Union, Dad would give speeches after work. We'd go for walks and he'd tell me our souls were scarred. He'd rest his hand on his heart, and say that didn't mean we were less worthy than other people.

"After hearing that story for years, parts of it sank in. I never did what Dad did, but I know what the union men meant to him." He gripped his coffee cup.

"Tell me more."

"Security came to some of his speeches and the police hauled him off to jail more than once. One time there was a scuffle and he suffered some minor scrapes, but before they put him in the cell, one cop yelled, "Anarchist," and sliced his forehead above his eye." Takami drew his fingers across his forehead. "No one saw him do it, so it was Dad's word against the cop's. Dad said his days in jail were about justice. He carried that scar his whole life like a medal of honor."

Nora watched the waitress refill his cup. She knew the answer to her question but was afraid to ask. "When did he die?" The question hung in the air.

Takami answered with difficulty. "There was a heart attack last year."

"Oh Takami," For a moment she couldn't speak but shook her head. "I have to tell you I've been dreaming of finally meeting my father." Her throat felt too tight to speak. She drank from her cup and waited. "When I was a kid, I ran away and took a bus from Michigan to Chicago with nothing but my violin. I believed if I became good enough I could earn enough money to travel to California to find him." She searched his face to see if he thought she was crazy, but he was listening. "All these years, I think I believed that everything would change if I could find my father. If I'd known about you last year – "

Takami looked uncomfortable.

"You miss the dad you grew up with and I want to know everything I can," she said. Nora tried to picture her dad leaving his home for a country where he didn't know the language, risking his life in a dive, shouting his moral convictions to other workers. "Do you have a picture of him?" She looked at Takami's dense hair parted on the left, wondering if she might possibly see a hint of what her father had been.

Takami hadn't thought to bring a picture. The family had some of them in albums at home, photos on vacations, with the kids, at holiday dinners. He brought out his wallet. "It's not the best." He removed one bent black and white photo of his dad in a diving suit, apparatus in hand.

"He looks so serious," Nora said, looking back and forth between the photo and his son sitting opposite her. "Was that the scar

over his eyebrow?" The picture was too far away to tell, even though she held it and studied it for some minutes. A half-smile seemed to cross Takami's face but he didn't answer. "I think you have the same ears," she said.

"I don't know. Dad says – said I have my mom's eyes." Takami contemplated. "You don't smile much, but your eyes do, like Dad's."

'Those shoulders." Nora said. "One of the few things Mother said was that he looked just like the heartthrob from a movie she saw, *Bridge on the River Kwai*. She'd get this faraway look when she talked about him." Nora wanted to keep the photo, but it was too much to ask.

Takami chuckled. "That would be Sessue Hayakawa. Dad didn't believe it when people said he looked like a movie star. Mom would tease him."

"And I can see you look like his picture."

"Not that it impressed my wife. She will have none of it."

"Did your dad have a favorite child?"

"Not a favorite. Only me." Takami looked at Nora, but she didn't seem offended.

"My grandmother had a favorite son, my uncle Daniel. He died of pneumonia, but she made it clear that he should have lived instead of my mother." Nora thought of her grandmother's rant against Kioshi but refused to burden Takami with more.

"I bet he would have loved it to have a daughter. We didn't play much music around the house, but he would have been proud of you."

Nora beamed at the thought of basking in a parent's pride.

After another coffee came more childhood stories, Startled when he looked at his watch, Takami admitted he had to get back to the human resources department. "I almost forgot the letter. My mom found it after Dad - left us and kept it in case Ruth's family ever found him. If I told Mom about you, I'm sure she'd agree that you should have it." He handed Nora an envelope, dog-eared and fragile, then reached for his jacket.

"Takami, do you have to go?" She looked down at the letter in front of her. "The picture, and now this - could you stay while I read it?" Nora asked.

"Wait a sec – " Takami went to the back of the coffee shop where there was a payphone to call his office.

My Darling Ruth,

So much has happened. Did your mother give you my last letters? I hope to hear from you soon. I hope this will be the last time they move me, so you can write to me here at the address on the envelope. Soon the war will be over and all of this will go away. As I said before, the food and conditions at the last camp made us sick.

My friend Aito's daughter was near death. Worry was hard on all of us. When I told the families in our cabin that we must tell the commander we need safe food, I was taken to the commander's office. I filled out a loyalty questionnaire. It was worded very badly. They said my answers were not loyal, and I was troublesome and unruly, so I was sent here to the isolation camp, Tule Lake.

Here we work in the fields all day as farm laborers. Now we are harvesting potatoes so work days are longer. It is crowded and dirty, yet we make our voices heard, even here. We work hard in the fields and show them this is what we do for our country. There are German and Italian prisoners here too and guards are everywhere. We are Americans! Yet they treat us no different from the foreign prisoners who fought against our country.

My dear, when I fall into my bunk at night so tired I don't even hear those around me, I dream of you and the time we will be together again. I will work with the railroad. You will find work in a beautiful California art museum and we will be happy you and me.

I hold you in my thoughts with love and devotion,
Kioshi

She gripped Takami's arm as she turned over the envelope and read her mother's name over her grandmother's Michigan farm address. In block printing across the bottom of the envelope, Grandmother had written: DECEASED Return to sender. The date was June 1945, years before Takami was born. Nora's mind swirled. The date of the postmark was the summer she lived in the barn with her mother, the summer her mother cried for Kioshi when she thought Nora was asleep.

"He didn't forget my mother, Takami."

He stretched out his hand to meet hers.

"I want to know more. I feel like I'm near the end of a Sherlock Holmes mystery when he reveals all the steps and everything becomes clear. Tell me another story."

"Wait a minute. Who cares about Sherlock Holmes? Haven't you read Matsumoto's "The Face?" Takami was dismayed that Nora shook her head. "I'll get you a copy. An English copy. You have to read "The Face."

Nora didn't argue, but she was more interested in prying open Takami's memories. "Okay, one more story." He drank and the waitress topped off his cup. "Here's what it was like having him as a dad. He'd tell us stories about his work diving around the warships, so when he got serious and told me it was time that he would teach me to swim, I was scared. What if I disappointed him? He was like the superhero of diving to me." Takami paused to make the memory as clear as he could for Nora.

"It was early morning at the public pool. The water was freezing but it was peaceful. He talked about a starfish from the *National Geographic* magazine. Be the starfish, he said. So I stretched out my arms. I looked into his face, so calm and quiet, and I imagined I was the starfish and it felt like a rippling blanket of water was holding me up. Dad screamed and scared me, so I drew in my starfish legs and sank like a rock. He picked me up and hugged me. 'My Takami, my Takami,' he said. 'You did it. You can do it again.' So we did."

Nora heard Takami's sentimental voice.

"Later when I'd get in trouble fighting at school or taking all the TP in the house to decorate a friend's trees, he'd be furious. I'd say, let's go for a swim. It worked at first, but then he knew I was just distracting him. I still can't go for a swim without thinking of him."

Nora imagined she was the starfish being guided by her father. She imagined how a father's hug would feel, what he would have said if he had known about her life with Grandmother, the school in Chicago, or if he could have heard her play with the symphony.

"You are a missing piece to my puzzle, Takami."

"This is unreal." Takami grabbed his jacket and stood. "Next time we have to go to the Japanese Museum. But first, you'll have to meet my wife. The noisy kids too."

"Name the time. I'll be there."

Takami shifted into his serious voice. "Not my mother, though. I can't tell her yet. It would kill her."

"But I was born before he met your mother."

"You don't know my mother."

"I can understand that. But I would like to thank her for the letter."

"Come to the house for dinner. I'll get out the old photo albums and you can see Dad bowling, making dim sum, diapering the kids - "

"Bowling?"

"He was on a team from work. He was pretty good too. He didn't have a lot of work friends, and this was one place he could almost be himself." Takami waved goodbye, admitting he was impossibly late for work.

Nora sat with her coffee staring at the letter. The photo of her father, now engrained in her mind, didn't look like the father in her imagination. It was like reading a book before seeing the movie. The movie actor was never the same. She refused to think about all she had done to find her father. But now there was Takami and his family – her family. Kioshi Iguro was her father. She was sure of it. He survived the camps, and still, he knew how to be a good dad. Nora folded the letter and held it close.

25

Nora
1970

"My birthday party's on Saturday. Can you come?" Susan snapped the latches on her violin casese at the end of her lesson.

Nora looked at Susan's mother standing at the door ready to take her home and didn't know how to respond.

"Susan has been talking about it all the way over here," Mrs. Walker said. "She'd really like it if you could come. I would too." Nora still hadn't answered.

"It's not just kids, the parents will be there too – just drinks and dinner, gifts and cake, that's all. What do you think?"

Nora felt uncomfortable, but she had known the Walkers for two years now, watching Susan grow into a promising young violinist. "How can I refuse?" she said to Susan. "Let's celebrate your big day."

Jae Kane drove, having had clients in the neighborhood. Neighborhoods like this were not concerned with equity, she said, but they liked art. The house was imposingly formal with tall columns and spiraling topiary trees lined the curved drive. "If I don't hear from you, I'll be back at eleven," Jae said.

Nora walked up the wide front steps and smoothed her dress. Inside, the foyer was already filled with adults in black-tie attire. Had they been invited earlier? Nora was relieved she had worn a simple black dress instead of something more casual, but she was puzzled by the lavish display for a child's birthday. From what she knew of Susan, a lover of her stuffed hound dog puppy and Little House books, this didn't look like her idea.

"Miss Nora, you made it!" Susan bounded up beside her with her usual energy.

"Happy birthday, Susan. I bet you're excited."

"Daddy said he has a surprise for me after dinner," she said.

The guests were making their way into the long dining room under light from chandeliers, each table setting marked with a name card. As guests found their places, nearly every seat was accounted for, but Nora was still looking for her name. Mr. Walker took her elbow and guided her, not unkindly, to the hallway. "Miss Nora, I hope you understand, when Susan invited you, my wife had already arranged for the caterer. It's $500 a plate. Do you understand?"

Nora realized she was supposed to say something. "What do you mean?"

"I don't have room for you here. You can eat with the children in the kitchen." He shifted on his feet and gave her elbow a pat. "Run along to the kitchen now." Mr. Walker didn't wait for her response. He turned and walked back to his guests.

Nora didn't know whether to scream or laugh. Maybe he wanted her to put on a uniform and help serve. Mrs. Walker asked her to be here. No, she could handle this. Making a scene at Susan's expense was senseless. This patronizing elbow patter was the problem, not her promising student. She could get through this evening for Susan.

In the kitchen were eight children tucking into plates of mac and cheese with little hot dogs. Dozens of waitstaff, one for every two guests in the dining room, left and returned in succession behind them. "You must be Susan's friends. How's your mac and cheese?" Nora was determined to be friendly.

"What are you doing here? You're supposed to be at the adult table," a serious boy asked.

"I was so well-behaved out there, that they told me I earned the privilege of eating in here with you," Nora said.

After a pause, the children laughed, and Nora did too. One of the cooks placed a plate of mac and cheese in front of her, and she dug in with gusto. Dinner table conversation spiraled into knock-knock jokes, then riddles. What is black and white, and red all over? The serious boy took a second helping of mac and cheese. "Jeremiah was a bullfrog…" Nora sang. The boy tapped the back of his fork and sang along. The others added "Joy to the world…all the boys and girls…" and the table was rocking with giggles and drum-like taps from children freed of dinner table rules.

"You've kept these kids better occupied than I could," one of the cooks behind Nora whispered in her ear. Tongs reached around her shoulder and a plump langostino landed on her plate.

As the children grew full, Susan's face peeked around the corner. "Please come into the gathering room for cake and presents," she said in her most shy voice. Nora noticed her smile was gone. Maybe the children's camaraderie looked more inviting to her than being the guest of honor at her father's table.

Nora told the cook how much she enjoyed the tasty crustacean and the cook returned her thanks with a wink. Nora turned to the children. "Let's go see the grand opening," she said, and the children bounced around her down the hall.

The gathering room was filled with guests holding their after-dinner drinks and making echoes of small talk between puffs of cigar smoke that drifted to the high ceiling. On one wall under a hanging lamp shooting byzantine spots of light and shadow beneath it, stood a table with a four-layer birthday cake bearing Susan's name. A few pieces had been cut and a woman in a dark dress with a white collar stood behind to cut more pieces. No one seemed to notice the cake. "At least there are two of us," Nora said to the woman behind the table. The woman, also Japanese American, looked directly at her and nodded without comment. From above, spots of light glared over her in harsh light.

In one corner backlit by floor-to-ceiling windows, a tuxedoed pianist played a gleaming grand piano. In the opposite corner sat Susan on a folding chair, opening gifts alone. "There she is," Nora pointed out to the children, as they discovered circuitous routes through the crowd to sit before her on the floor.

Susan tore into wrapping paper now that her friends were near and thanked the children for the contents of the boxes. "This one's from Miss Nora," she announced. When she pulled a wooden obelisk from the box, the children were puzzled.

"What's that?" A girl with glasses asked, settling a Madame Alexander doll in her lap.

Susan knew just how the wooden piece worked. "We use this during my lessons. You set it like this." She set it on the end table beside her and removed the wood cover. After a careful pause, she slid the weight down the pendulum. Holding the top carefully, she wound the key on the side. "It's a metronome. It's beautiful, Miss Nora. I love it."

Nora smiled as the measured click of the mechanism resonated around them.

"What is that sound?" Her father appeared. "That's most annoying, Susan. We have guests. Turn that thing off. What kind of a gift is that for a child?"

"But it's from Miss Nora," Susan said.

"Turn it off now." Mr. Walker gave her a look and hurried off.

Mrs. Walker came to sit with Susan as she opened the last few presents. She put her arm around her daughter. "Your father would like you to play your violin for everyone now."

"Oh, Mama. not here." A look of panic crossed Susan's face. "What should I do?" Mother and daughter looked at Nora.

Nora tried to figure out why a father would treat his daughter like a show pony. Was this the surprise he had promised her? Her mind cataloged the pieces Susan had practiced. "Susan, remember that Bach concerto in A major? You liked it so much that you showed me how you had memorized it."

"But what if I forget?"

"You'll have a piano to fill in for you. Let's go talk to the pianist." She took Susan's clammy hand and gave it a reassuring squeeze.

Mr. Walker tapped his glass with a spoon from the bar and announced that his accomplished daughter would now play for their entertainment. Waitstaff brought in folding chairs like the one Susan sat on and within minutes, everyone was seated in uniform rows.

Nora tuned Susan's violin while she gave some instruction to the pianist, and he nodded. "We're ready when you are," he told Susan.

Nora registered the fearful look on Susan's face and fought the desire to rush to her and enfold her in her arms. Instead, she handed her the violin. 'You know this," she winked.

Susan remembered the shortened version of the concerto with reasonable accuracy, the nimble pianist filling in the rest and ending the piece with a few grand chords. The guests applauded with polite but tepid enthusiasm.

"And now," Mr. Walker stood before them like a carnival barker and cleared his throat without a word to Susan. "My daughter's teacher, Miss Nora will perform for us. Miss Nora is a principal violinist with the Los Angeles Symphony, and she has a great piece picked out for us. Miss Nora?"

Nora was stunned. He may as well have asked the bartender to make a flaming drink before his guests, or the chef to prepare a pufferfish on the spot. She had to remind herself that this was Susan's day, not her father's. "I have something else in mind," Nora joined Susan and her father in front of the piano. "Do you have a second violin in the house?"

Nora had heard that lawyers never asked a question they couldn't already answer, and she knew there were two violins. Susan

talked about how her mother had played in high school and college. "I'll get it for you," Mrs. Walker stood up and headed to the foyer staircase.

"Susan, do you remember our duet from last month? The variations on "Turkey in the Straw?"

"I love that one!" Susan beamed.

Mr. Walker cleared his throat. "That's not what I meant."

Nora continued addressing the guests and ignored him. "I'm sure you're familiar with this folk tune, but our version is a little different. See if you can find the tune in our variations," she told the guests as a teacher would.

"I told you." Mr. Walker pointed at Nora.

"Ah, here it is," Nora held out her hands to accept Mrs. Walker's instrument.

"I haven't played in a while, but I tuned it as best I could," she said.

Nora nodded to the pianist. "Key of C," she said.

"Let's have some fun," she whispered to Susan. Nora lifted the right-handed instrument and played a long, exaggerated first note for comic effect, then ripped through half of the melody with breakneck speed. She stopped and looked at Susan, who picked up the tune, tapping her foot to the beat. Nora noticed Mr. Walker paced behind his guests, hands folded behind him, looking ready to burst.

The second variation had a waltz-like lilt, and the two of them sashayed from side to side animating the rhythm with their dance and their violins. The pianist, not to be outdone, began swaying on his bench as well. Nora remembered to smile and the pianist, with a few simple chords, seemed to be relaxing into the rhythm as well. Glancing at Susan, she saw the fear recede as the girl concentrated on the dance and her fingers, instead of her father's friends.

For the last variation, the two of them stood like wooden soldiers in a cuckoo clock, bending their knees in alternate rhythms all the way to the harmonic last note. When the echo ended, they each plucked two strings and took elaborate bows. Nora turned to Susan to shake her hand, clearly enjoying what was more of a game than a performance. Nora heard the laughter of the guests as well.

Once more, Mr. Walker appeared beside them with a quizzical look. "And now Miss Nora will play – "

"I'm sorry, Mr. Walker, but I really must go." Nora turned to Susan. "Happy birthday, dear. Our duet was so much fun."

Susan looked up with grateful eyes. Nora ignored Mr. Walker's entreaties and made her way to the telephone in the kitchen for her ride home.

Jae Kane noticed how quiet Nora was on their drive back to her apartment. Nora's hands were clasped and her shoulders rounded.

An earwig crawled across the car windshield. Trapped inside the window, Nora slammed it with the heel of her hand.

26

Nora

1970

Nora placed full blame for her ordeal on guest conductor Von Karajan, who ruled the podium like the Austrian *Anschluss* officer. Ruby, the violinist next to Nora, also worked as a translator. In a nervous whisper, she called him a *Heckenschütze*r. "What's that?" Nora asked. "He's a sniper. He's ready to ambush us," she whispered.

Rather than draw feeling from his musicians, he preferred to bully it out of them. In a capricious tantrum, he demanded Nora play a solo over again, railing about her incompetence after each repetition. Von Karajan believed in his command of English but the orchestra struggled to understand his accent, especially when it was barked at them. He would circle his finger in the air and say, "It depends on! See?"

As closely as Nora and the orchestra listened, von Karajan never revealed what it depended upon. He shook his head and mumbled, "My woman before ten years," or "My woman make task." Ruby believed he was talking about his wife, but couldn't be sure.

Tension built up to the seventh repetition. Nora glared at Von Karajan and he locked eyes with her. He returned his gaze to the conductor's stand and tapped his baton, ruffling pages of music. After they played the passage one more time, Von Karajan declared Nora's solo sublime and the rehearsal ended.

Relieved, Nora relaxed her aching arms and whispered to Ruby, "Wasn't that just like the first one I played?"

Before Ruby could answer, an extra viola player hired for this concert approached Nora. "You know, the way you stared him down, there's not a lot of Japaneseness about you."

"Japaneseness?"

"Yeah, you know, you don't act Japanese."

"And how would I do that?"

She fidgeted with the hem of her blouse. "Oh, that didn't come out right. I'm so embarrassed."

Ruby turned to look at the woman, but Nora stayed silent.

"Can you forgive me? I really didn't mean to sound that way."

It's all about her, Nora thought. She looks in the mirror and sees her birthright-to-be-forgiven reflection. "We're all more than our heritage. Sure. It's okay." This woman would never know the feeling of passers-by who instantly looked away, or worse, stared as if she had grown another head.

The woman's hand flew to her breast as if a priest had absolved her with Hail Marys. "Thanks." She gave a confused smile and waved off.

Dragging herself home, Nora unlocked her door, kicked off her shoes, and poured a glass of wine. Pushing away her laundry basket of yesterday's clothes from the dryer, she plunked down to read her mail. A colorful postcard caught her eye and she pulled it from the bills and ads. Bursts of blossoms covered the trees and picnickers sat beneath them on blankets. Puzzled, she turned the card over.

Greetings from NYC, the card read. It mentioned a picnic in this place, a botanical garden in the Bronx, and compared it to Huntes Garden where she had walked with James after the *Black and White* performance. His crabbed signature read, *Thinking of you, James.*

Nora sprang from the sofa and looked at her door, the one he had slammed shut years ago. She pulled the chair from her desk and gathered paper and pen. The garden on the postcard wasn't tropical, but it did remind her a bit of Huntes Garden. She wrote a page, then tossed it in the basket only to write another.

Their university basic harmony class came to mind and she wrote without stopping, It was a killer 8:00 class and she usually studied in the library across the street for an hour in the morning so she didn't wake her roommate. Taking 19 credits that term made her chronically tired. Professor Sanderman taught from a lit stage with a piano and a chalkboard on rollers. His hundred students sat in the audience seats beneath him. More heads would have nodded off, except for his seating chart method of calling on students at random throughout the lecture. "I said, Miss Iguro, what about the exposition in Beethoven's violin concert?"

James turned to her and elbowed her awake. "Some called it the crazy quartets in Beethoven's time," Nora babbled while she thought up an answer. What had Sanderson asked again? "Some refused to play it because of so many runs in high registers. The double exposition or ritornello in the first movement is in 4/4 time."

"Correct, finally, Miss Iguro. Furthermore ..."

Nora blinked at James as the lecture continued. He smirked

back. That night they drove to the 7-Eleven to get a Slurpee, but they waited in the car until Donna Summer's "I Feel Love" was over. Nora listened to James explain what a Moog synthesizer was, but she didn't want to let on that she'd never heard of one and moved the conversation to feeling invisible in her music classes. James didn't care if she didn't know a sine wave from an oscillator. He listened.

"These are the seventies. We have to open the blinds so they'll see us," she said with more conviction than she felt.

More than a few glasses of wine later, she had written the pages she wanted to send. She looked back at the postcard. There was no return address.

27

Nora
1970

Her hand was poised to knock on the door when it flew open. Nora blinked. "You're Takami's wife. He told me so much about you," She dropped her arm and felt like she had struck out already with a greeting as lame as that.

The short, wiry woman, looked her up and down. "Call me BL," she said, her dark eyes peering at Nora.

A chill ran up Nora's spine. BL snatched the flowers Nora had brought with her and disappeared into the kitchen. Alone in the front hall, Nora didn't know whether to follow BL or try to find Takami. Then she heard the kids' voices in the backyard and found the back door that would lead her to them.

"Give it back."

"I won't. You took it."

"Whose is it?" Nora asked about the ball between them.

They looked up. "Who are you?"

"I'm joining you for dinner." She took a seat around a picnic table. "Your father invited me. I'm Nora." She wasn't sure if Takami had revealed anything more, so she kept it simple.

"Nora, Tak took my soccer ball."

"Did not. I found it. The neighbors kicked it over the fence." He pointed. "Finders keepers."

His little sister frowned and folded her arms.

"Lili, you think if you make that face you can get your way. It won't work." Tak said.

"I see you've met the kids," Takami said, closing the door behind him.

Nora could see his shiny hair and assumed correctly he'd just gotten out of the shower. "I've met BL, Tak, and Lili," Nora shifted around the bench to face him.

"Why'd you invite her, Dad?" Tak asked.

Nora felt out of place with Tak's question. Her eyes scanned the backyard as she thought of making a run for it.

Takami took in a breath. "I'm glad you asked me, Tak."

Nora wondered if this might be one of the most uncomfortable evenings since Susan's birthday party. Maybe BL had just gotten the news too.

Takami sat on another picnic bench around the backyard table and drew his children near. "Let me tell you about Nora – "

The children forgot about the soccer ball and listened to every detail as their father relayed the story of how he met his half sister.

He took their grandfather's picture from his wallet and told them this was Nora's father too. "Now look at Grandfather's eyes and Nora's eyes. They're the same."

The children and Takami studied Nora's eyes and looked back at the picture. They nodded.

Lili looked into Tak's eyes. "They're your eyes too, Tak."

"Are not," Tak shook his head.

"Now when you miss your grandfather – "

"But Grandfather is – " Tak interrupted.

"As I was saying, you can look at Aunt Nora's eyes and think of him being right here in our hearts."

Nora melted at those words. Her desire to flee vanished. The look on the children's faces convinced her she wasn't leaving for anything.

"Aunt Nora," Lily said the words, getting used to them. "Does that mean she'll be around for my birthday?" Lili asked her father.

"If she wants to be," Takami answered.

"Does that mean she has to give us Christmas and birthday presents?" Tak had a new spark in his eye.

"I don't know," Nora looked thoughtful. "I've never bought gifts for children before. I might pick out the wrong thing." She winked at Takami.

"We can give you lists," Lili offered. She looked at Tak and he nodded.

Nora laughed and it was decided. The children had a new aunt. BL would be another matter.

28

Nora

1970

Takami and Nora weren't sure what to expect at the Japanese Museum. It was only open on Saturdays and Nora had an afternoon practice followed by a concert, so their time window was limited. They walked up the slate steps to face two imposing hand-carved doors. The round windows beside them reminded Nora of owl eyes. Inside were shoji screens and a mixture of old and new Japanese art.

The assistant at the information desk was talking on the phone, so they paused before an embroidered silk art mural. Nora marveled at the thousands of tiny stitches, like grains of rice that told a story - people at a river, warriors engaging in battle, a tea house scene with a bridal couple in elaborate ceremonial dress. A card on the wall explained the work. With an elbow to Takami's side, she pointed, "Look – 900 years old."

The assistant ended her call and welcomed them. Nora half expected her to wear a more traditional dress, but she wore street clothes as they did. At their request, her greeting changed to a look of heightened awareness. "Come this way," she said.

Down a narrow hallway lined with silk ink drawings was the desk marked "Supervisor." Before they sat down, the supervisor asked them what they needed. Nora and Takami repeated the background
information about their father and mentioned every relevant detail they could remember about Kioshi. The supervisor nodded and looked back and forth between them.

"Here's his picture shortly after his internment was over," Takami removed the black and white picture from his wallet. She held the picture carefully and studied it. Without a word, she disappeared. On one wall were photographs of Japanese American soldiers from WWII. "Takami, I don't understand. They fought in WWII?"

"Tens of thousands of Japanese fought while tens of thousands of others were in the camps. The fighters were called the *'Nisei'* soldiers, I think. I didn't listen much when Dad explained about them. Hard to figure, isn't it." They sat for so long that Nora thought the supervisor had forgotten about them.

At last, she returned carrying a faded, green ledger book. "You saw the Niseis?" she said as they turned their attention from the wall photos.

"Dad said *Nisei* meant yes/no."

"Yes/no was the answer the soldiers wrote on loyalty questionnaires. Some questions could be used against them whatever they answered. In the end, over 30,000 Japanese men served in Europe during the war," she said. The supervisor turned to the ledger and with a practiced hand, gently turned the pages to the year 1943. "Let's see what we can find." Her finger traced names down a page.

"Tule Lake had 74 residential blocks. In each block, there were 14 residences or barracks." She turned a few more pages, her finger tracing down the page. The camp was supposed to house 12,000 people, but more busloads came, and at one time, there were over 18,000 housed there, mostly US citizens. Some were German prisoners. Overcrowding meant a high risk of infectious diseases."

Her hand stopped at the list of names in cabin 14-L. "Here we are - Kioshi Iguro Barracks L. It looks like he was transferred here. Tule Lake was one of the harshest internment camps. He could have angered a previous camp director." She looked up at both of them. "By no means does it suggest he was a criminal."

She turned the book in their direction so they could read the information for themselves. Takami noticed someone familiar among the list of names. "Jack Soo!" Takami's eyes widened. "Is this the actor? He was in the same barracks as Dad?"
The supervisor nodded. "One and the same."

"Who is he?" Nora looked at Takami.

"Do you ever watch the TV show, *Barney Miller*? Jack Soo plays Nick, the officer who makes the terrible coffee." Takami chuckled. I love watching him. He doesn't play some token sensei or evil samurai. He's just a funny, regular guy.

The supervisor smiled. "He's known for that. He only accepts acting roles as an American, not a stereotype."

"Dad never mentioned him. I wonder if he knew?"

The supervisor closed the book. "Come with me to our library. I have some books that might be more helpful to you."

The library was small, the size of a bedroom, with four walls of shelves, piled high with books of all sizes. The supervisor invited Nora and Takami to sit at a table while she perused the room, fingers on spines, pulling one book for the table and then another. When she finished, seven heavy books were displayed before them.

Takami sneezed from the dust and the two of them looked up to her for a hint of where to start. "Check the indices first. Look for your father's name, the year, and the name of the camp. Here." She pulled one book to start with. "This gives information for the individual cabins."

Nora didn't notice the supervisor leave them. She found a page about their father's cabin 14-L. "Takami, look – medical records." She pointed to the page. "The *issei no-nos* staged a hunger strike due to complaints regarding medical care. They were penalized an hour a day extra work in the fields farthest from the cabins."

"It looks like most everyone got vaccines for typhoid. They were overcrowded. Look at the other diseases and infections - measles, smallpox, polio, valley fever, whooping cough..." Takami pointed to a list of patients in the infectious disease infirmary for September 1943. "Look - these are the dates he was in the infirmary." Nora pointed to the black ink on the ledger paper line.

Together they scanned the page for more information but found only lists of names. "So he never told you about it?" Nora asked.

"I don't remember him saying anything. Mom didn't say anything either." They stared at Kioshi's name on the page, part of a long list. "When I was young, I'd sit on his lap and touch the scars on his face. I'd ask him where the holes came from. He said they were parts of him that bad people tried to take away, to remove his *seishin*, his soul, heart, his spirit. Then he'd laugh and hug me. "It didn't work, did it? My heart and spirit are here with you."

Nora reached for Takami's shoulder and gave him a hug that surprised them both. "I really must go," she said. "I'll be late for my practice."

"Just one more thing." Takami found another book with a report about the hunger strike. "It looks like Dad started the hunger strike. Look at this." He pointed to the next page. *"...assigned to segregation area for 30 days for disloyalty. Instigated hunger strike."* But look at this part *"Released after ten days. Assigned to infirmary. Smallpox."*

29

Kioshi
Indiana, 1946

With relief, Kioshi looked out the window from his seat on the bus. He could leave the heavy weight of the hunger strike and smallpox behind. When an interviewer from Earlham College in Indiana came to Tule Lake, Kioshi saw it as a chance to escape and find Ruth once more. The officials at Tule were happy to be rid of him. Earlham, a Quaker college, made arrangements for 24 Japanese American students to study there.

Kioshi felt grateful beyond belief. From his talks with some of the men in the barracks, he decided on pursuing a mechanical engineering degree. The long bus ride to Indiana gave him time to think about a new future with Ruth and his career. He daydreamed of developing new methods of propulsion on the ships from the naval yard, similar to one of his barracks mate's careers he had heard about during internment. Kioshi had never dared to hope for such a career, but now, maybe it was possible.

The week of final exams after his first term at Earlham was far different from his experience at Michigan State College. His life on the California docks and through internment gave him a new determination to excel. Kioshi had found new friends, not only among the other Japanese Americans who shared similar stories but among some of the students who invited him to study groups at the library.

The tone of the school was subdued but cautiously hopeful with so many men still returning from the war. He knew better than to talk about unions, wages, or politics. It was a struggle, at times, to resist discussing such things, but he knew his freedom to study depended upon it. On the other hand, he relished the Quaker beliefs of ethics and equality. He would still be at Tule without them.

"Okay, we have to remember that Grant's decision to pair the wooden ships with the ironclads and force their way into the southern port of Mobile, Alabama was a turning point in the Civil

War." Philip, a sophomore who organized the study group and invited Kioshi, gathered his papers to leave. Their final exam in American History 201 was an essay exam, and Philip reminded them to purchase a blue book for their writing. "Professor Hubbard is all about the war's turning points."

"I need to remember that Farragut led the ships after the ship ahead of him was torpedoed," Kioshi said. "Remember 'Damn the torpedoes! Full speed ahead!'"

The young men in the group looked at him in wide-eyed surprise.

"Oh, I meant darn the torpedoes," Kioshi said.

The others laughed in good spirits as they left the library study room. Kioshi swallowed the lump in his throat.

On his way to the campus store to purchase a blue book for his exam, Kioshi froze. A young woman running down the steps of the Runyan Arts building, wavy auburn hair shining in the sun, looked at him. From across the street he watched books and folders drop from her arms and her frantic scramble to gather loose papers. The way she looked when she held her books came back to him. Could it be Ruth? His heart pounded. What would she be doing in Indiana? She was more beautiful than he remembered. Kioshi ran to help her.

30

Indiana, 1946

Ruth smiled to herself as she walked from the front door of Runyan Arts and into the sun. "Ruth, I'd like you to research and write the introductory speech for Eames' lecture on the convergence of art and design. This is important. Are you up to it?" Miss Simmonds the curator asked.

Ruth was ecstatic at her good fortune. Ray Eames was at the top of her field when most famous designers were men. Even if Ruth's assistant curator job was part-time and lasted only a few months, it felt exhilarating to be among college students, working next to the art curator, researching artists and their works.

Conversations with art professors intoxicated and delighted her. Her husband Samuel said he hadn't seen her so happy since they came to Indiana. He found ways to be disagreeable and expressed his displeasure with the hold Earlham College had on his wife.

In her excitement, Ruth ran down the front steps of Runyan, holding tight to her research folders. When she reached the bottom step and looked up, the folders dropped from her arms. She couldn't breathe. It was Kioshi. She was sure of it. He tried to find her. His letters got lost. They could be together! She could run to him now and tell him he had a beautiful daughter, just as she had imagined countless times. Even across the street, she could see his expression. He saw her too.

Her eyes blinked in case she was imagining what she saw. With each blink, a new worry raced through her head. She thought of her fine house, her husband, and his promotions. Was it worth giving it all up for love?

Then she saw Kioshi step toward her from the other side of the street. He broke into a run and she was rattled. Swooping down, she grabbed her folders and ran between buildings far and fast until she was sure he wouldn't follow. One more corner and she ducked down a side street. A panicky look back confirmed he was nowhere to be seen. She stopped to catch her breath, her back against a brick wall, pushing against it, willing herself to disappear. Ruth looked up at the sky and told herself she refused to go back to a life of struggle.

A tear slid down her cheek. Ruth was the different one - the pregnant one, the homeless one, the one married to a Jewish man who weighed each word she said, the one with an Asian daughter who garnered scowls wherever they went together. Here at Earlham, she felt that her work had value. Miss Simmonds approved of her.

The sun beat down, but she stood still as a stone. Surely life with a Japanese husband would never make her feel as if she fit anywhere, despite her work. At least Samuel could pass for a Christian man at the neighbor's barbecue or at the movies. He hid his faith over the risk to his job. Kioshi would never be able to blend in like that. The heat from the brick wall intensified on her back. In her mind, Kioshi's lean body ran toward her. Samuel's double chin touched his chest as he fell asleep in his easy chair. Ruth drew the back of her hand across her eyes, petrified by her decision.

31

Part II

Nora
California, 1975

Nora had taken an extra gig playing in the African Methodist City Hope Church mostly because they told her to play whatever she wanted. "I can back you up on whatever you decide to play," the pianist told her on the phone. She told him her church gigs were usually specific requests, but he responded with a good-natured laugh. How curious! Nora told him she had selected a traditional spiritual first sung by the Fisk Jubilee Singers in 1870, something with history. She anticipated this first performance since paying off the instrument, yet writing the last check seemed like closing the door on any hope of ever seeing the stolen sable violin again.

She expected the church to be a 19th-century towering structure, but this church was small and new. Maybe she should have chosen more contemporary music. Standing alone in the narthex she looked up at two tall windows where light played in geometric angles across the walls and ceiling. She was startled by a strong hand resting on her shoulder. "You must be Miss Nora. We're so glad you're here. Welcome to City Hope and the first service in our new building!"

Nora turned to the group behind her and introductions were made all around. They discussed the piece and the pianist nodded. "That's fine. I'll follow you whatever key you're in," he said.

She walked behind the wiry man who hopped up the steps to the chancel and slid onto the piano bench.

"It's a Bosendorfer," Nora said. "With a sound like this, my violin could be squeaky and asthmatic and we'd still sound phenomenal."

"She's a beauty." The pianist's left hand reached the extra octave at the bottom of the keyboard and struck Beethoven's 5th Symphony notes *Ta Ta Ta Dah*!

The resonant tones filled the small sanctuary. Nora watched the glint of his wedding band as his fingers raced across the keyboard in an arpeggio

"My piano teacher, God bless, is a concert pianist and he donated his personal piano for the new church building."

They had time to run through the song before the worshipers arrived in small groups at first, then in numbers enough to fill every pew. Hers was the first song in the service, "Sometimes I feel like a Motherless Child." Nora wished she had chosen something happier, but the pianist surprised and delighted her with rich, complex harmonies he hadn't used during their run-through. If he knew his wife the way he knew this piano, she must be a very happy woman.

Their melodies encircled one another and echoed throughout the church, imparting a burning despair so real, that Nora felt her heart rearranged. She looked over the worshipers as the last note sighed with an echo and she could see it in their faces too. Instead of ending, the pianist bashed the keyboard like Elton John in "Benny and the Jets." He followed the resounding chord bursting into "Every Time I Hear the Spirit" pushing the rhythm faster.

Nora watched as the congregation rose and began to clap and sway in rhythm. He nodded, inviting her to play along. Music that began as soulful and reflective ended in a celebration of kinship and connection, or *kyosei* as Saiko taught her. Before she took her seat, she caught the pianist's eye. She whispered, "you breathe music through your fingers."

His eyes crinkled. "You too."

With a nod and a smile, a choir member gathered her robe to make room for Nora on the bench. A muscular man with a resolute expression nearly floated to the lectern in front of her, his billowing white robe and rainbow-hued stole trailing at his back.

"One drop." Pastor Jeremiah pounded the lectern and the sound echoed.

A few *Amens* rumbled.

"In the early times when violence enslaved us, one drop of Black blood imprisoned you, confined you, locked you up, an enslaved person in this country."

He looked around the sanctuary. "What choice did we have? We could fume, seethe, storm, boil, rant, roar, sputter? Blow a fuse, have a fit, go off the deep end?"

The congregation shook their heads. *Unh uh.*

"When our church burned," he slammed his fist on the pulpit once more, "that was violence pure and simple. But here we are, our spirit rebuilt with hope, courage, and a testament to overcoming suffering. We gonna breathe fire, be wild, spit feathers?" He looked around the room. "Lawd no! What good goin' back? Violence is evil. We go forward with one drop – one drop of forgiveness. Forgiveness comes back to ourselves, our souls. By the grace of God, we are still here. They could not break us."

Nora stopped listening. It was too much. They had their church, their place of renewal and affirmation, destroyed. Yet what she saw in their faces inspired her. The people refused to give up or give in. Music catapulted in her mind, this rising up feeling. If she was anywhere else, she would have dashed to find her pencil and staff paper, to capture these faces in musical notes on a page.

"This highway that splits our neighborhoods? The city planners say it clears out blight. What blight? These are people's communities. Family businesses were cared for with pride. This is how our neighborhoods get lost and spread out like the diaspora after the Civil War, Go find another place to live when redlining says no you can't live here.

"This urban renewal is urban destruction. And it's not just here in Fountain Valley, no! It's in Syracuse, New York, and Flint, Michigan. Miami could have followed an old railroad line, but no, they slapped down their freeway right through the Harlem of the South. Nashville, Montgomery, Washington D.C. too. These were solid neighborhoods - blocks of family homes gone." Pastor Jeremiah shook his head. "They run highways through our homes." He looked up and reached his hands out. " But our church is still here."

That afternoon, Nora slapped a piece of staff paper on her desk and sharpened a pencil, ready to write the notes that might re-create the weight of the pastor's sermon. Her fist slammed the desk as the pastor's fist had. She brewed tea and paced the floor. Still, no musical notes journeyed from her mind.

32

Nora

1975

Dinner for one wasn't her favorite way to cook, but Nora pushed herself to experiment with new foods when she had an excuse. The farmer's market had an endless array of fresh produce, in all its vibrant colors, and she wanted to sample it all. On her way home from a rehearsal, she decided to stop off and browse the market for something different.

Tonight Takami had invited her for a spur-of-the-moment dinner after Lili's first soccer game of the season. Nora decided to take a fresh fruit salad, like one she'd made earlier just for herself. When she thought she had chosen everything she'd need, she smelled jackfruit. She was sure Tak and Lili would love it since it smelled like Juicy Fruit gum. As she waited for the vendor to cut a thick slice of the heavy fruit for her, she saw an elderly Asian woman with her cane walk up and sniff the air.

"I smell rotten onion and pineapple." She wiggled her nose.

"I smell bubble gum," Nora said.

The woman watched as the vendor wrapped the shiny slice with its nubbly skin and handed it to Nora. "My brother grows these in his backyard in Okinawa. I hope they taste better than they look."

Nora told her it would be the star of her fruit salad. On the way to her own apartment, the bags of fruit swinging from her hand, she was afraid she'd missed the soccer game. In the kitchen, she whirled from sink to chopping board to bowl, rushing to make it in time for Takami's dinner.

"Lili, what's going on?" Nora was surprised to see Takami's daughter greet her at the door with Rocky in a cage.

"Oba-san Nora, let me tell you!" Lili took Nora's arm and the cage handle with the other. She led Nora to the living room.

"No chickens in the house," BL called, whisking Nora's salad out of her hands as she and Lili made their way to the backyard.

Rocky examined the grass for bugs and pecked through the grates of the cage.

Lili told Nora to sit down on the picnic bench. She stood before her and held Nora's hands. "It was show-and-tell. I brought Rocky and talked about how chickens can be friends with kids. Mrs. Evans let her out of the cage and everyone stood around and started petting her. She was polite, she really was. She walked around to my friends and made her little gurgles. Then Jimmy Puff came up and she started chasing him!

"Uh oh."

"Yes. She knew! Jimmy is mean. He makes fun of me. Somehow Rocky knew and started chasing him around the room. He ran like this. Lili raced across the patio, dodging potted plants and a chaise. All the kids in my class laughed and it was so awesome. Ms. Evans told me to put Rocky back in the cage."

"Then what happened?"

"I looked at Jimmy Puff, and he looked scared. The best part was he didn't say anything to me all day. It was the best day ever!"

Nora laughed. "Lili, I'm so glad it was the best day ever! Jimmy Puff doesn't know what he's talking about. You are beautiful."

"Mama says Jimmy Puff is a jerk and some people are always gonna be like that, but today was my day. I love Rocky!"

After dinner and a replay of Lili's soccer prowess, Nora saw the lunch boxes she gave the kids perched by the kitchen sink. She heard BL's voice in the den asking Tak and Lily pointed questions, nudging them to finish their homework.

Running hot, soapy water, she washed Tak's sticky Batman lunchbox, removing the half-eaten peanut butter and honey sandwich and a few grapes on a stem. When Tak's clean box rested on the drying rack, she reached for Lily's My Kitty lunchbox. It had fewer peanut butter smears but held a torn piece of notebook paper. *I love you from Brice,* it said. A heart was scrawled over the love. Nora dried both boxes, returning the note to Lili's box.

"I see what you're doing," BL appeared from the den. "You just saved me a few precious minutes tomorrow morning. I have to return Rocky to Saiko's backyard before work."

Lili appeared in her pajamas and Tak shortly after. They darted from their dad to Nora, collecting hugs goodnight. Tak raced to a corner bookcase where his He-Man action figure waited. Tak always slept with He-Man. BL rounded them up for a bedtime tuck-in. When the kids were in their rooms, Nora asked, "So who is this Brice in Lili's class?

BL turned her attention from straightening sofa pillows and frowned at Nora. "What have you heard?"

Nora described the note. "I wondered if Lili talked about him."

BL shrugged. "If he passed the Rocky test, he must be a good boy."

That night she returned home much later than she'd planned. Despite the hour, Nora decided to sort through a three-day stack of mail and found a letter from Flo Johnson in Chicago. Their letters had continued since Nora left, and the sound of the paper as she sliced the envelope lifted her spirits.

After skimming through several hand-written pages, she read them a second time. Flo, never short on opinions, commented on yet another postcard Nora had received from James, again with no return address. *Might he be a bit passive-aggressive?* Flo suggested. She wrote about Nora's teen days in the orchestra when James would tease, and Nora knew just the way to tease him back. *He called you the music teacher's pet, and you said if he didn't bother you so much, he could be too. You told him his violin playing made you look good. Back then, you fought fire with fire.*

33

Nora
1980

Saiko decided to have a party at Huntington Beach before the orchestra's next concert. "Four arms are better than two," Saiko said. Nora fastened her seat belt and grabbed the shopping list from the dashboard.

"Did it have to be this early?" Nora said.

Think of it as a celebration. You finally paid off your violin, didn't you?"

A celebration was overdue.

"Here's the *dalgona* candy stand," Saiko said. They each chose a ten-cent disk from the market vendor. Nora pointed to a cooled star from the finished candy, Saiko had an umbrella, heart, and flower. They watched as the stall cook waved a thin layer of the sugar mixture into the pan until it was golden brown. He slid the melted sugar mound mixed in baking soda and plopped it onto parchment. Covering it with oiled parchment, he flattened it with the skillet and pressed in the cookie-cutter design. Nora waited to see if the stall cook would give her a pin to try and carefully piece out the star. "Hey, Saiko, you have a pin?"

If it came out in one piece, she'd get free candy.

"No free candy. Just for kids," the shop owner waved his hand. They moved away with their treats, smacking their lips.

"Wait until you see the fish at this hour," Saiko said. "I found a recipe for poaching it in foil right on the beach grill. It's early enough that we should find the choicest selection."

The market was lively, as it was on many Saturdays. Fishmongers sang, *"Cazon, Cazon Mejor Precio!"* or *"Atún mas fresco!"* In Spanish voices with color and texture and spring, they called out competing prices. A flash of blue caught her eye from a fish held high by its tail in a wild, pendulous swing. The Spanish phrase *el duende* came to mind - a reaction to art, whether it was joy or pain, chills, or pleasure. The fishmongers were like actors on a stage, plying their art with every fish. The expression on customers' faces, hers included, almost promised they'd be back for more. Nora couldn't smell anything fishy at all, even though she was surrounded by varieties of fish - including sea urchins. So unlike a Michigan farm market, this was. She remembered tagging along with Grandmother, the bland root vegetables, and the fishy smell of lake perch. Fountain Valley market fish smelled fresh like the sea.

On a corner in buckets of ice were containers of seafood ceviche in all its tomatoey magnificence. Nora could see the rings of calamari in the containers and backed off. James loved the stuff, but she could never get over the idea of the ingredients. In another stall hung lengths of fresh pasta draped from a wooden pole.

Below them were trays of ravioli stuffed with either cheese, mushrooms, or Italian sausage. At the end of the aisle, a guitarist backed a young woman swaying in a long, colorful sundress. She belted hokey covers of pop songs into a microphone. They stopped in front of a stand to sample wildflower honey on sourdough bread.

"Hey, Nora, you think this bread would go with blue cheese?" Saiko asked.

"Hey, hoe kiss my aura, Nora!"

Nora turned to glare at a man in a black AC/DC shirt. "And you can kiss off!"

"Hey, she speaks English!"

A spray stung Nora's eyes. Saiko grabbed her arm and pulled her back. Wet drips fell from her hair and clothing. "I can't see. My eyes - " Nora's arms reached in front of her. Saiko led her behind the sourdough stall near the owner.

Two voices followed them. "Go home, Jap bitches."

"Dog eater yellow monkeys – "

"Here," the shop owner, a Polynesian woman, gave Nora a towel soaked with water. "Wipe your eyes quick. It's Lysol cleaner they sprayed. They're gone and there's no sense in trying to find them. They know how to disappear in the crowd. They've been harassing us since the news about the auto industry." Nora soaked her eyes and the painful sting made her keep them shut tight. "Saiko, are you here? Are you alright?" Nora asked.

"Just keep rinsing," she said.

The stall owner rinsed the towel in a bucket of water and returned it to Nora's hands. "Again," she said.

Nora blinked her eyes enough to recognize bright flowers on the stall owner's muumuu. The cool water made her eyes feel like she could open them more fully. She was angrier at the harassers than the irritation.

"You don't know, Nora. He might have had a gun. Be careful what you say," Saiko ran her hand through her hair, shaking out her own spritz of Lysol spray. She pulled her t-shirt, now clingy with Lysol, away from her body. Nora looked Saiko over, checking to see if she was hurt in any other way. The stall owner rinsed and handed over the dishcloth. "Again."

"At least we're together," Saiko said.

"This is my fault, Saiko."

Saiko stopped her from her apology. "It's not about fault or blame. I'm sick of it all, the duality, everything. I don't want to talk about it."

Nora ignored her. "Takami loved that movie *Blade Runner* – where the Japanese buy everything and take their jobs. No matter what, we're permanently unforgiven." Nora thanked the stall owner again and held the rinsed cloth to her eyes.

"The factory workers thought their cars would always be number one." Saiko fluttered her t-shirt again. "Their pride was wounded. It's *Jisonshin o torimodosou to suru*. They felt justified in lashing out like Lost Cause Southerners after the Civil War trying to gain back self-respect."

Nora turned to the stall owner and bought two loaves of sourdough. "So they terrorize Japanese women shopping in a farm market."

It was at times like this when Nora returned to the apartment alone that she missed James, the listener. He would have been attentive to her story of the fishmongers, the sourdough, and the Lysol spray guy. James would've liked the black AC/DC shirt. If he was still here, she would have bought that seafood ceviche. Restless, she reached for her violin to fill the quiet room with sound, to fill the hollowness like a recapitulation in the music she practiced, coming back and back again with no end.

Things vexed her like that high school basketball t-shirt James wore for years with its frayed neck and holes on the sides, the one he left in the bottom drawer. From time to time, she slept in that shirt even though she was itching to throw it out. Maybe her decision to stay in California was wrong. The kitchen clock reminded her there was just enough time to make the dish for Saiko.

Everyone but the two of them had left the beach party after the brilliant red-orange sunset dipped its fire below the skyline into the ocean. By the time Saiko and Nora checked the beach for plastic cups and forgotten sunglasses, a few stars were shining. "I'll take these into rehearsal tomorrow," Nora said with her grocery bag half full of miscellaneous containers and one knee brace.

On the drive home, Nora opened the car door at a stop light and tapped the sand out of her beach shoe. "The beach party was a great idea."

"It worked out," Saiko said. "We needed some time out of the rehearsal hall. At first, I thought the June Gloom would ruin the day." Saiko talked about the overcast skies that sometimes overtake the California seaside. "The sky cleared in time and the ocean was a windless calm. We were in a party mood."

Saiko popped a cassette of *Saturday Night Fever* in the player and they sang "Stayin' Alive."

"I'm going to fast forward to Evonne Elliman's tune, "If I Can't Have You." Nora pushed the button. "By the way, your Mahi was delish. The beach grill worked out too."

"Les Harding raved about his fish with mango and a pickle." Saiko laughed and glanced at Nora, who was staring at the road with a glazed expression. "What's the matter?"

"I'm not sure. I think about rehearsal tomorrow, and the next concert, and the next. Remember when you told me I'd better watch out if I lost my passion? I'm trying, but something is missing."

"What's that supposed to mean?"

"It's just that I miss that anticipation before a concert, all the feelings ready to pour into the music. Faking it just won't work. I want my old desire back."

"It's work, Nora. No musician is crazy about every piece of music."

"Remember the composition James made with me? That's the feeling I want back. I need to create music that means something. Maybe with a light show or dancers."

"It's enough for me to make music, but for you, I know it's not enough," Saiko said. "You want to break musical rules and pick up where words leave off, not play notes that someone else wrote. It's the thing you do to take you out of yourself, yes? Like Dorothy's martial arts, Maki's plants, and Jae Kane's welding."

"When I hear a *Black and White* performance, it can't be held or displayed on a shelf or eaten like food, but it can be possessed inside a person anyway. Like the memory of a good book, it can be a part of them." She put her hand on Saiko's arm. "Here's an idea. How about – "

"Don't think about asking me to write. You'd be better off getting the chickens to help you."

34

Nora

1980

Nora arrived at the sound of pounding in Dorothy's spotless kitchen. Maki and Jae took turns with their *kines* pounding the rice dough with an even rhythm on the square butcher block.

"Good timing, Nora. We're almost done," Dorothy said. "Next time you'll do the pounding."

"So what are we celebrating?"

"Jae, did you tell Takami's kids we were making mochi?"

"They'll be over later. He said, 'Isn't mochi a New Year's thing?'"

"Yeah, but who wants to wait until New Year's?"

"Nora, we'll teach you the steps. You missed out on the washing, soaking, and steaming. I started that two days ago. Here. Take the rolling pin." Dorothy cleared a spot on her kitchen counter, carrying away the bowls and measuring spoons left from the dough.

"I don't do pastry."

"Quit whining and take the rolling pin. We've got twenty-four squishy rice balls. Keep them round but roll them flat and even. We're stuffing them with homemade ice cream." She placed a clean pastry cloth on the counter and set to work cleaning the bowls and measuring spoons in hot, soapy water.

Nora took the rolling pin in two hands but pushed down on a ball instead of rolling it.

"What are you doing, you bozo? It's called a rolling pin for a reason." Dorothy's voice betrayed her irritation.

Nora ignored the attitude. "Hey, Jae was pounding it just a minute ago."

"Hurry up, Nora, the ice cream doesn't stay solid as long as the store-bought stuff."

Everyone was waiting for her with their ice cream scoops ready. Clearly, they had done this together more than a few times before, and she was wrecking the production.

"Give me a break. I'm new to this." Uncomfortable with all the attention, she slowly rolled out the dough ball. "Okay, here's one." She peeled the wobbly circle off the pastry cloth and held it out like a soiled rag.

"Oh, no," Maki said. "The ice cream will break through. Try it this way." Maki moved closer to the butcher block. She stood on one foot since standing for long periods was never comfortable for her after the garden pallets episode. With experienced hands, Maki rolled a few times and the dough circle was just thick enough.

"Who's got strawberry?"

"That's me." Saiko scooped a perfect round of ice cream, plopped it in the center of the sticky rice, and sealed the bottom so neatly, that Nora couldn't tell it had a seam. Into the freezer it went, on a cold jelly roll pan.

Dorothy had dried and put away her bowls and spoons with quick efficiency, mumbling about the mess and vowing never to host mochi-making again. Her voice became a shrill accusation. "Faster, Nora, the ice cream is melting!"

Nora was ready to give up, but Maki talked her into rolling the remaining dough circles as the others scooped balls of chocolate, strawberry, or vanilla ice cream into the centers. She paused with her rolling pin, "So did they ever settle the husband's lawsuit over the oleander from your greenhouse, Maki?"

"Still pending," Maki frowned. "He has a new lawyer and they've asked for an extension."

"Is it a flower?" Nora asked.

"It's a tree. They're all over California. I'll show it to you when you pick me up at the greenhouse for the rights protest next week," Maki said. Maki wasn't one to close her shop early for anything.

Jae talked about her protest sign. "End the Violence or Facts not Fear?"

"How about "We are Not a Virus! Racism Is?" said Maki. "What's on your sign, Nora?"

"I'm still deciding. How's this?" She dropped a perfectly flattened ball into Maki's waiting hand.

Dorothy grew quiet. "It's not New Year's, and this isn't a celebration, but the mochi is to make Li feel better."

"What's wrong with Li?" Saiko said.

"It's a buddy from back in Vietnam. Y'know during the war Li didn't even realize Michael was hittin' for the other side if you know what I mean. Not that it mattered to him, but now he has AIDS. It sure mattered to Michael's family. They won't speak to him. So Li goes over to see him once a week and I give him a casserole to take. He doesn't have much of an appetite, but it's something. Michael gets weaker and Li gets madder."

Dorothy passed a sponge under steaming tap water and scrubbed the countertop where it was already scrubbed. "These past weeks hit him hard and Li wanted to do something. He met up with this bunch of California guys who were going to make an example of Jesse Helms. Helms wants to hold up money in the Senate for AIDS research. Li took a few days off work and traded off driving a van with these guys all the way down to Helms' house in North Carolina."

Dorothy had a mischievous smile. "Li said it did them all good, swapping stories all the way to Raleigh. When they got there, they made sure nobody was home. They unfolded a big inflatable they'd made to fit over Helm's house and pumped it up. Li and the older guys held the front. The younger guys hopped up on the roof, then they pulled it down the other side until the house was fully covered. It was a big yellow condom that said something like "Helms is deadlier than a virus" right in the front.

"A giant condom," wide-eyed Maki looked at the other women. "Did they get arrested?"

"They were just finishing up when a cop car pulled up. The cops laughed and didn't arrest anybody. Their rental van was parked too close to a No Parking sign, though, so they got a parking ticket."

"What did Helms say about it?" Jae asked.

"They never saw him in person, but he was furious. He ranted on the Senate floor, calling the guys radicals." She scrubbed the countertop. "It helped Li, ya know? When he told Michael the story, Li said his face lit up. Li had to do something and he fought back, my radical husband."

Nora looked at the faces around her. After all this time, Dorothy could still surprise her.

The back door opened. "Is somebody making mochi?" Tak asked.

"Wash your hands, kids, before you do anything," Dorothy said. "Here's the soap."

Lili saw Nora and raced to her side. "I made the varsity soccer team."

"Fantastic, Lili! You worked so hard. I'm so happy for you." She almost slipped and asked how the violin practice was going. When BL told her that Lili had taken up the violin, Nora was so tickled that she'd nearly mentioned it more than once. BL told her to wait. Lili wanted to improve on her own and then she'd tell Nora when she was ready. Nora tilted her head to touch Lili's without losing her dough-rolling rhythm.

"Next year I'll take driver's training. Then I won't have to wait for Tak to drive me around." She rolled her eyes. "I can listen to 'Teenage Wasteland' all I want instead of his dumb cassettes."

"Okay, now wash." Dorothy led Lili to the sink. "Tak, you're driving? Oh my god! I hope you make it home."

Lily joined her brother who handed her the soap. Dorothy checked their hands before passing them a towel.

"I'll have a chocolate and a strawberry," Tak said.

"Strawberry, *please*." Lili wasn't going to miss out on mochi in the absence of a please or thank you.

35

Nora

1980

Nora, Dorothy, and Jae Kane added their homemade protest signs to the trunk of Saiko's car. Saiko gripped the wheel, annoyed that their drive to pick up Maki at her greenhouse would make them late. When the car pulled up, Nora first saw bags of peat moss, garden stones, and young fruit trees. But as they neared the sign over the door, Enchanted Garden, she marveled at a collection of oleanders. "Look at these blooms," she said to Dorothy.

"Beautiful and poisonous," Dorothy countered. "Hey Maki, what's with the oleanders?"

Maki came to the doorway, wiping her hands on her smudged apron. "They're still good sellers," she said. "Nora, this is the tree that created the lawsuit we talked about." She surveyed the other plants as she talked, removing a broken leaf. "The husband claims it's not murder because I sold him the plant."

Nora tried to imagine how blooming trees could cause a lengthy murder case.

"Before I sell one, I have buyers sign a waiver explaining all parts, the flowers, bark, and leaves, should be handled with gloves only. Touching a leaf, let alone eating one, can lead to illness or – " Maki gestured a knife across her throat. "I have his verified signature."

"Sounds clear cut to me," Dorothy said.

"This case isn't close to ending," Maki said. "We'll have to wait and see." Maki carefully broke off a bare stem from a red and purple fuchsia hanging over her head. "Can you look around for a few minutes? I'm almost done with this terrarium. A customer came in wanting one five minutes before closing, and he can't wait."

Nora wandered through the greenhouse reading labels of plants she'd never seen. True to its name, the greenhouse did have an enchanted feel. From tiny Hobbit jade to pink Medinilla, wherever she looked, a jungle of green, an Eden of surprises. Nora held the tiny orange and pink pindot leaf and gently swept back a long banana plant leaf blocking the walkway, her sandals finding their footing on the pebbles as she walked. A wisteria cascaded in the corner, too big to ever leave the greenhouse but providing shade for the sun-shy coleus below.

She could hear the others talking outside. Making her way further into the greenhouse under a vine-covered arch, she was drawn by the sound of falling water - a collection of flat stones cantilevered into a pool of water lilies and hyacinths with intense, sweet scents. Nora wanted to stop and take it in, but they were already late. The curving stone walkway lined with tiny-leafed ground cover ended at a round stone fountain with just enough moss here and there to make her feel as if she'd just come upon an ancient grotto. Under the highest peak of the greenhouse, a sculpture of a child looked down from the fountain's center, flowers in her hand, releasing a miniature cascade of water that made a calming patter as it fell to the pool below.

"It makes you slow down, watching her, doesn't it?" Maki came up behind her with two small terrarium plants in her hands.

"That's it. She's soothing. I love it here, Maki."

"Thanks." She juggled the plants in her hand to pick up a third small moss plant in front of Nora. "You saw the old wisteria when you first walked in?"

Nora nodded.

"After battling with it the first year, I realized it was past the point of bending to my will. But the ficus here," she pointed with her elbow, "is still malleable. The three trunks I can braid into one trunk - teach it to be stronger and more beautiful as one."

Nora turned from the fountain to look at the ficus with its even braids, about as tall as she was, the picture of leafy grace and strength.

"Now help me finish up so we can get out of here, will you?"

Nora followed her to the potting bench, wincing at the sight of Maki's left foot, still misshapen from the pallets.

Maki gave orders and the women gave up their hopes of hearing the beginning of the rally speeches. Dorothy swept soil, which she said looked like dirt to her, from the cashier area. Saiko trimmed the leggy inch plants that had wandered into the freckle faces below. Nora worked around Maki, under a fragrant pudding pipe tree, gathering the plant waste below Maki's workspace and piling it on the compost in back.

As soon as Maki's terrarium was planted and the sale complete, she made her way to the front to usher the customer out and turn the front door sign to CLOSED.

"Hey, what's the deal?" A woman on the other side of the door looked irritated.

"Sorry - we closed ten minutes ago." She pointed to the hours listed on the door. "See you tomorrow!" Maki waved her off.

Parking near the protest was tight and Saiko finally found a spot on a side street blocks away. They gathered their signs and walked toward the sound of the crowd.

Chants and voices grew louder as they passed more protesters with signs reading, PROTECT ASIAN LIVES, THE EMBARGO HURTS US ALL, THIS IS MY HOME TOO. Dorothy pointed to her favorite so far: LOVE SUSHI - LOVE US!

They carried their signs for blocks. One organizer's voice chanted for a call and response through a bullhorn: STOP ASIAN HATE.

"Maki and Jae, you are courageous to have your own businesses," Nora said. "When people look for someone to blame – "

"We didn't have a choice," Jae said. "When no one will hire you because you're female and Japanese, you start your own business."

Dorothy changed the subject. "I don't need to work, and Li likes me at home." Then her voice changed. "But sometimes I wonder what it would feel like to make my own money."

"Ching chong chink," a child on the sidewalk laughed and pulled the corners of his eyes up with his fingers, staring directly at her.

Nora looked away and thought about Jae's words. The sounds of the protest grew louder. She looked up at her sign "Remember Vincent Chin."

"You know, this isn't our first protest," Jae Kane said. "When was our last one?" She looked at Maki.

"I think it was five years ago," Maki said. "That's when the Toyotas started really selling here. People bought them, but they sure blamed us for it. Do they know American workers build Japanese Hondas in American factories?"

Nora remembered hearing about that weekend. She was playing with a chamber group in San Francisco.

The sounds of anger and yelling grew louder in Nora's ears. The crowd was backing up and she couldn't see what was happening. Police with helmets and bullhorns told people to go home and she could see the top of an officer's baton repeatedly beating down. A collective gasp rippled through the crowd. Only those in front could see, but Nora knew a human being was on the pavement taking blow after blow.

The swell of the crowd pushed her like a rogue ocean wave as she tried to find Saiko or Maki. Where were Jae and Dorothy?

Sounds changed to screams and an invisible wall of teargas blanketed the crowd. Protesters ran in all directions. Nora couldn't see through her burning eyes. She coughed and rough hands grabbed her arm jerking her away. Someone punched her throat and then her stomach. She doubled over and tried to face her attacker but couldn't see. Gasping for breath, she lost her balance when someone pushed her. She kicked and elbowed the air, robbed of her sight. A hand from a vehicle grabbed her arm and pulled her in before she fell to the pavement.

Gradually, Nora regained some sight and squinted through watery eyes around the interior of the police wagon, looking for her friends. Faces like hers peered back, only strangers' faces. Few words were spoken and the faces appeared as stunned as Nora's. "Anybody need a doctor?" a man asked.

The driver turned a sharp corner and shoulders collided. Mumbles of "I'm sorry" echoed through the van.

"So what's that on your sign?" a woman asked.

Nora took a breath and looked down. Through all the upheaval, she gripped her protest sign. "Victor Chin was celebrating his upcoming wedding." She paused to clear her scratchy throat and the gut punch made her feel sick. "He was murdered by two Detroit auto workers." She swallowed. "They blamed him for taking their factory jobs." Nora tried to say more but coughed instead.

"Yeah, the dirty bastards who did it got three years probation," a voice from the front of the van answered for her.

"He was a draftsman... had nothing to do with the factory," another added.

"What will they do with us?"

No one could answer. The erratic driver turned more sharp corners, made quick stops, and forced the packed protesters into one another. They focused on bracing themselves and then another quick stop left bumped heads and sore shoulders. Those who murmured apologies from the first sharp corners gave up as they neared the police station.

The following afternoon, Nora had tea with Takami at a Japanese restaurant and tried to field the questions he fired at her. "Why didn't you call me? I had to find out from Saiko. If she hadn't called, you'd still be in jail." He opened a honey packet into her tea and the waitress set a bowl of chicken soup on the table in front of her.

"There were so many of us. I shouted for a phone call but I was one voice in the crowd. And one toilet just out there in the cell with dozens of women. There wasn't room for anyone to sleep and it was too noisy anyway." Nora's hand was shaking as she picked up her teacup. "What is that you're eating?"

"Tuna sandwich. Pickled radishes and cucumbers." He swallowed. "So I get it, you couldn't get a phone call. What about the judge?"

She grabbed the other half of his sandwich and took a bite. "When I got to see him, I thought I could explain free speech, and that would be the end of it. Then he asked if any of my family was involved in un-American activities."

"Nora, you didn't – "

"I told him our father was unfairly interred. The judge looked at me like I was a Nazi."

"Oh no."

"That was when he whispered something to a clerk and had me sent back to the cell for the night. By then the women from the van were gone. I was so tired, and with more women gone, there was enough room to sit against the back wall and I dozed a bit."

Takami looked at her. She had definitely slept in these clothes. "I thought you saw the judge again."

"I woke up when the jailer grabbed me and took me back to the courtroom. I asked for breakfast, but he said, not so fast." She spooned the soup from the edge of the bowl. "The judge said, your father Kioshi Iguro was arrested for promoting a union vote on company property like it was a criminal offense. I told him the protest wasn't during working hours.

He looked at the papers, not at me. "Anarchism splinters by design into powerlessness and obscurity." Then the clerk came in with a message probably that you were there. Thank God. Did I tell you how much I love that you're my brother?"

Takami grimaced. "I'll take that as a thank you."

"I told him I'm a member of the musician's union and organizing outside of work hours is legal. Anyway, he read the note and he dismissed the case."

"I contacted the ACLU. They were all over it and called someone at the court. Maybe that was the message.

"Jae Kane and your friends were beside themselves when they could finally see again and noticed you weren't with them. They called the police stations but no one would give them any answers. They didn't feel they could do anything, but thought I might be able to help."

"I kept telling this cop that I was allowed one call, but he just yelled." Nora finished half of Takami's sandwich, but he didn't say a word. "And at one point he screamed in my face." It hurt to talk and any movement made her belly sore. "I was looking down the jaws of a brute. I could smell the alcohol on his breath."

Takami saw her wince. "You should go see a doctor." He knew she wouldn't. "Will they ever find the thug who pummeled that guy?"

"It happened so fast and I couldn't see. The first officer who put me behind bars said it was for my own safety, but then when they asked me about Dad, it became another matter entirely." She took a sip of tea and her hand shook.

36

Nora

1980

"That's wonderful, Saul! I'm sure you'll love Interlochen." Saul's surprise visit told her he had made up his mind.

His path to music school had taken some convincing and Nora's letter of recommendation to Interlochen had just made the deadline. "C'mon in. I just have to stir the chili but I want you to tell me about it."

The late afternoon was unusually cool and with the still-raw memory of the jail cell, she wanted the comfort of chili.

Grandmother hadn't been much of a cook, but in the fall and winter, chili showed up packing a punch in the rotation of flavorless meat and potato dinners. It was the only thing Grandmother made that Nora looked forward to eating. She scoured the back of the refrigerator and brought out various sauces, tomatoes, and a zucchini. In the freezer, she found a half-pound of burger, which she put in a stew pot with just enough water and heat to thaw. She diced a plump, sweet onion along with a few garlic cloves and tossed them in with the thawing meat and seasoning, stirring and savoring the aroma. Adding kidney beans, tomato paste, and fresh diced tomatoes wasn't enough.

It needed more liquid, something more flavorful than water. In the refrigerator, she noticed the half bottle of Lambrusco. The sweet, dark burgundy would cut the tomatoey acid perfectly. She kept pouring until the consistency of the chili was the texture of Grandmother's. With more sprinkles of chili seasoning and cayenne powder, she set the chili to simmer, but she was hungry. The wine, tomato, and onion smelled irresistible, but she forced herself to set the timer for 30 minutes. There would be enough left for tomorrow, and if her memory served her, it would be even better the second day.

Saul followed her into the kitchen with a look of thrill and torture. "It's Mom and Dad. They just can't get through it."

He held the acceptance letter with the school logo on the envelope. "Saul, it's Interlochen! You can't pass up this moment. You've earned it. You have to go!"

Saul's parents were grieving the death of his little sister. A birth defect hastened her short life. Saul was torn between having the opportunity of his life with young people from all over the world and feeling duty-bound to stay with his grieving parents.

"I hear what you're saying, Saul. People work through their grief differently." Nora wanted to comfort him but she knew he would love Interlochen. Then her stomach growled, distracting them both. The spicy aroma drifted from her kitchen.

It was almost like Saul could read her mind. "Gosh, that chili smells good."

"Would you like some?" she offered.

She ladled them each a bowl, toasted some naan, and they talked about Interlochen. By the second bowl, she had convinced him.

Soon after Saul left, Saiko called. "If you don't come over and tell me what happened in jail, I'll come over and frog-march you!"

Nora had to admit that chicken therapy sounded just about right. Saul's issues pushed the distress of jail to the back of her mind for a while.

As soon as Nora sat at the patio table in Saiko's backyard, a glass of iced peach tea appeared in front of her. The poet Basho's *Narrow Road to the Interior* lay open. As she leaned over to read the name of the poem, a new generation Hen Solo flew up and settled on her lap, fixing feathers and warbling. Nora automatically patted the hen and shared Saul's good news about the scholarship. "I have some vacation time coming in a few months and I think there might be time to fly to Interlochen and hear Saul's first concert," she told Saiko. The iced tea felt cool on her recovering throat. "While I'm out there, I may as well fly to NYC for some sightseeing."

"This is Saiko you're talking to. What are you really flying to New York for?"

Nora didn't hesitate. "I'm going to look up James."

Hen Solo had enough and hopped from her lap to join the brood. "Did I ever tell you about James' caramel cake? I can't help it. These memories recur like phantom limbs."

"What about it?"

"He knew I liked *dulce de leche*, and when I came home one day, this cake was in the oven. I'd had a tense day, and I just listened to his excitement about the two layers, one of chocolate, the other, a caramel mousse. He explained the science of how the cake layers would trade places during the baking, the dutch chocolate layer falling to the bottom, and the caramel mousse layer rising to the top. He held me talking like a professor about flour weight and oven temperature and that damned cake smelled so good. He dipped his finger in the caramel bowl by the sink and I licked it off. It would be an hour before the cake came out of the oven, so I took his hand – "

"Okay okay."

"Okay and then some – but we joked about getting married that day, and what it would be like meeting his family." She watched a ladybug fly from the condensation on her glass and sipped the tea. It tasted so much better when Saiko made it. "Then all hell broke loose. He said he didn't want to get married. When I said it didn't matter, that made him mad too. He was a grump the rest of the night."

"Men. Then what happened?"

Nora shook her head. "The next day it was like nothing had happened. It was just his mood, I guess."

"On again off again. That's unsettling."

"The funny thing was, the next week he started again, saying *we could go to New York for our honeymoon.* I made a face at him and said, *Are you kidding me?* Then we both started laughing."

The chickens interrupted with a dirt bath kerfuffle, each squawk and flutter creating more dust in the shade of the wisteria. Nora watched their pecking order until she noticed Saiko's strong hand on her wrist. "I'm so sorry. In all the confusion we couldn't find

you at the protest. And to think you spent the night in jail. We drove to the police station but they wouldn't tell us anything. At last Jae Kane thought to call your brother. I still don't know how he found you. We were all so worried."

Nora hadn't thought much about how Saiko would take it. "It was the ACLU. Takami has a friend who works for them." Her frown returned, as it had for most of the past few days.

"But that man who was being beaten, Saiko. He's in intensive care with a skull fracture. All that anger and violence. It was supposed to be peaceful but it's just more confusing. What about fairness? Whatever is my neighbor's right is my right. Isn't it WE, not US and THEM? I felt cold and sick when we passed the angry faces along the boulevard. Remember the mother waving the Confederate flag and her little boy screaming?"

Saiko nodded and held her head.

"Remember the rows of squad cars? Protesters wore swim goggles as if they expected teargas. When we walked by that candy store the owner scowled. He was boarding up his store window like we were criminals. Then the sirens. Saiko, what good did our protest do?"

"Nora, at least we did something instead of nothing. We showed them what we're looking for."

"Don't look for vegetables in the dairy department."

Saiko stood up and circled her arm around Nora's shoulders in an awkward hug. "It's like the undertow of the ocean pulling you down." She pressed her cheek to Nora's head.

37

Nora

1980

"Dorothy, I want to ask you something."

"What are you doing here?" Dorothy checked around her porch and looked past Nora as if she was embarrassed to have someone at her door.

"I wanted to do something after, you know, what happened, and spending the night in jail." She paused. "May I come in?"

Dorothy checked for spies once more and reluctantly stood back from the open door so Nora could walk into her living room.

The room was neat and no-nonsense, like Dorothy's kitchen from the day they made mochi. One overstuffed La-Z-Boy recliner occupied a corner opposite a color TV, probably Li's. "Your house is so neat. It's more organized than mine," Nora said, trying to put Dorothy at ease.

"What do you want?"

Since there was no invitation to sit down, Nora walked back to the dining room where a floor-to-ceiling cabinet stood. Instead of dishes on display, there were trophies and medals for taekwondo. "Look at these! You really have developed your skill."

Dorothy's tone changed. "Some of them are Li's but most are mine." She pointed out a few awards she was particularly proud of. "This one's from Fresno last year. It was some tough sparring against women from four different states and I came in second."

That's just what Nora wanted to hear, but she wasn't ready to ask just yet. "What's this picture? Who is that shaking hands with Li?"

"That's from a few years ago. She's Yuri Kochiyama. You don't recognize her?"

Nora shook her head.

"She was an activist, a friend of Malcolm X. She worked for desegregating schools in New York and pushed for reparations for Japanese-Americans in the internment camps. Li met her at a Vietnam Vets convention a few years back. He said she really inspired him."

Nora barely listened. Her focus was on the awards for taekwondo. "Dorothy, could you teach me?" Dorothy said nothing. "I can't stop thinking about that night and I feel like I need to protect myself, but I need some direction. What do you say?"

Dorothy folded her arms and walked to the window. "Are you sure?"

Dorothy kept her back to Nora as she spoke. "You know, you're cool. You are charming with your half-white, half-Japanese self. Have you seen the way men look at you? But no." She paced across her living room. "Instead you hang on to Saiko, Jae, Miko, and me. Look at you. You're middle-aged and still looking for someone you can play daughter to."

Nora was astonished. "What are you talking about?"

"Advice. I'm talking about every issue you have, you come running to us like we're supposed to fix it." Dorothy sneaked a quick look to see if any of this was sinking in. "Now you want help with self-defense, right? Isn't that what you want?"

At times Nora thought she understood Dorothy and still found it hard to talk without running into a wall. "I want to learn self-defense, yes," she said. "I'm not looking for a mom."

"It's funny, isn't it," Dorothy said. "We gravitate toward people who are like us, look like us." She opened the cabinet and lifted out the ribbon and medal from Fresno, holding it like it was Olympic gold. "Now, you and me, we're half alike, since you're half white, but your face looks like Saiko, Jae, and Maki, so that's what they see." She looked up. "But in that storage unit, it didn't matter who was who. All there was between those three guys with their gun and knife and us, was each other. We're all we had."

"Do you know what my arm looked like the day after? You really hit hard." Nora could feel Dorothy ramping up and tried to defuse her.

"So go to work. Build up that namby-pamby violin-playing arm. Wax on, Wax off!"

Her words triggered something in Nora. "Dorothy, you don't think you pander to Japanese people just because your husband is Japanese?" She saw Dorothy's eyes narrow and felt more determined to strike back. "Go ahead and make fun of Miyagi like everybody does. The writers made sure his *Karate Kid* life didn't matter. He was there to serve others. Just like nobody in real life cares about internment camps, those movie characters never tried to know Miyagi, know that his wife died in childbirth in Manzanar. Is that character as good as we Japanese people can get in movies?" Nora faced down Dorothy and pictured her as an immovable force, like those bristly white pines she remembered that stood up to the blustery Chicago winds.

"Look." Dorothy's voice tensed. "I'm saying what you need to hear." She pointed to herself. "It's not just the Japanese thing or the Taekwondo thing, Nora. Every day I ask Li *do you love me.* Every day he answers, *So far.* It's day by day." She shrugged her shoulders. "I ask myself can I hold it together one more day for him? Everything about him irritates me. Then I tell myself, how could I ever find another man so beautiful, one who loves bird watching, be-bop music, Korean food, and Fred Astaire movies like Li does? Nobody, that's who. He sparks of beauty and those sparks get me right here." Dorothy's fist pushed into her chest.

"You and Li – "

"Beauty has rules – stifling rules, but those sparks escape the rules. It's not what you think or what so many people are drawn to. Your brother Takami. Does he ever ask how I am? No! Does he ever give me a call just to talk to me? Or Saiko. When you two get together without me do you think to talk about me? Wonder what I would say about your conversation? Just because a woman no longer follows the rules, does she lose her beauty? The spark, the spirit is still there, still bearing fruit."

"Dorothy – "

"Don't you interrupt me. I'm not finished! I hate it when people talk over me. The spark, the spirit is still there still – "

"You just said that."

"That's it. You're making no sense. Here's the phone number." She scribbled a number on notepaper and held it to Nora's face. "Just leave."

"I can see I've upset you, Dorothy." Nora took the note. "Thanks. I'll see you later."

The front door hit Nora's arm on her way out. She felt like a dog scolded for tipping over the trash. Not all friendships were easy. Some were irascible and intense. Nora pulled the scrap of paper from her pocket. The phone number was barely legible, but she could read it. More questions without answers came to her mind. It was a long, slow walk home.

38

Nora

1980

Jae Kane's van was packed with art. Nora had second thoughts about agreeing to play her old Japanese Music City Pop cassette tapes to accompany the sculptures.

"How much farther?" She asked. She barely had enough room for her violin and an overnight bag with all of Jae Kane's artwork.

"Where's your patience? It's all about the journey. I-5 is a beautiful drive."

"I've rarely been to San Francisco since high school. I bet it's changed."

"San Francisco has more bookstores than any city in the US."

"Bookstore? I thought this was an art gallery."

"Well, yes, but it has rare books and wine tastings. They do things differently in San Francisco."

"How rare?"

"They have Jack Kerouac's scroll of *On the Road* displayed right now. This is opening weekend for it."

"Really?" Nora wasn't a Kerouac fan. She wondered if some of the students from her old school might be.

The bookstore held seven floors of books in a building that looked like it hailed from Gold Rush days. In the back of the main floor was an oversized carved oak bar with a dozen bar stools and an old-timey mirror behind the bartender. She was going to improvise around Japanese synthesizer music from the 80s in this place from the last century?

"Miss Nora," a young woman shook her hand. "I'm Hyacinth. We look forward to your synth music here at Bookinalia. Please follow me and I'll show you where you can set up."

Hyacinth motioned to an alcove with a music stand, a microphone, and a small Marshall portable amp. Clearly, the bookstore hosted other gigs such as hers. "It will get noisy in here tonight, so we want to be sure you're heard."

Nora put her jacket over a tall chair and looked at her surroundings. Across from her was a collection of anime books, old and new, from Astro Boy to the latest comic books and magazines.

"I'm over here!" Jae Kane waved. The area saved for her art backed up to the far wall, much larger when compared to Nora's spot. Nora watched as Jae paced across the area, hand to chin, appearing pleased with the eclectic venue, mentally placing her constellation of art pieces.

"I'm double-parked in front. Can you help me bring the sculptures in?" Jae Kane asked.

Together, Hyacinth, Nora, and Jae made quick work of the placements, and Jae Kane was directed to a prized parking spot for her van down the street. Soon several groups of visitors wandered in. Teens, parents with strollers, and professor-types with capes and caps mingled and conversed. Nora arranged her Music City Pop CDs in the order she thought best and hit "play."

The first one was Miki Matsubara's "Stay With Me." Her improvised live riffs wrapped around the pop music with its funky, bubbly vibe. After checking out Kerouac's plexiglass-covered scroll in the back, visitors would stop to listen. There was no time for dinner, but Nora and Jae nibbled on a wide array of appetizers, bubble tea, and cola.

During a break, Jae checked on Nora. "Good crowd," she said. "You know I really thank you for coming. Your music adds to the whole experience of the place."

Nora assured her she was enjoying the people-watching. "Are you getting any buyers?"

"Two so far, which is pretty fair. I've given out a lot of business cards too. One woman was interested in the "Untitled" from our adventure in the storage unit." She looked at Nora. "I'll be glad to see it go."

"You look so animated when you describe your work."

Jae Kane smiled. "I hope everybody I talk to goes away with a bit more understanding. Oh - here's a new group. Gotta go." Jae threaded her way back to her art.

"Nora, is that you? She heard a familiar French accent and turned to see a distinguished older man with a tweed scarf over his jacket.

"Monsieur Bernard! What a pleasure to see you!" Nora was astonished to see her admissions director from the San Francisco Youth Symphony standing before her, white wine in hand.

"Please call me Henri, Nora. What brings you here to one of my favorite places in the city?"

Nora explained that it wasn't her idea, but her friend needed some musical back up and now she was pleased she'd agreed to come. Jae Kane's music could wait for this man who orchestrated her career. She delighted him with a story about the Los Angeles Symphony and hinted at the expansions into new areas.

But Henri had a question. "Whatever happened to that young man, your friend?" One of his caterpillar eyebrows raised.

"Oh, James?" Nora said. Could Henri have remembered that they were nearly inseparable in those days? "He left for New York. He pursued other – interests."

Henri quickly pivoted to other subjects including a viola student he was trying to get an audition for with the Honolulu Symphony. "It sounds like you have some promising students, Nora. If they need scholarships, we always have room for the best."

She nodded and promised to send Henri her concert schedule. He had friends coming in from Lyon who might enjoy her *belle musique*.

Nora would have spent more time with the distinguished Mr. Bernard but caught a look from Jae. She said her goodbyes and chose a new CD beginning with a low-key song, "Plastic Love." During the introduction, she plucked a few strings to check the tuning.

A quick look confirmed that Mr. Bernard was still on the spot where she had left him, listening without moving. After relaxing into the piece winding to its end, she rested her instrument and was surprised to see he was still there, his face so serious. "You were one of the few." He reached for her hand and kissed it. "One of the few."

Hyacinth closed the doors at 11:00. Nora harmonized to the last chord on the CD's playlist and bowed to Jae's applause. "We did it!" she announced. Two art pieces had been sold and taken home by their owners. 'Untitled" was too large, and the buyer would return with a van to pick it up the following business day. "That hotel bed will feel awfully good tonight," Jae sighed.

"Not yet," Hyacinth hurried back to them. "I was hoping you'd come to the open mike night at the Purple Onion. It's, you know, music, comedy, we could have a few drinks and a few laughs."

The Purple Onion was a cellar room at the bottom of a craggy stone-walled spiral staircase. Hyacinth opened the door and a raucous roar assaulted their ears. A comedian waved from the stage soaking up the cheers and applause.

The three women wound their way through a labyrinth of tables and smoke to find the last three seats near the bar in the back. A waitress in a short purple dress and curly hair took their drink order.

"Sangrias – make it a pitcher," Hyacinth told her. "The drinks are watered down, but the Sangria's the best."

"Do you come here often?" Jae asked.

"I'm trying to get enough courage to do an open mike. You have to sign up early, though, and I usually work late." Hyacinth revealed that she was a spoken word poet and had competed in high school. She wanted to try out some of her works in progress.

"What do you write about?" Nora asked.

"I have some relationship poems, breakups, mother/daughter issues, the cosmos, that sort of thing, but the one I really want to share is about my friend Marda. We've been friends since elementary school and she's going through a lot. People don't know how their hateful comments take their toll on a person. How those comments can ruin someone's life. I helped her find a doctor who didn't treat her like shit. But what can they do outside of pain meds? So I wrote a poem. One day I'll get on that stage and read it. It's something I can do for her."

A group that called themselves Straight Ahead took the stage. The bass player was tall and trim, the guitar player, stocky with ringlets of hair that fell in his eyes, and a young woman dressed in black played flute. The woman, whose wild red hair reminded Nora of the musical *Annie*, grabbed the mike. "We'd like to play Dave Brubeck's "Take Five," she said.

"What about that man you were talking to?" Jae asked.

Nora explained that Henri was somewhat of a mentor for her and seeing him was the best part of the day.

"He's a regular at the bookstore," Hyacinth said. "We all know him."

"If it wasn't for Henri I probably wouldn't be with the LA Symphony," Nora said.

"Meaning you wouldn't have met Saiko or me, and you wouldn't have been at the bookstore at that place and time," Jae said.

Hyacinth filled their glasses. A poet recited a heartfelt prose poem filled with loss and longing. Hyacinth added what the poet should have included and left out. Next up was Joe Barker, another comedian. He began by barking like a dog. "Let's look at

Shakespeare," he said. The audience groaned. "No, I mean this guy knew what we go through every day, know what I mean? He paused. "He has that Hamlet guy talk about the 'thousand natural shocks,' and he's talking about all those little miseries we put up with, day after day. Am I right?"

The audience wasn't listening yet, but Nora was.

"Those miseries can add up. And then what?" We wanna grab a sword and start swingin' that's what!"

The side conversations quieted.

"Just the other day I was on the California St. Line. Been standin' there for five minutes when this punk kid gets on and grabs the seat before I can sit down. Now normally I wouldn't make a scene, but that day was like *Alexander's Horrible No Good Very Bad Day,* you know? I'd already suffered my thousand natural shocks. Let me tell you – "

Joe Barker retraced his humorous litany of slights and offenses of the day, truly funny to Nora since they didn't happen to her. The laughs grew until Barker ended his routine. "The thing is, I coulda ignored this kid on the cable car, no problem. But with the thousand shocks under my belt, I'd had it. I barked. I yelled for him to get his skinny ass outta that seat before I threw him off the car. And ya know what?" The audience was quiet. "He got up and I sat down."

Joe seemed to look straight at Nora in her seat at the back of the room. It was as if he was talking to her and she took his routine as personal advice. She could take those looks people gave her, those comments, the night in jail, all of those natural shocks, and put them to use.

The women at Nora's table held up their sangria glasses to toast him. Nora liked to think the kiss Joe Barker tossed to the audience was meant for her.

39

Nora

1980

Nora opened the door in a strip mall, with the name "Taekwando Demetrius" on the glass. This was her second visit since Dorothy had scribbled her note with the phone number on it. The first time she spoke only with the receptionist, finding where to purchase a uniform or *dobok*. She had yet to meet the man whose name was on the door.

Small talk with three other beginners abruptly stopped when Demetrius appeared barefoot before them. The women looked up at this formidable giant of a man who frowned at them, and their mouths closed. His head was shaved on the sides with a stripe of black, curly hair down the middle.

Demetrius was a friend of Dorothy's husband and they had covered each other in Vietnam. Nora laughed to herself over her reaction. He wore the same uniform as they did, white cotton pants and a tunic top, but it was divided by a solid black belt. She stared at the belt. Everyone knew what a black belt meant. Even though the uniform was loose, no one could deny the muscular strength beneath it.

"*Chah-ryut*," his voice boomed. "After me. *Taekwan*. Now bow."

The women followed. Demetrius bowed back.

"Before we talk about our purpose and goals, I want to say I have an idea of what you're thinking." He paced before them. "All of my beginning students think that I'm a monster, a giant because I am black and I am big. But I'm not a monster or a giant. I am your *Sahyun,* your teacher. *Sahyun* means I have studied to become a master 8th-degree black belt. There is only one degree above me, and that is a *Saseong,* a grandmaster. I am here to teach you to protect yourselves from harm, not to harm you."

He stood still and looked over each of them. "Some criminals believe women are easy targets, that women are weak and fearful. Add to that, if women are Black, Mexican, or Asian, some criminals believe they are justified to attack a woman who looks different. You and I cannot change how people see us. But you are strong. You will have the element of surprise on your side, and you will prevail."

For the next hour, Demetrious explained the martial arts in words that chipped away at Nora's anxiety. She thought of the practice as an exercise, a series of kicks and punches. By the end of the hour, the women practiced a few beginning moves with each other. One of the women, a short, energetic Mexican, spoke to Nora as they were ready to leave. "I was afraid at first, but I think I like him."

"Me too," Nora nodded, ready to say more, but the woman walked out. At the door, she put on her shoes and turned to say goodbye to her *Sahyun.* "Did anyone ever tell you that you look like Mr. T?"

Demetrious looked up to the ceiling. "All the time," he said.

"Oh, *Sahyun,* I did the same thing to you that people do to me." She reached for his hand and squeezed, but he didn't respond. His look was quizzical.

"We're expected to represent every person in our culture - all Asian people are alike and I am Asian so I represent all Asians. It's the same with you, yes?"

"If you mean I'm one Black man myself, and people don't see me as different from my friend or my brother, yes, you're right."

"That's it." She studied his face. "Sorry about the Mr. T thing."

"It's a daily dread. People don't understand. This is my job." He lifted his hands and motioned around the room. "But it's not me. You know I'm a bird watcher? And model railroads - love 'em. I have one in my garage."

"Oh, have you been to Huntes Gardens? It's a great place for birds – except for that cat."

Demetrius gave a low-voiced chuckle. "I'm gonna watch out for you Ms. Iguro. You're one to watch out for!"

40

Nora

Michigan, 1980

Nora stepped off the plane into the Cherry Capital airport near Traverse City confident that her weeks of preparation assured that nothing was forgotten and everything would be perfect as planned. She arranged for a short ride to her lodging, the Stone Hotel, just off the Interlochen campus.

At the lodge, she picked up her key from a student with big curly hair. He grabbed the pencil in her hand to draw an imaginary map in the air, directing her to a cabin, not unlike the ones inhabited by the student campers. Logs snugged the outside and knotty pine inside, a look she would describe as rustic. But the view from the front window was spectacular. Once in the cabin, she dropped her bag and parked her travel-weary self at the picture window, taking in the tall pine forest and winding path before her. She waited for the coffee she had set to brew moments before, sniffing the air for its roasted, nutty aroma.

Last night after she had tossed some last clothes in a bag at home, she felt free and relaxed. Grabbing a pencil and staff paper, she sat down to write. Sketching some notes of a short motif, she picked up her violin to see how it would sound. How exasperating her writing was! She put down the violin and returned to the notes, erasing, rewriting, adding some contrast, and trying again. Her violin sounded pedestrian, lackluster, and trite. Her cries of exasperation stalked and taunted her around the apartment. Why couldn't she write the music in her head like she did when she and James wrote together? She sat and picked up the pencil again, scowling at her motionless hand.

Nora sipped her coffee and took a closer look at the trail outside her window. It was a far cry from Fountain Valley and a welcome change. She freshened up in the spartan bathroom and changed into jeans and a sweatshirt, ready to take on that trail outside her window to see where it led. Time had lost its meaning. A vacation contentment overcame her when she opened the door and heard distant saxophones, trumpets, and violins, students practicing scales, harmonies, clashing notes climbing atop one another, percussive and competitive.

The trail and the scent of pine led Nora around one curve, down a hill, and up the next root-tangled, rock-covered point, until at the end, she found sunlight again, snake grass, and a weatherbeaten sign on the sandy beach: Duck Lake. She kicked off her running shoes and walked out into the shock of cold northern Michigan water, oblivious to the gentle waves lapping at her jeans.

"Hey there, did you forget your swimsuit?"

Nora turned to see a man in a jacket and rumpled blue corduroy pants, the uniform of teachers at Interlochen.

"Oh, am I in the wrong place?" Nora asked. "I just walked down the trail in front of my room at Stone House, and this is where I ended up."

The man walked his blue canvas shoes to the tip of the water's edge. "Not a problem. I think you're in just the right place."

A sunfish, late for this time of year, flipped up from the water and disappeared, the ripples extending to Nora's legs. "Even the fish are friendly here," she said, shifting her weight to keep her legs from paralyzing with cold. "So, I'm supposed to see my student's concert tonight at Kresge Auditorium. How do I get there from here?"

"Your student?" He rubbed the back of his head and tried to clear up the confusion. "I'm Jay Michaels, the violin instructor for the World Youth Symphony. My students are playing tonight's concert."

"Well, Mr. Michaels, my student is Saul Levy from California. Maybe you know him. I came to hear him play." Maneuvering her numb legs across the stony lakebed to face him, she felt the stones shift in the sand under her feet. Instantly off balance, she plopped into the frigid water with a shocked yelp, the heat stolen from her body. Jay leaned in with a hand to pull her out. She didn't take it at first, wanting to save some shred of do-it-herself dignity. But her muscles refused to do as they were told. Her shaking hand dripped and she reached for his warm one. Once her toes were wiggling on the solid shore, she looked up and saw Jay's ice-blue eyes, looking back at her.

He shrugged and took off his jacket, covering her shoulders without asking. "You came all the way from California to hear your student play a concert?"

Nora threw her head back and laughed. Was she flirting? "I had some vacation time. I'm headed to New York the day after tomorrow." Damn. Was she shaking from the cold or because she found him so attractive?

"Saul Levy. So you're the one who taught him that quick switch from coloratura vibrato to a consistent wrist vibrato. He told me his teacher helped him figure it out."

Jay's smile warmed her. "Coloratura vibrato – like a mezzo soprano sings? I've never heard it called that." Nora ignored the goosebumps and the two musicians fell into comfortable conversation.

"You'd best get back to Stone House to thaw out before dinner. It's cafeteria-style, and you want to be one of the first in line. This is chicken piccata night, and the sauce gets a little sticky if you're not at the beginning of the line."

Nora picked up her shoes and waved goodbye to Jay. "Maybe I'll see you after the concert." Only then did she notice she still wore his jacket.

That evening, she followed Jay's directions to Kresge Auditorium, the chicken piccata laying heavily on her stomach. Nora was one of the first diners in line, but Jay didn't mention that the piccata was thick with egg noodles. Then there was the matter of her wet jeans hanging on the shower rod in her bathroom. If only she had brought another pair. She'd be lucky if hers were dry by morning when she was supposed to climb the sand dunes with Saul's family. She saw hands waving in the audience and a smiling Mrs. Levy hopping up and down to gain her attention. It looked like the Levys were able to find joy in their son after all, even at a time when they grieved the loss of their daughter.

Mrs. Levy pointed to a seat they had saved for her. Nora arranged Jay's jacket on her lap, in the hope she could return it to him after the performance.

"I'm so excited for Saul and proud too. He wouldn't be here if it wasn't for you," Mrs. Levy said, patting Nora's arm. They perused the program and noted that Saul's name was in the upper third of the violin section.

Nora assured Mrs. Levy that it was his work ethic that brought him here. Even so, as the lights dimmed and the students took the stage, his mother's proud words warmed her.

After *Symphonie Fantastique* and *Fanfare for the Common Man*, Nora looked at the program to see what was next. She heard an intake of breath from the audience and thundering applause. With his leg braces, Itzhak Perlman walked onto the stage. Nora gasped along with them. She had only heard Perlman in recordings, never in concert. Focused on Saul, she didn't check to see who was the featured soloist. "Can you believe Saul is going to play back up for Itzhak Perlman!" Nora yelled to Mrs. Levy, her eyes wide.

All Mrs. Levy could do was smile and nod. She kept applauding too.

After the last piece on the program, the conductor returned to the microphone. "We have a special encore for you, written by one half of a composing team who is in our audience tonight. Please enjoy *Black and White* by Nora Iguro and James Roberts."

Shocked, Nora turned to Mrs. Levy who didn't seem surprised at all. The conductor raised his arms and the opening notes sent chills up her back. Nora stole side glances at the crowd. She'd never experienced *Black and White* as part of the audience before. Multi-colored faces with expectant expressions reflected light from the stage. Her shoulders tensed. Terrified that they would hate it, she pushed those thoughts aside. The cymbals exploded in their introductory rhythm and an older man bounced in his seat with a cough. A young girl behind him, probably a little sister of a musician, leaned forward. Maybe she was hearing this at just the right time in her life. A woman two faces down sat emotionless. Nora imagined the music offering her comfort or escape. A man in a seat by the aisle listened with a portable oxygen tank by his side. The concert could be a way for him to feel like everyone else for an evening.

She listened, touched by the careful notes the young musicians played. Nora could spot her contributions in the lines of melody separate from James's work – like a mother spotting her child in the crowd running out of school at the end of the day, the sun in his hair. Her memories entangled across time, thrilling at the grand parts, nostalgic at the delicate ones.

Too soon, the final capitulation sneaked up on her, where she and James set their competitive spirits aside and wrangled the final measures. She felt a connection with that delicate last tone, that final note from a musician's heart. There was something in the sharing of this creation, this world they inhabited within the music. She joined the audience in applause and realized she'd held her breath, shoulders almost to her ears during the performance.

"I hope you don't mind." Mrs. Levy confessed. "I told them you'd be here and asked if they'd play it for you."

Nora stared wide-eyed at her not knowing what to say.

"Go on up there and talk to them." Mrs. Levy motioned to the musicians on stage. "They're about to leave."

She sprang from her seat, dodged the audience as they moved out of the amphitheater, and climbed the steps to the stage, shaking hands and speaking to the conductor.

After the concert, the Levys and Nora had arranged to meet Saul on the entrance path in front of Kresge. It was a starlit night and in the shadows, Mr. Levy was first to see his son stepping forward to shake hands.

"That was absolutely remarkable!" Nora told him, stepping in to reach her arm around and pat his back.

"Mr. Perlman talked to us this afternoon, so we knew just how to play with him. He said we'd make him sound good. We were scared of him at first because he's so famous." Saul brushed a mosquito from his arm. "But he knew about the torture we go through every Friday during our auditions for chairs. He was cracking jokes with us."

"Good job, Levy," a familiar voice joined in. Yours was one of the better concerts this year."

"Mr. Michaels, I think it was the best concert this year." Saul was beaming at all of us. "Uh – " Saul's attention was suddenly taken by a girl about his age who stopped in front of them. "Mom, Dad, this is Adrienne Claire. She's from Abidjan in Côte d'Ivoire. She plays the cello."

"*Bonjour, je suis tres heureux...*I'm happy to make your acquaintance." Adrienne smiled. She bounced on the balls of her feet and tossed her lustrous black hair from her shoulder.

"C'mon, let's go to the junction, Adrienne. There's not much time." Saul said, taking her hand and walking off with other students down a path different from the one Nora had taken to get there.

"Well, that was quick," Nora said.

"You have to understand," Jay said, "They're going to Harmony Junction before lights out. It's the only time couples can have some time together before they are sequestered in their cabins on opposite sides of the camp. Not to worry," Jay addressed Saul's parents in a serious tone. They're supervised with flashlights and bells. "A little hand-holding, a hug, a peck on the cheek, that's about all there's time for. They're escorted back to their dorms."

Mrs. Levy smiled and nodded. Mr. Levy said, "Harmony Junction, eh?" They said goodnight to Nora and agreed to meet for breakfast the following morning before their hike over Sleeping Bear Sand Dunes to the Lake Michigan shore.

"So, you're not only a composer, I liked what you did with *Black and White* by the way, you're going to hike the whole dunes, all the way to the lake?" Jay asked.

"Why do you say it like that? It's just a sand dune. I grew up in Michigan." Nora bristled in defense, although she'd never walked a dune before.

"I guess you'd better turn in now. Can I walk you to Stone House?" Jay said.

"I'd like that," Nora linked her arm through his and forgot her annoyance.

They passed the Fredrick's statue *Two Bears*. "The black bear and brown bear are natural enemies," Jay explained. But here, Fredricks has made them peaceful, sort of friendly."

Nora circled the bears.

"By the way, that recapitulation in the end - it splinters into all directions."

Nora wanted to know more about his reaction. "Exactly! Like a clash of cultures where the instruments outside of the violins and basses think they're right and the others aren't listening to anything but themselves."

"No, I meant it was - uncomfortable."

"I didn't mean for it to be comfortable." Nora kept walking and looking at the bears from different angles. "That ending clash is intentional discomfort and misunderstanding. During the premiere, we had art and photography projected behind the orchestra. It's different tonight just hearing the music." Her fingers touched the face of the biggest bear. "But in a way, there's a stronger focus without the art. I liked it that way." She looked at Jay, daring him to disagree.

"It's about people, isn't it."

"That's me. I can't find the words, so I use music."

Along the way, Jay pointed out trees lit with tiny lights in the dark along the path. "This stand of white pines is really something," he said. "When I first came here five years ago, they were as tall as I am. Look at them now."

Nora looked up at the soft needled trees, easily twice as tall as Jay. "It has a cozy feeling. Interlochen is like a wonderland of forest."

"Trees are poems the earth writes upon the sky."

"Kahlil Gibran. And FDR said forests were the lungs of the land." Nora looked above the trees to the starry sky and heard Jay take a deep breath. "My friend Saiko told me about *shinrin-yoku*," Nora said. I think I said that right. It's Japanese for forest bathing. It means taking in the forest and savoring nature with all of our senses."

Jay nodded. "Maybe that's part of the reason why I come back here every summer, year after year."

Nora's thoughts returned to Saul. "I'm glad Saul found a friend, someone he can take to Harmony Junction. Good for him. Someday he'll have this Interlochen romance to look back on."

Jay took his jacket from her arm and placed it over her shoulders again. They walked the lighted path through the trees back to Nora's room at Stone House. Nora asked about Perlman and Jay said the famous violinist impressed the students with the importance of finding a balance and making relationships outside of music. He felt Perlman's message resonated with them.

They stopped at the steps of the hotel with its overhead beams and stone-columned porch. "This will be our Harmony Junction," Jay told her. "I'll hold your hand," he took her hand and raised it to his lips. "Give you a hug," reaching around her back, he held her close. "And kiss your cheek," he whispered in her ear before a chaste brush of his lips on hers.

"Oh no – " Nora sighed and relaxed into his embrace. "I'm not ready to say goodbye," she shook her head.

"All the more reason to make a memory tonight," he said.

Nora stole a quick glance to see if the Levys were within eyesight. She winked at Jay and led the way to her cabin.

The shoreline of Lake Michigan grew smaller as Nora's plane descended toward New York. She barely spoke to her seatmate, lost in thought as the last glimpses of the blue waters were obscured by filmy clouds. The Levys were avid hikers and although she'd lived in Michigan growing up, she found the dunes were a challenge. She was grateful for the crisp, cool fall day. Few tourists were climbing in

October. She didn't expect the sand would find its way into her shoes and socks.

"I'll go first," Mr. Levy instructed. Saul's friend Adrienne had never climbed before either, so he talked to both of them. "Put your footprints in mine where I've already flattened the sand. You'll get more traction."

Nora and Adrienne did as they were told, but still, Nora was gasping for breath at the top of the first dune.

"You look a little flushed, dear," Mrs. Levy said. "Are you breathing enough? Be sure to breathe deep before you start the next climb."

They continued on their climbs and descents of the sandy trail, past occasional scrub trees, thistle, and beach grasses. More than a mile later, they ascended the last dune to the spectacular expanse of sparkling Lake Michigan. Nora felt light-headed but relieved to reach the water. She basked in the sun that peaked out from clouds over the great blue lake. "It's not California," she said. "The hike was tough going, but worth it."

"C'mon, Adrienne, Saul said, kicking off his shoes. "I'll race you."

"You are a crazy man. *Homme fou*," she said, pulling off her last sock and chasing him down the dune to the water's edge.

The Levys and Nora watched Saul and Adrienne run down the dune and into the bracing water, squealing with laughter.

"Hey, are you Japanese or Chinese?" Nora's seatmate had asked her a question.

Jolted out of her memory of the day before, she looked at him. He was a solid man with a short haircut. Maybe military. "I was born in Indiana. Why would you ask such a question?"

"Yeah, you say that, but how do I know? Prove it. Let me see your license."

Nora ignored the man and opened her book.

The man raised his voice. "I said, let me see your license."

At that point, other passengers summoned the stewardess who walked by with a few words for him. His face folded into a sock puppet of agreement and he turned his head to the ceiling. The stewardess looked at Nora with an inscrutable expression.

Returning her gaze to the window, Nora thought about Jay, the way he moved, his voice. What was she thinking? It was so unlike her. She hardly knew him. It was the way he whispered in her ear, his touch, electrifying, thrilling. Jay laughed and told her he really wasn't the kind of a man who invited himself to a woman's room, especially a woman he'd just met.

"But I invited you," she reminded him.

Mr. Muscle kept making quick, restless movements next to her, pushing his shoulder into hers, then his elbow. She leaned forward and checked the shopping bag at her feet with its cuddle-sized stuffed bears for Takami's children - jet black and caramel brown with shiny noses. Were they too old for stuffed animals now? They couldn't be. What time would this plane land? Not soon enough.

Her thoughts returned to Jay and the memory they had made that night. Jay laughed at his own sweet clumsiness around her, and Nora confessed how embarrassed she was that he had to pull her out of the lake that afternoon. Those awkward feelings evaporated when she thought of the time she spent nestled in his arms.

41

Nora

New York, 1980

Nora had been in New York for two days before she finally tracked down someone who knew where James might be. Every request required an appointment, and the appointment was always the next day. She didn't mind spending her time wandering around the Empire State Building and Rockefeller Center Plaza with its golden, striving Prometheus, as she searched for James.

She took in an afternoon matinee of *Phantom of the Opera,* gasping when the chandelier nearly crashed upon the heads of the audience in front of her. Thoroughly smitten with the musical, she hummed "All I Ask of You," all the way from the F train to the East Side, and found Dosankos, a Japanese noodle shop. She was starved. Within ten minutes she had a steaming bowl of oniony soy noodles and vegetables before her, complete with her favorite baby corn.

"*Hajimemashite*"

A Japanese man sitting opposite nodded and talked to her. She wished Saiko was there to translate, but all she could do was nod and smile back. Diners were seated family-style in long rows and she felt a familial comfort eating shoulder to shoulder with strangers.

After one dead-end appointment - the New York Musical Society had never heard of James - she decided to walk to the Public

Library. Along 42nd Street, she passed the 1930s-era Nat Sherman clock. Assuming it was a bookstore, she wandered in to discover warm wood-paneled walls and the familiar sweet scent of cherry pipe tobacco. Several men in the store stopped what they were doing to look at her. "May I help you, miss?" a clerk asked.

"That scent. My grandfather smoked the same tobacco." She approached the tobacconist behind the counter with the zeal of a New York tourist. "What is it?"

The tobacconist gave her a look. "That would be your Captain Black," he said, reaching behind to pull down a silver and red packet. "It's a blend of Virginia and Cavender tobaccos. Very mellow. " He placed it on the counter in front of her. "That'll be $7.95."

She watches Grandfather with one hand on the steering wheel of the pickup truck, smoking his pipe through the cold, dark night. Later he astonishes her with a rare visit to her third-floor attic room, urging her to keep playing her violin.

The evocative scent of his tobacco brought it all back. Nora nodded her head and smiled. "Here's a ten," she said.

The walk along 42nd Street by Central Park relaxed her. When she was on the edge of sleep, tonight, she would think back on this day and her first thought would be to share it with James. Even now. She wondered what it was that kept her in California. The men she had dated couldn't come close. There was the man who liked video game music, the older man who couldn't quit talking about his kids, and the one whose eyes darted to the Raiders game on the TV screen behind the bar whenever she tried to explain what she did for a living.

Not one of them was as vulnerable as James when they first moved in together, or as unconquerable either. The blame she harbored for James' leaving had long passed. She opened the bag of pipe tobacco and breathed in. Survival skills could be repurposed, some even let go, like Grandfather when they worked in the barn and he said he would try again to get a new grip with a rusty wrench.

A black sedan drove by with a bass-heavy melody that she repeated to herself and matched her steps to its rhythm. Right here in James's city, she felt him with a fierceness as if he was walking beside her. Maybe he had found another violinist in New York, a whole, complete unbroken woman without baggage, one he could laugh with, and kiss, have exceptional sex with, one who didn't challenge and puzzle him, entice him to scribble music on a page with her. She carried the weight of him when he left, like the book she read, *The Unbearable Lightness of Being.* Nora felt connected to Thereza who fell in love and compartmentalized. Tomáš's love of work and passion for the uniqueness of sex with multiple women overwhelmed him to rationalize its meaning. Tomáš saw no contradiction. Sex isn't love! Two different things! Over time, Thereza forgives. The weight seems lighter, like a fragile porcelain vase lovingly repaired, but the crack remains, the fragments of glue holding tight.

Church bells chimed and Nora spun around looking for a cathedral, but it must've been blocks away. She had once been hired to play for an Easter service at the First Congregational in Los Angeles, arriving for practice at the time five bell ringers were preparing their peel. They invited her up flights of spiral steps into the bell tower and explained that a peel was a rare celebration – three hours of music.

Nora listened to these New York bells down the block, feeling them in her core. She knew the bell ringer felt more than the note that rang from his bell. She marveled at the thought, to be able to produce a thrum of feeling from the pull on a rope tied to a pulley and a thousand pounds of cast bronze. If only she could write down this feeling in notes with other street sounds and turn it into something other people could feel too. She sighed and laughed at herself for all the ideas she had in the shower or in the middle of the night that vanished by the time she could turn them into music.

Her thoughts wandered to working side by side in the apartment with James, his counterpoint, his laugh, the raw feeling of their creation, an accordion of paper on the table spread in front of them.

What about real composers – did they ever get distracted? Pencil in a diminished chord when they meant to write an augmented one, but the dog needed a walk? Then do they reconcile it like the artist who turns it into a pretty little tree, while the rest of us cover our lives' little blunders with revamps, redos, and tweaks? A composer's mistake won't kill anybody, not like a heart surgeon who messes with the wrong artery. But when the composer chooses the right note, the perfect fit, it can transport a melody into a memory that stays with us for the rest of our lives. A truck cleared its throat, and a bus beside her hit the brakes sighing to a stop like the rounding brush backbeat on a jazz snare drum. A new tune popped into her head that somehow included smoke from cherry pipe tobacco.

Everything surrounding her was James' life, and she didn't fit in it any more than she fit into her brother Takami's family. It could have been guilt or inspiration that made her feel like stealing from their traditions to make them fit, trying not to feel like an impostor, an interloper. Or maybe her curiosity kept her knocking on doors waiting to be let in.

Finally, at 5th Avenue and 42nd Street, she looked up at the formidable lions at the steps of the library, the ones from the *Ghostbusters* movie. Not one to believe in ghosts, she imagined the ghost woman inside the library, reading a book and shushing her. Through the front door, she stopped to look up at this grand tribute to the written word.

In California, they had the beautiful new Disney Concert Hall and the Broad Contemporary Art Museum, but those buildings were for entertainment more than enlightenment and preservation of thought and ideas. She passed a room with walls and rows of card catalogs. The Rose Reading Room was the biggest room in the library, and she tiptoed the length of its tile floor while readers under table lamps poured over books on long desks.

Further on, Nora found herself in Gottesman Hall, the treasure room. Hanging from the ceiling was a partially open umbrella. Searching the wall for a label, she found it belonged to P.L. Travers, the author of *Mary Poppins*. The introductory paragraph on the wall boasted 4,000 years of history in one room. Further back was Jefferson's copy of the Declaration of Independence, handwritten. Underlined were passages that were cut from the final version denouncing slavery.

Curious, she walked to a plexiglass display lit from overhead. Two young men had their eyes galvanized on a Nabokov manuscript but dispersed as she approached. Nearby, was a James Baldwin first edition from his Paris days. By the wall was an old wooden desk and chair that belonged to Charles Dickens.

She had an idea. At an information desk, she asked where the map room was.

"First floor, room 117," the clerk pointed to the stairs with an outstretched hand.

As she rounded the corner to the map room, she looked up to blue walls and magnificent century-old chandeliers. A Broadway-handsome librarian smiled at her and gave her a quick idea of what she might find there. He casually mentioned some parts of the collection dated back to the 1500s. Nora looked into his steel-gray eyes as he spoke, but a wild-haired patron at a table beside them scowled, turning the page of an oversized map book on a study table in front of him. He cleared his throat and glared as if the two of them were singing "Springtime for Hitler" from *The Producers*. Her handsome librarian lowered his voice.

"Do you have maps of Central Park?" Nora asked.

Broadway-man led her to a cabinet of map books and traced his finger along their titles. He pulled out one and carefully opened it on the laminated surface of the cabinet. "You might find this of interest. You can see the change in the park over the years. It ends in 1955 when they tore down this area and started to build Lincoln Center." His hand circled an area west of Central Park.

"I haven't been there yet, but here it looks like a residential area."

"It used to be San Juan Hill, home to jazz kings like Thelonious Monk. But developers razed the neighborhood, and the jazz bars to make room. Mostly Black and Hispanic families. Immigrants brought Caribbean music, Zora Neal Hurston wrote there, the groove, the energy – "

"All sacrificed for Lincoln Center."

"They called it urban renewal. It was urban removal. But look." He carefully turned pages back to maps labeled New Amsterdam, the earliest moniker for the colony of New York. "Now

New Amsterdam was north of Central Park, but you can see what came before." He traced his fingers across the map.

"Those walls – were they to keep out Native people?"

"The Lenape tribe lived on the island when the Dutch came." He explained. "They sold it for $24. in beads and trinkets. Today there are no Lenape Natives in the area. They were moved to Oklahoma."

"Moved?" Nora looked at him.

He closed the book and handed it to her. "You can find out more about it in the back, after the maps." He walked away to assist the throat-clearing man, a New Yorker in a hurry.

Although it was cool, the library's outdoor reading lounge overlooking the park was unlocked. She found a chair, carefully set the map book on the table, and started on the first page. A light breeze ruffled the pages as if a ghost passed through. Pages detailed walls, Natives, and Dutch settlements. She imagined what their music might be like.

The park names were amusing – The Ramble, Sheep Meadow, Great Lawn. Over time, New Yorkers had greeted one another in dressed-up Sunday strolls, taken carriage rides, and bird-watched here since the end of the Civil War. Fascinated with the maps, she looked over the rail to see the park of today and imagine what it might have been like before Lincoln Center and before the Dutch pushed Native Americans away.

Toward the back of the book, she found the history of Central Park. It was Seneca Village, a neighborhood of over 200 homeowners, mostly African American, with churches, cemeteries, and their own schools. The Seneca name could have come from a tribe, or the wealthy, powerful Roman statesman. At the end of the war, Seneca land was purchased under Eminent Domain for the park, and residents were pushed from their homes. Nora looked again over the verdant expanse of the park before her and thought about the park planners' takeover of the Village. What was gained and what was lost?

She thought of her father and the thousands of Asian families forced from their homes. Why hadn't she learned about the land taken away from Natives or Black people like the congregation at City Hope Church pushed from their neighborhood? She hadn't learned about the internment camps until she found out her father was in one. All were made to leave their homes, their shelter, and their souls' comfort. If we had learned the truth, would we have done better?

Nora knew that German students were taught about the horrors of Hitler. The Germans had a proverb, *to change and to change for the better are two different things.* Her head began to ache at the thought of untold stories, like her father's. From her seat above the railing, she watched a young family walk under the trees in the park, Dad pushing a stroller, and a young girl holding a bright balloon.

Her last full day in New York was her third appointment. Even though she had many destinations yet to see on her list like the Central Park Zoo, and Times Square, she had no time left to see them. She gazed out at the crisp, gray morning from her hotel window and picked up a sweater from her suitcase. Next to the in-room coffee maker were teabags, so she filled the carafe from the bathroom sink and heated the water. She settled back in the one comfortable chair in her room and picked up a book she'd found in the airport - *Wild Swans*, about the Tiananmen Square uprising. She read chapter after chapter, wrapped in her sweater, sipping tea and nodding in agreement. She thought of the protest she attended with Saiko and the others. When people in power fear losing it, innocent people pay.

The administrator she was meeting came highly recommended, and this time she was more hopeful she would locate James. Despite her leisurely morning, she arrived an hour early and perused the recital hall, listened in on practice rooms, and checked out the lobby's photos of famous musicians before her appointment.

"Nora Iguro?" A woman with shocking white hair slid a folder from the side of her desk. "I know that name. You wrote the composition the Los Angeles Symphony did with James .... Did you not?"

"That depends. Do you consider it innovative and ground-breaking or a ho-hum piece of tedious lackluster?"

The woman let out a hearty laugh. She introduced herself as Margaretta Taubman. "Please, call me Metta. James has told me all about you. I think every time he speaks of you he misses you more. You know – " She tented her hands under her chin, "You could divide your time between New York and Los Angeles. It's not an uncommon thing for musicians to do. The best of both worlds – East Coast, West Coast?"

"I'm happy where I am, thank you." Nora was stunned at Metta's words. "I came to ask you where I can find James. I've done some detective work trying to track him down, but – "

"Oh no! This is the movie *Wild Complications* all over again. Have you seen that one?"

"Can't say I see too many films, but what about James?"

"That's the thing. In the movie, Starla realizes she loves Markus and travels to Paris to find him, only to find he's traveled back to Houston to find her. Isn't that crazy? The same thing has happened to you two."

"I don't understand."

"It's James. He's in Los Angeles right now, meeting with a violin soloist for our fall production. He was going to look you up while he was there. Isn't that hilarious?"

"He was going to look me up?"

"He's flying back tomorrow. Can you stay until then?"

"I have to leave tomorrow. We start our new rehearsal schedule." Nora stood up to go. It was suddenly impossible for her to talk to this woman any longer.

"Look, I'm sorry things didn't work out." Metta realized this wasn't a laughing matter. "I'll tell James that you were here."

Nora continued to edge closer to Metta's office door. Everything was so quick and efficient here. Could she have a moment to process all of this? She put her hand on the door handle to steady herself. "Tell James I said hello. He has my address," she said. He had been in this office and probably sat in the same chair. She thanked Metta, who gave her a few encouraging words and invited her back any time.

Nora didn't realize how she exited the building and ended up back in the brisk fall weather, people in a hurry passing in both directions. What had just happened? Tell him she said hello - of all the things she could have said! She started walking and found herself on 5th Avenue overlooking Central Park. It was her last afternoon in New York.

A man on rollerblades with a boombox hit her shoulder and kept going. Off-balance, she rubbed her shoulder and stared after him. No fear! Her Taekwando classes gave her confidence and she gave a mental thank you to Demetrius. But Metta had just seen James a few days ago. What are the chances that James was in LA at the same time she was here? And Metta said he was going to look her up. It had been years since the argument, the job offer he couldn't refuse. She was a different woman and of course, James would be different too.

An autumn breeze picked up and she buttoned her trench coat instead of just tying the belt. She heard a clicking sound in the park and turned to look at a swirl of russet leaves. Beneath the trees was a group of jugglers tossing and catching fast-spinning pins. She stopped a moment and sat on a bench to watch the intricate patterns. A woman passed by with a baby carriage. Inside was a bright-eyed terrier listening to the woman who seemed to be having a pressing conversation with the dog.

The long walk and muddled thinking brought her no closer to any decision. Maybe it was a waste of time to come here. But there before her stood the Metropolitan Museum of Art with its grand steps and trio of majestic front doors. Once Nora bought her ticket, she marveled at the huge sprays of fresh flowers and didn't know what to see first. Wandering past Henry VIII's armor, she found an antique piano dating back to 1720. Slowing to look at a Stradivari violin, she stopped when she came to the Amati. The Amati Kurtz violin was known for its elegance and incomparable craftsmanship. Nora imagined what it would be like to play such an instrument.

The day before she had explored another Met museum, the Medieval Cloisters in Washington Heights. A group of seven Renaissance unicorn tapestries from the Netherlands graced the high walls. What a mystery! A myriad of colors, flowers, hunters, ladies in medieval dress, and of course, unicorns. According to the museum label, the unicorns possessed the qualities of freedom and magic. She was excited to give Lili and Tak the plush toy unicorns she found for them in the gift shop.

42

Nora

California, 1980

"I saw the bears and unicorns and thought of you two," Nora told Tak and Lili. They sat in the living room on a Saturday morning with Takami and BL listening to Nora's travel stories. As soon as she took them from the shopping bag, she knew she'd made a terrible mistake.

"What was I thinking?" Nora looked at the two teenagers and regretted the stuffed animals. "I have to realize you're growing up."

"That's okay Oba Nora," Lili said. "I'm never too old for stuffed animals." She rose from her chair, all long legs, and long hair. In one swift move, Lili kissed her aunt's cheek and whisked the gifts off to her room.

Tak looked around and with a soccer player's moves, spiked his unicorn, bouncing it in the air. "Thanks, Oba." He hugged the bear to his side and disappeared into the kitchen.

BL and Takami looked at each other.

"What's going on?" Nora said. "Is it about Saiko talking to James while I was gone? She told me."

"I have to tell you something." Takami was clearly ill at ease. "I wasn't exactly honest with you, Nora."

"What do you mean?"

Takami shifted uncomfortably and stood up.

"I told him to come clean with you, but he said he had a responsibility to obey his father's wishes," BL said. "Say it, Takami."

"Just give me a minute." He stared at the floor and then walked to the window. "I know I should have told you. So many times I almost told you, but I promised Dad."

"Promised who? What is going on?"

Takami released a flood of words and somewhere in them, she heard *father* and *alive*. "I told Dad about you, that he had a daughter, but he refused to see you until he was healthy and at home, not a weak old man in bed. Now he is very ill and realizes his time is short." Takami looked at her to gauge how angry she was. "I finally convinced him to see you. I've been trying all these years. You have to understand in our culture we respect our – "

"I thought I could trust you. You let me believe a lie." Nora found it hard to catch her breath.

"I told him," BL said.

"Don't make it worse," Takami said. "Believe me, it was hard to get him to agree. I've tried."

"No." Nora stood and blocked his way. "You've had years with him. You wanted to keep me from him. Did you tell him about me at all? You robbed me of years I could have had with him. " Her heart pounded in her ears.

"I did tell him about you – your concerts, our dinners together, how the kids love you, I told him everything, even your night in jail. He would refuse. The – staff wouldn't let you in." He had never seen Nora so angry.

"That's it. Take me. I want to see him now."

In the stark, spare hospital room, gray clouds outside the window failed to reflect the mood of the frail, wrinkled man. Her eyes were his, welled with tears and glistening. Unable to look away, she walked to his bedside. She felt his hand on her cheek and squeezed her eyes shut, feeling his touch.

Kioshi's hand shook. "My pearl, my daughter."

Her anger softened. With so much to say, her mind raced.

"Talk to me," Kioshi said.

She started with the homeless walk through the Indiana countryside with her mother and thought better of it. She talked of living with her grandmother but saw the hurt in his eyes and shifted to a softer story.

He smiled about her school in Chicago and the orchestra, and how she had saved her money to find him. "Look at you, so brave, so independent. Your music brought you here and we are together. Takami tells me you make your violin sing. You must bring it and play for me."

It seems they were both trying to keep parts of their lives from one another. She held his hand and took in every detail of his face. Besides, the wrinkles were the cheekbones that gave his smile a jolly look, the scar on his forehead, a proud souvenir of the long-ago protest, and his steely gray hair that looked like it had been cut with scissors. When he got better, she decided to take him to a good barber.

"Tell me about meeting Mother?"

Oh, I remember the first time I saw her at the church. She sat right next to me and I could feel electricity just being near. I knew right then that she was the one. She was the American woman I had found my pearl for, dived so deep, beauty for beauty – inside too – a beautiful person." His gaze drifted in reverie with his smile. "And out of that love, we made you. If only I had known – if only she had told me, answered my letters." Kioshi's voice grew softer. He tried to catch his breath. "I was working to make a good life for us – working hard – when they sent me to the camps."

Nora gripped his hand and held it to her cheek. She looked to Takami who shifted uneasily in his seat. Maybe this was the first time he'd heard this story of her mother.

"Let me tell you about the broken stone," Kioshi began.

"Oh, *Otōsan,* not that sorry old story," Takami said.

"What story?" Nora asked.

"Today, there is a *Sessho-seki* left from a mountain volcano, a demon stone in a Japanese village."

"Yeah, a stone from like a thousand years ago."

"Takami, stop!" Nora wanted to hear whatever her father had to say.

"As I was *saying,*" Kioshi's eyebrow shot up at Takami, "*Sessho-seki* means killing stone in Japanese.

Nora winced at his smallpox scars. She held his smooth hand and her struggles seemed small in comparison.

"The stone holds the spirit of a demon from long ago. It is the spirit of the fox with nine tails, *Tamamo-no-Mae.* The fox appeared as a beautiful woman and she conspired to overthrow the Mikado,

Emperor Toba, the father of 14 royal children. A brave warrior heard of the plan and brandished his sword – "

Kioshi raised his arm with effort, swirling figure eights with an imaginary sword in his grasp, " – killing her before she could carry through with her violent deed. After the conflict, Tamamo-no-Mae's fleeing spirit became trapped inside the *Sessho-seki* of volcanic stone forever. To this day the myth warns that the spirit in the stone is so strong, it will kill anyone who touches it."

Nora tightened her shoulders. "So the story has survived through hundreds of years. What does it mean?"

"Ah – even our long-ago ancestors wrestled with good and with evil. There are times when we have evil perpetrated against us." He looked at Nora as if his frown could will that evil out of existence for her. He sighed. "But we Japanese don't talk about bad luck. Better to trap the evil in stone. Too many bad vibes, yes?"

Nora nodded.

"Old stories like this one, the omens, they inspire us to fight against evil, to conquer it. So even though the evil spirit is trapped, if the stone ever breaks, the evil would be released into the world. This is always a possibility, yes? So we live with possibilities. Always possibilities." He looked into his children's eyes.

"I want you to know – both of you – what things were like in Japan and why I left." Kioshi's voice grew raspy. "Life was very difficult. The Great Depression here was severe, in Japan too." Kioshi covered his mouth and coughed.

"My family had little money. I didn't want to ask for a new pencil for school. My mother plucked chickens to earn money to feed us. There were no jobs and never enough food. My clothes were ragged and I had to wear the neighbor boy's shoes when he outgrew them. I put newspaper inside to cover the holes in the bottom.

"People laughed. But when I dove in the water, people didn't see my clothes." He smiled. "You see, I could do something that not everyone could do, and I was admired, no mocking. So many dives to help feed my family. So I kept going, diving deeper, finding more pearls, always looking for a pearl better than any other man's."

Nora looked at the dark veins crisscrossing his hand. "The pearl on the ring my mother always wore. That was from you. I never saw her without it."

Kioshi's eyes looked up, fragile and defenseless.

"*Otōsan,* you're getting too tired. We'd better go," Takami said.

"No no – just a while longer. I need to tell my daughter," Kioshi said. "Just when things started to improve for Japan, the military took power over the leader we elected."

Kioshi paused and breathed. Nora wanted him to rest, but couldn't tear herself away.

"We had new rules on what we could say, where we could go – very restrictive, rules that required us to call truth a lie, to be loyal to death. All children were forced to train using wooden toy guns with real bayonets. We were told to cut each other, to make us strong. I hated the training."

Nora shot a look at Takami. His face told her that he hadn't heard about this before.

"The newspapers didn't tell us we were taking over parts of China. The people were given no choice and we had no power to stop the military. I had to leave. I had a grandfather in California and – " Kioshi coughed, a rattling sound from deep in his chest.

"Things are better in this country for you, Takami. Nora, you are half white. They will listen to you. Correct things, repair the wrongs." He looked at Takami. "Remember that's why I'm here. I rocked the boat."

Takami explained, "Dad worked for migrant farmers and the Farm Workers Union. He'd work with lawmakers to make California farms safer. It was tough and he made some enemies, but – "

"Nora will find a way to make things better." Kioshi turned back to her. Nora swallowed hard.

A nurse appeared at the door. "You must leave now. Mr. Iguro needs his rest." She walked in and stood by the bedside waiting for them to leave.

"No rest." Kioshi was gruff with her. "I have things to say to my children."

"My father's a little cranky," Takami hoped the nurse would leave, but she stood unmoving

"I'll come back tomorrow, father." Nora savored the sound of the word in her voice. "We'll talk more tomorrow."

"Yes yes, tomorrow." Kioshi smiled a wan, round-cheeked smile.

"You too, Starfish," Kioshi looked at his son.

"Like you say, Dad, fall seven times, get up eight," Takami nodded.

Together they walked down the long hall with slow steps.

"Dad told me to do something. There has to be something I can do for him but I'm not so good with words. Takami, people need to know." Nora drew her sleeve across her eyes. "His bravery, his strength – "

Takami placed his hand on her shoulder. I know it was wrong not to tell you. He had his pride."

"I'll think of something."

"You're your father's daughter. He had his pearl diving. You have your violin."

At the corner, they saw two brown-uniformed men watching them. They looked like they belonged at a prison gate, not a hospital. Nora walked faster, half expecting them to cuff her and take her back to jail. She pushed the elevator button and took one last look at them through the closing doors.

The next morning was Sunday. Nora had agreed to play at an early church service with a small chamber orchestra, but afterward, she would go directly to the hospital to see her father. She opened the door to leave her apartment and there was Takami. The look on his face told her everything.

In slow motion, she moved back from the door nearly tripping over her own feet.

Takami gently took her wrist and led her to the sofa. He brought her a cold glass of water from the kitchen. "There's more I haven't told you." His face was haggard and his voice, flat. "For years our lawyer has tried to free him. He's been in prison, Nora. That's why he didn't want you to see him all these years." He sighed deeply and his shoulders rounded.

Nora looked at the change in him. "The ACLU – "

"Now you know why I knew who to call when you were in jail. We were so close to getting him home on parole too. But then before the election, Congressman O'Rourke came out with his hair-raising TV ads about cracking down on dangerous offenders - meaning neighbors from different ethnic groups. O'Rourke won by a landslide. Dad's speeches for unions and equity were called criminal incitement. Un-American. There was a riot in a nearby neighborhood after his speech. They claimed *mens rea*, or guilty mind. The chance of parole looked more like one in a million after O'Rourke won."

"Free speech is free speech."

"He never gave up hope, Nora. And once I told Dad about you, he really believed he'd live long enough to greet you as a free man. I couldn't deny him that and I wanted to believe it too. But then when they put him in the hospital, when he knew how close he was, he knew he had to see you. He swallowed his pride."

"It looked like any hospital room to me."

"He made a deal with the guards. They knew he was close to the end. He arranged for the guards to be down the hall when you came. Dad kept his pride right up to the end. He got to see you as if he was a free man."

She couldn't listen anymore. With a shuddering breath, Nora reached her arms around her brother and they sat huddled together, her face buried in his jacket, and the scent of leather.

"I never knew I could feel so empty." Takami held on and rocked her side to side.

43

Nora
1980

After her student left, Nora made a PB&J sandwich while she waited for her next lesson. A resounding knock on the door ten minutes early startled her, and when she opened it, Tak charged in. "Tell me what to do!" His voice, now low and powerful, would have been a fine singing voice without all the anger.

"You want a quick PB&J?"

He nodded. "I can't talk to Mom and Dad. They just don't get it. Everything is my fault."

Tak had been the subject of a few tense conversations with BL. His mother said he had dated so many girls in his class that she called them his flavors-of-the-month. But Danielle's self-confident, adventurous nature demanded more of him than the acquiescing girls he'd dated. With playful wit, she commanded that he try to understand her, whether he agreed with her or not. He found her onerous sparring irresistible.

Nora guided her nephew to a chair at the table and pushed him to sit, placing the sandwich plate in front of him. "Start from the beginning. It's Danielle, isn't it."

"All I did was make a few suggestions about our plans after the
prom and all hell broke loose. She says I never listen to her. Now she's letting some guy take her home from school in his new car."

"So listen to her."

"I never get my way."

"How about a compromise?"

"That means I don't get my way!"

"So Tak, do you want to feel closer to Danielle, or do you want to have your way and be miserable?" His mouth was full of sandwich so she continued. "Look, nobody's trying to tell you who to be or what to do. But you like Danielle, right? She tests you. You know you'd never be happy with some girl who only agreed with everything you said, right?"

He nodded and swallowed. "I guess so."

"Maybe she just wants to know that you hear her, that you weigh and value what she's saying."

His fist hit the table. "Whose side are you on?"

Nora sighed. "She listens to you, right? Tries to understand?" Tak chewed the sandwich and glared at her.

"How about reading an inspiring novel? Something with a different worldview." She reached for the peanut butter and started a sandwich for herself.

His voice cracked. "Are you kidding?"

A knock at the door signaled her next student had arrived.

"What guy reads an inspirational novel? Oh man – the more I talk about this it just gets worse."

"Just hear me out. I've seen a few of my high school girls with this book, and they say it's really good. From a pad by the phone, she pulled off a sheet of paper and started writing. "It's called *Siddhartha*. Check it out."

"How lame is that! You're no better than Mom. Tak batted away the paper Nora held out to him. "Danielle read that one too. I think that's part of what our problem is. No lame book is going to do anything!"

The second knock sounded louder this time and Nora headed for the door.

"Tak, if you didn't care for Danielle so much, you wouldn't be so angry. Think of the novel as a peace offering. Then discuss it with her and don't argue!"

"All this listening and understanding – it's just stupid, Oba Nora. You don't understand. Nobody understands."

"Your grandfather talked about identity. Some seek identity with a career, a watch, a car, and for me, it's the wonder of music. Tak, some guy with a car has been taking Danielle home. You don't need a car or a watch to mend things with Danielle. Show her your identity." Nora took his hand and squeezed it. "Let her know who you are."

She tucked the slip of paper in his t-shirt pocket and patted it. "Think of what your grandfather would want you to do," she whispered. Tak stalked past the surprised young student in the hallway. She hated being on Tak's bad side, but knowing Tak, he probably owed Danielle a concession.

44

Nora
1980

Nora opened the door and with an anxious habit, smoothed her black skirt. The small group gathered in the sunbeams of the sanctuary. She stood close and nodded to the pastor who began with solemn words. Nora loved the warmth of his voice and the company surrounding her, the baby's snuffles and coos bringing smiles to their faces.

Tak had Danielle's arm in his. She caught his smile. Did he read that novel after all? Lili carried a camera, ready to capture the day for her new little sister. One face was unfamiliar, a serious, older woman. Could it be Takami's mother, the woman her father had married?

Her mind wandered from the pastor's words and she tried to imagine Takami as a new father again. His goofy smile almost made her laugh out loud. His arm reached around BL with baby Isla in her arms, her face typically inscrutable. Nora heard the pastor say her own name and bounced back to his words.

"Do you, Nora Iguro, by word and example, pledge as Isla's godparent to watch over this child and uplift her life in faith?"

She cleared her throat. "I do."

After the ceremony, she nuzzled the squirming infant. Spinning her in a circle, she stopped to look into her dark, blinking eyes and told her stories that sounded more like a fortune teller than a godparent. Isla's eyes were Taiwanese like her mother's, and her chin may have resembled her US Navy father. Little Isla would be half of two cultures, like Nora. Takami's and BL's adopted daughter stopped squirming and cooing to listen.

"Look at that," BL told Nora. "I hope she listens like that when she's thirteen."

Lili snapped photos and Nora turned. "Can I ask you something?" Nora tugged Takami's arm.

He linked his arm in hers and they walked out of the church to pause under an old rosewood tree, saved from the landscaper's excavator when the church was built.

"You haven't decided to work in New York, have you?"

"Let's just say I wouldn't mind going back for a little research. I have some ideas for the symphony." She caught his puzzled look and laughed. "I'm Isla's godmother now. Somebody has to make sure she's properly spoiled, and that has to be me." A breeze whispered through the leaves above them.

"I'm thinking of that day in the hospital, the last day with our father," Nora said.

Takami nodded.

"For me, it was one of those 'remember exactly where you were' days, like where I was when I heard about Neil Armstrong's walk on the moon. I can see the look in Dad's eyes when I told him about the pearl. It's indelible. I'll never forget it."

"I know it was wrong, Nora. I should have told you about Dad."

"Like you said, he was a proud man." Opening her shoulder bag, she pulled out an envelope.

"I have the letter with me. Kioshi's letter that you and your mother gave me. I thought your mother would be here and might want it back now. Do you think she would talk to me?"

Takami felt awkward. At a loss, he put his hands in his pockets while he tried to find words.

"We're a family, aren't we?" he said. "I remember Dad saying we can have purpose in life, and we can make our own meaning. First, your purpose was to find Dad, and you found us."

Now Nora didn't have to ask about the letter.

Takami looked up when BL approached. His mother walked next to her with baby Isla in her arms.

"One last thing, Nora," Takami looked at her. "You've got the purpose, now go for the meaning."

"Picture," BL ordered, showing Lili where to stand to get the shot she wanted of Takami and Nora under the tree.

"Wait," he said. He took his mother's arm and brought her into the picture on his other side.

"Oh look. Isla's hand is up in the air. Lili, take it now." BL said.

Lili kept clicking her camera, advancing the film, and focusing again while Takami nudged Nora's shoulder in front of his. His cheek pressed to her forehead and their forced smiles gradually felt more real.

"C'mon back to the house?" BL said. "Everybody's bringing something. Nora the head honcho auntie must be there. The kids insist. We have miso soup, pickled vegetables, macaroni, and Takami's grilling some fish."

The auntie comment warmed her heart. She may not know a thing about mothers, but she could be a head honcho aunt. "But I didn't make anything."

"Nora, just come over." BL sounded exasperated, but Nora knew better.

"One more thing," Nora turned back to face Takami. Lili wants to play violin at Interlochen. She asked me to remind you that it would be the opportunity of a lifetime."

"Nora,"

"I'm just telling you. She's determined."

"I hear you." Takami scratched his head. "It's like your *densho* - passing your music on to the next generation."

The food at Takami's was plentiful and so beautiful that Nora took way too much. With her plate full, she approached Takami's mother and asked about some of the foods she had never tried before. They made a date for lunch.

When it was time to leave, the phone rang. "It's for you Oba Nora," Lili said, handing over the phone. "Thanks for talking to my dad," Lili whispered. "He's going to think about Interlochen." She threw her arms around Nora's neck and ran off.

"We're making mochi at Saiko's," Dorothy said. "You in?"

Over the phone, Nora noticed the naturally sharp edges of her friend's voice sounded smoother since her father's death. Surely it wasn't easy for Dorothy. Nora welcomed her effort.

Late afternoon was an odd time to make mochi. On the other hand, Nora didn't want to go home to an empty apartment right now.

45

Nora

1980

Before Nora could knock on the door, Saiko opened it. "Come to the back." She led Nora through the house.

"You've painted the whole wall this time. It's the color of Native American clay."

"Terra Cotta," Saiko said.

"Where is everyone? What about the mochi?" Nora asked.

"First things first," Saiko opened the sliding door. The table held the familiar pitcher of spiked iced tea and two glasses. A man in a facing chair turned to look at her.

Nora stood in a frozen stare. James didn't look needy or desperate, just a softer version of his younger self.

Saiko nudged her out the sliding door and closed it behind her. She watched as Nora sat, but she could only see her back. Was she angry? Probably not. Where would they start? Finding her father? James's postcards with no return address? Nora's night in jail? Saiko's desire to eavesdrop made her linger to adjust her curtains and watch the animated gyrations outside the window. James handed over a glass of tea. They both spoke at once and Saiko unwillingly retreated to another room muttering *koi no yokan*, the inevitability of what would happen between these two.

An hour later, Saiko brought out sandwiches. She made sure to knock on the glass before she opened the door. "Ahem, Nora, he was so insistent. I hope you don't mind. And there's no mochi. Dorothy lied."

James said he had something to show them. "Don't go yet, Saiko. I want you to see this too." James stood and reached into a bag behind his chair. Out came a battered violin case.

Nora drew in her breath. "It can't be."

James was holding the case with the tacky sticker from the Chicago Preparatory Orchestra on it. Without a word, Nora smoothed her fingers over the case and set it on the patio table. The latches sprang with their familiar flip and the cover complained and gave way. She dried her hands on her skirt and gently lifted the sable violin to her chin. Settling into the familiar fingerboard, she drew the bow across the strings, listening to the sound of its familiar tone, just as she remembered it. Maybe better. The truth in the sound sang to her with the passion of a human voice. She saw beauty in the dark wood surface of the violin that had endured by her side through so many sorrows and joys. It was all she needed.

"Still sounds good," Saiko said.

Watching her, James took a moment to speak. "I had it restored and restrung. It wasn't in too bad a shape, but you wouldn't have wanted to see it that way so – "

As she listened, her eyes blurred.

With the violin clutched in her hand, she skirted the table and threw her arms around his neck, nearly spilling their drinks. He told her how he spotted the sticker on the case in New York and chased a guy down Doyers Street offering him money on the spot. His arm reached around her. "I had to bring it back to you."

Nora's watched a sigh rise in his chest and imagined what it might mean. She sighed too, not in any hurry to release this clumsy embrace that felt like a cymbal crash, a long note held in a familiar harmony that overwhelmed her even after the song was over.

Nora stood, tucked the violin under her chin to rip a spirited arpeggio with a flying spiccato.

"Hey, take it easy. You're shredding it already!" Saiko said. More than a few of the new horse hairs from the bow had split, sent in different directions from Nora's athletic playing.

She stopped and examined the bow with a regretful glance at James, but he was laughing. The laugh lines surprised her, but that tousled hair with a few flecks of gray still created butterflies.

"I've got my reasons," Nora countered. "It's pent-up energy." She raised her bow to Saiko who had already disappeared behind the sliding door.

"You know, I wasn't exactly living like a Trappist monk in New York. I saw a life coach, the same one as Metta. Still do. She told me to come back and face you, to be wildly vulnerable, she said."

"You New Yorkers and your life coaches. All I need is Saiko's chicken therapy. Was that therapy after – "

"After I found your violin."

"So what does that mean, wildly vulnerable?"

"I'll tell you. I'm feeling relief, warmth, anticipation…and you?"

"I don't know. What am I feeling? Like a pulled-out rug is being put back under me?"

"That's not a feeling."

"James, you show up here and we never talked like this before, and – how do I know?" She threw her hands up.

"You look like you're anxious."

"Anxious? What do you mean anxious?"

"Take some time." He slid his hand over hers, his voice with its soft fire. "You'll figure it out."

He was going to say more, but Nora motioned for him to listen. Inside the house, Saiko was playing Stevie Wonder's "Overjoyed" from the album *In Square Circle*.

"Perfect." Nora smiled. They listened all the way through to the end.

James picked up a sandwich. "I'm here for two weeks," James said between bites. "Is Naugles still around? We could see the old orchestra crew, grab some tacos and take a walk in that park we liked."

Nora set the violin on its case, looking between it and James. "This is not a small thing. James, it's all so much." Was she talking about the violin? She pointed her finger. "For one thing, you have to know Naugles is Del Taco now."

James didn't respond. "You look fantastic, Nora." He touched his glass to hers; the ice in both glasses long melted. His look became serious. "I've played this moment over in my mind a hundred times - what it would be like to see you again."

He listened to her measured words, her life's quick fall, and the slow climb after he left, finding her father. James responded in awkward ways, impatient as if he was on some mission. He'd told her about New York's breakneck pace. "I'm glad you had a talk with Metta when you came to New York. She likes you and didn't bat an eye when I dropped my summer music event work to see you. And here I am trying to turn lost years into minutes." He frowned and looked at her as if he was trying to figure out her expression.

She waited. "What are you frowning about?"

"So I'm thinking if you could spend your next vacation in the city there are people I want you to meet?" He said it like a question. "We have a chamber music group. Wait until you meet Juan our bass player - we practice in his apartment. And Min, the flutist. We've got funding to produce a series of outdoor summer concerts in parks around the city. We could use your ideas." Without a doubt, New York was home to him. "Nora, there are so many places I want to show you. Red Hook has a park where we can watch the sunset under the Brooklyn Bridge and it's like the windows on the buildings catch fire." James' fingers raced over the condensation on his glass and he waited for a word from her. "Seeing you again, I miss you in my life."

Nora was settling into the initial shock of him and tried to listen. He seemed different. This is what significant time does, despite the familiar mannerisms of that annoying boy who sat next to her in the Chicago Youth Orchestra. "You never married. You didn't have children."

"No time. No space. No regrets. The things I thought were so important when I left? Not so much. Except I should have invited you to come years ago."

"You can be proud and stubborn that way." Why did she say that? Talking together felt so good and she could tell her comment stung. So he didn't have children after all. "Isn't it funny, I call my students my kids. I flew to Interlochen to see one of them perform. That was on my way to see you in New York."

"Metta told me."

"And there's Lili and Tak, James. I have a niece and nephew, and who knew I could love children so much? And now I have a goddaughter, Isla." She could tell him about her darlings. Things invariably spilled out when she talked to James.

46

Nora

1980

"They'll be multi-sensory with ensemble voices, instruments, dance, and a projection screen." James's voice brimmed with energy as he told her about his new collaboration for outdoor summer concerts.

"How about telling a broader story – the story of Central Park?" James's words sparked an idea. Nora stood and paced across the patio. "Did you know there was a village of Black survivors of the Civil War working from their own homes in their own village?" Nora told him about the map room at the New York Public Library, the purchase of Manhattan from the Lenape tribe, and suggested they use music to tell the story.

James noticed that she said *they* tell the story. "But," he paused, "We're not Black or Indian."

His comment shocked her. The Lenape was about history not a transaction. "I don't have to be Black to feel for displaced people. I don't have to be all Japanese to feel for my dad's life in the camps. I don't seem to fit in your culture or my brother Takami's, but music doesn't exist in just one culture, mine or yours. It's not static. We can find something new in the mix.

"Maybe music can pick up where protests leave off. The left-handed, the brown-skinned – who hasn't felt like the odd man out? Like John Lennon's song *Imagine*. That song still helped inspire the Czech Velvet Revolution. They took back their country without firing a shot." Her pacing picked up speed. "I want to make music that wakes up people."

"Yeah, I remember when that song came out in New York. You couldn't find a radio station that didn't play it. I couldn't escape it."

"That's power. Besides, his wife – "

"Yoko was Japanese. Everyone blamed her for breaking up the Beatles."

"But she inspired Lennon. He credited her with most of the *Imagine* lyrics. Not many people realized that." Nora poured more tea. Had they been talking for minutes? Hours? Time folded in on itself.

James picked up the thread. "Iconic like Marvin Gaye, yeah, what's going on – "

James stood and danced around the patio, clasping her fingers as he sang the words. " – Tell me what's – what's that chicken looking at me like that for?" He let go and stood back.

Nora noticed a California Grey, cocking her head and peering at James. "That's Egg Nog. She doesn't know you, that's all. Look, we can go further back. We need native instruments from the Lenape tribe. Maybe Native musicians, and drums, and native wind instruments. I'm thinking sounds through the fields outside Seneca Village. We can incorporate parts of their dance rhythms in conflict with Dutch and British folk tunes. You know Lenape means authentic, true people?

"So we'll need an authentic choreographer. Slow down, will you? You've had time to think about this. It's new to me – "

"You're the one who started this. I'm itching to write again, James. It's new to me too. I haven't had an idea like this since well – I know we argue but we can build something beautiful from riffs and scraps of tunes. I want to do this for the Lenapes and the Seneca Villagers, and for my dad."

"Now it's way beyond Central Park and you're doing this for *you*." James recognized the familiar charge in her voice. "What makes you think we can pull it off?"

"I'm ready to write my music now." She pointed her bow at him. "You are my muse."

"Uh, I'm a guy. Muses are women."

"Not so. Kerouac had Cassady. Frida Kahlo had Diego Rivera."

"Okay, then." He folded his arms on the table. "I'll be your inspiration to come to New York."

Nora swallowed hard. "When I talked to Metta, she had an idea: a two-state solution."

Instantly, she regretted the big decision of Metta's idea. It was so much more comfortable talking about music. "Our themes could speak with the volatile rage of Beethoven, the soul of Irma Thomas, the passion of Puccini."

"You've said that to your students, haven't you?"

"It's that decisive, slow burn, the force – the salvation of music." She played for James and the strings sang her jail time beneath her fingers, the Lenape of Central Park, the jazz masters of San Juan Hill, the rebuilt City Hope Church, her father's days of internment, all of it, singing beyond words.

James leaned back to listen. "Play that last part one more time, Nora."

"I need staff paper, a pencil – "

James looked at her. "I won't forget."

Again she whipped through the new passage with kindled senses and put down her bow. "I want our LA orchestra to play it too - in New York. We have a Japanese composer who transcribes some of our work and he was telling me that minor chords that sound sad to American ears have no such connection to the Japanese, just familiarity." She tapped her bow. "You're picturing what it will sound like, aren't you, this coming together of so many cultures? Colors splashed behind us when we play, maybe Native artwork or photos, you think?" She looked at James' face and felt her own ideas burst like popcorn. "Picture a joining like bridges – feeling connected." She turned to him. "I'll agree to your chamber orchestra, but our LA Symphony has to be the group to play it in New York."

They sat down. She saw James' thoughtful nod and could tell he was making his own plans.

"And the Yokohama Concert Hall near the bay where Dad dove for pearls."

James shook his head but he was smiling.

"Metta said she liked what we did for the LA Symphony," Nora said.

"There's Wynton. He could direct us to some tunes from bluesy New Orleans to New York broody jazz – "

"You're not talking about Benson Wynton?" Nora was awestruck.

"Hey, I know some people." James pulled a face along with his name-dropping. "Have you heard his oratorio *Clearing Fields*? He loves video games too. We played Pac-Man last week."

"My nephew Tak plays Pac-Man. His mom keeps limiting his arcade time and then he walks around humming the tune. You could ask Wynton about his New Orleans experience. The jazz roots part?"

"Anyway, I think we could talk to him about getting our music out to a new generation. Gamers can be hard-core. It could be powerful."

"Let's work in a skosh of shimmery Japanese Music City Pop for my dad. We'll call it *Beyond Seneca Village*."

"Nah, how about *The Seneca Opus*."

"I'll fight you for it! We'll need more than this if we're going to pitch it to Metta," Nora said.

The sun was lowering and Nora saw the spark of amber in his eye growing darker. Nora felt a raindrop and looked up at the graying sky. She clasped his hand, pulling him up from the table. "Come back to the apartment." She grabbed her Chicago violin and hugged it. "We'll brainstorm all night." After a few gusts of wind came more rain. "Out of all the peaks and valleys, booms and busts, and Icarus moments, I love what I'm feeling right now."

Rain began to soak through them. James pulled her close and her arms wrapped his body, softer than the taut torso she remembered, but then hers was softer too.

"You feel like the rain on my dry ground." He kissed her the way he used to.

She blinked and understood exactly what he meant.

"If you have enough butter," James whispered, "I can make croissants for breakfast."

47

Nora

1990

Backstage, Nora was securing her violin after their first concert of the season. An usher approached her with a note. "From a tall man in the lobby," the young man told her. "He said he'll wait for you there, but he's in a hurry."

Nora thanked him and unfolded the paper: *Loved your concert. Can't wait to see you – Asher*

Could it be? "Look at this. *Fushigi.*" she handed the note to James and practiced a word from her adult education class in Japanese.

"It's been a long time." He stopped arranging the pages of music in his hands and looked at Nora. "What are you going to do?"

"What if it's really him? I have no idea. Just wait here for me, will you?" She threaded her way through after-concert well-wishers to scan the faces in the lobby. Her brother was tall. Recognizing him wouldn't be easy. Her eyes were drawn to a man who towered above a mixed group of people. He turned as if he was drawn by her gaze and his face broke into a broad smile. "Nora!"

She rushed up and nearly collided with him. People in the lobby tried not to stare at the Japanese principal violinist running to hug an American man.

Nora felt Asher's strong embrace through to her core. "It's really you."

"Your voice – it's the same." Asher said. "I'd know you anywhere. Look at you. And you're with the symphony for god's sake. I loved your concert. The *Bolero* – "

"Asher, did you get any of my letters? Did Mother?" Nora looked at him fully, unable to believe, grasping his arms to make sure he wasn't an illusion.

He shook his head. "You know, Nora, I was so young and we moved around a lot. I don't know what happened. I couldn't say." He scooped her up in another embrace. "But we've got to talk. I'm flying back to work in Indianapolis. Give me your number and I'll call you." He reached in his pockets for paper and pen. "Better yet, Mom's 75th birthday party is coming up in two weeks." He gave her the paper and she started to write.

"You should fly up and surprise her. That would be the best surprise she could possibly get for her birthday."

Nora looked at him with a skeptical glance.

"I'll arrange everything – your tickets, the hotel – you can stay in the same hotel where we're having the party."

"Mother is alive?" Until this moment, she wasn't sure Asher was alive either. "Are you sure she'll want to see me?"

"She'll be thrilled. But this is mostly for me. For us. We need to catch up. Let's not ever get lost from each other again." Asher looked as if he'd just solved an issue of existential proportions.

"Asher, I'd love to spend some time with you. I'm just not sure."

"Say yes, Nora. I've got to go, but I'll call you when I get back. You'll have time to think it over."

Nora gave him a last look and squeezed his hand in both of hers. "My little brother," she smiled and watched him weave his way through to the door. Already she missed him, the pull of family. She had so much to tell her mother and maybe it was time to forgive. She ran to tell James.

48

Nora

Indianapolis, 1990

Ruth motioned other family members away. In low tones, she told the story behind the pearl ring to Nora alone. Nora sat barely moving as Ruth recalled Kioshi's pearl diving, his vow to give the ring to his future wife, and his journey from Japan to the US. The found threads that wove the two young lives together turned into a patchwork of youthful intensity. As she recalled those days, Ruth's memories took her away from everyone in the room.

"Things don't work so well." Mother looked to both sides and leaned forward talking softly to Nora in the here and now. "It's painful. I'm ugly."

"Oh, Mother." Nora's chest squeezed. It might have been a hint of remorse she saw hiding behind her mother's half-smile. But Nora was afraid it was just her own wishful thinking. "I have a letter for you."

Asher glanced back at the two of them from across the room, feeling wary of their conversation. After the concert, he was ebullient to see Nora again, but now there were some thorny issues. He asked a work friend in HR about an investigator. He hadn't used one since the divorce, but he had to be sure that Nora was who she seemed to be. On the plane back from Los Angeles he began to have second thoughts about inviting her to their mother's birthday party, but the invitation was made. The best he could hope for was damage control. So far the family hadn't reacted with anything more than a few questions. Before yesterday, anyone else with proof that Mother had a half-Japanese child had taken the secret to their graves.

He still had two kids to put through college, and alimony to pay their mother. When he married a younger woman, he didn't think about kids. It annoyed him every time he was with them and people called him Grandpa. He planned to put his kids through graduate school, just like his parents put him through Indiana State and Wharton Business for his graduate degree.

Asher fielded questions about Nora's authenticity from his father's side, the only relatives he had left. With calm ease he didn't feel, he assured them that she wasn't a charlatan. Asher made off-handed comments about the ongoing investigation of his half-sister. Nothing had yet materialized beyond a night in jail for disorderly conduct at a human rights protest. He would come off like a brute if he shellacked her for a protest like that. So he regaled them with antics from their childhood, making his cousins laugh by telling them stories of sock puppet shows he and Nora would perform for his mother, filling in the details he was too young to remember. Yet much could have happened in their life apart. He wouldn't feel at ease until the investigator's final report came back.

When he noticed Nora stand abruptly and walk away from Mother, he wasn't sure things had gone as she had hoped. He motioned to his daughter and son to approach her, in case of an argument. Surely she wouldn't come down on a man in front of his own children. "Nora, I'd like you to meet my kids, Asher Jr., and my daughter. We named Nora Anne for you."

Nora looked tired but produced a reserve of energy to greet her namesake niece and nephew. The siblings couldn't have been more different. Asher Jr. with his affable voice inherited his father's smile. Nora Anne stood like a block of wood, her face ready to scream in boredom. Asher Jr. told Nora he was a musician too. He was curious to hear about her path to the symphony.

"After playing with the SFSYO I went to music school at UC Berkeley on a scholarship. I still know people at the Youth Orchestra if you're interested. It's a great place to start. After graduation, I tried out for the Los Angeles Symphony and I've been there ever since. There I'll stay. They'll have to throw me out."

Mother had been watching. Nora saw her sip champagne and set the glass on a cocktail napkin. If only that napkin could catch fire and burn to charred bits. Mother looked ready to say something and thought better of it.

Asher laughed. "In that case, our family will have to come visit you. I have a meeting in LA next month. Can you get us tickets?"

Nora told Asher and his son about the pieces they were preparing for the concert when Nora Anne broke in.

"I'm not going anywhere to see you." She stared at her father and then at Nora, unable to contain herself. "I hate that I was named for you. The only reason you're here is to mess with our family. I see who you are. You just show up like you're a part of us."

"Nora Anne!" Asher held his daughter's arm.

Guests stared, but Nora Anne pulled her arm away. "I know everything and you don't know anything."

Asher tried to move her away from the angry block of wood who was his daughter, but Nora stood resolute. "I hear your spite, dear, but life is too short for it." Nora thought of the summer in the barn with her mother, her interloper status at music school, the search for her father, and now her friends in Fountain Valley, the ones she needed and who needed her, friends who wouldn't question who she was, not even Dorothy. Saiko was right. Family could be whoever you wanted them to be.

She looked at Nora Anne and saw an impenetrable force in a new generation. "It's too late. I've heard enough anger. I lost my mother because of such anger." Nora gave a pained glance at her mother engaged in conversation. "I lived through years of anger from your great-grandmother who let me know every day that I didn't belong. I choose to free myself from all of it right now." She turned to leave.

Nora Anne came at her, but her father held her back. Escaping Asher's grasp she turned. "When you ran away, Great Grandma never looked for you." Her voice was loud and shrill. "She told Grandma and Grandma never looked for you either. Never. You were the secret shame in our family."

Nora headed for the door and Asher caught up to her.

"I'm so sorry. This is unconscionable." Distraught, Asher looked back at his daughter and then at Nora. Clearly, his mother had told Nora Anne more than he thought. "This is all new to them. I only told the kids about you last night. Really, I don't want to lose my sister again. Things take time."

Nora looked at her brother and saw through him. He had two weeks since they reconnected, not to mention the years before, for Asher to tell his family about her. Without a word, she pushed the door and let it close on its silent hinges behind her. She had done what was expected of her and said what she wanted to say. For years she had lived without knowing if her mother and brother were alive. Now she knew all she needed to know. It was midnight, and her steps had newfound energy. She found a lone cab outside the hotel lobby.

On the plane's descent to Los Angeles, Nora looked out the window at the twinkly lights. There on her hand was the pearl ring. After all the years it had graced her mother's hand, she felt it smooth the shards of the night, felt her father and his strength, diving deep with hope. It was a fair trade, she thought, the ring for Kioshi's letter to

Ruth. The initial searing pain of her mother's new betrayal was subsiding. When Ruth told the others she needed to talk to her daughter alone, Nora braced herself. But this time she left on her own terms. The memory of the pearl on her mother's hand was now replaced by the few moments she spent with her father. The letter would be forgotten, written to a woman who saw love as an arrangement, a deal.

Nora thought about her life growing up and the way people looked at her. She had assumed all people looked at one another like that. But James didn't. And her Japanese friends who were now her family didn't. Her first visit to the farmer's market with Saiko came to mind. Nora learned which vendors looked past customers like her, but not all were like that.

But after her mother's birthday party, she understood. When she walked into the hotel that night, she wasn't sure what to expect. She couldn't brush off their scorn as misinterpreted when it came from her own family. If Nora Anne were as stubborn as her great-grandmother, a herculean effort couldn't turn her around.

Recounting the *almosts*, she slipped the pearl ring on and off her finger – almost patching the holes in her childhood, almost reaching an understanding of what a parent is for, almost close to the secret of her abandonment being washed away, so close, but not quite. Being half of something wasn't a whole anything.

There was something elemental about the California women and her feelings for them. What would Saiko have to say when she told her about her mother? Dorothy would weigh in with something prickly and painful, but still worthwhile, no doubt. Maybe they would say her mother did the only thing she knew of to keep them alive. Asher had named his daughter for her, even if he had kept the reason a secret. And maybe she could defy her mother's demand that forbade all contact and meet with Asher, invite him to a concert or two.

Inside her, old dreams evaporated and new dreams took root. There was the way James had found her again and their *Beyond Seneca Village* composition found its way to both coasts, Japan too. Listeners had sent letters from home and abroad about their music that healed or inspired, calmed or woke them up. One listener said it made him feel like he'd been a part of something all along that he never knew about. But now he knew, and it could never be taken away. Another asked if Nora would send her a new CD after she left hers too close to the fireplace.

After a new performance, she would find letters, some in Japanese. Nora had Takami read them to her, but her classes in Japanese were helping her to read them herself. She saved every letter and thought of traveling to Yokohama to walk the streets where her father had walked. She liked to think the song for her father could never be erased.

James would tease and ask her if she loved him more, or the music they made together. On her left hand, she looked at the wedding ring he had slipped on her finger eight years ago. How terrifying and exciting was that simple ceremony in Saiko's backyard. The plane touched the tarmac with a satisfying bounce in this destination she had shaped into home. When she walked in the door, she figured James would offer to bake for her, tuning her heartstrings to a perfect pitch.

Song of the Pearl and Oyster 239

Afterword

The woman on whose life Nora was loosely based passed away in 2021. Her mother, on whose life Ruth was loosely based, died after her at age 103. The farmhouse on Hill Road still stands. The existence of the Eleanor Roosevelt letter was rumored in the family, but no document has been found. Names, characters, places, events, and incidents in this book are either the product of the author's imagination or used in a fictitious manner.

About the Author

Patty Duffy is a teacher, flutist, and music lover. Her first novel was *Give or Take*. *Song of the Pearl and Oyster* is her second novel. She is the mother of three amazing children and lives in Michigan. She can be found most spring and summer days hiking and biking Michigan trails with her partner, Ralph.

Reader's Guide Questions for *Song of the Pearl and Oyster*

1. What decisions would Ruth have made today that would be different from the ones she made in 1945?

2. Kioshi makes quick decisions and to his detriment, sticks stubbornly by them. What personal qualities does Takami share with his father?

3. Was Ruth's quick decision to marry Samuel made to protect Nora or herself? What makes you feel that way?

4. Presentism is the tendency to interpret past events with present-day values. Do you feel sympathetic to Nora's grandmother? Is her treatment of Nora justifiable or heartless for the 1950s? Why? Are you reminded of someone you know who creates division by hanging on to the past?

5. When Miss Bird teaches violin to Nora, it becomes more than a love of music for her. What does the violin mean to her?

6. An old Japanese proverb is "Fall down seven times, get up eight." What are some of the instances in which Kioshi has fallen and gotten up?

7. We first see the competitive spirit between James and Nora in their fight for first chair with the Cuban director Joe Freyre. Is their competition more helpful or hurtful? Explain.

8. What should James and Nora have discussed before James left for New York? What was left out of the discussion that could have changed the outcome?

9. What qualities do you see in Kioshi that were also present in Nora? Did Takami share these qualities?

10. After the storage unit conflict, Maki, Jae, Dorothy, and Nora all cope in different ways. Is there a common thread in their behavior? Describe it.

11. At Interlochen, Nora is a member of the audience as she listens to the performance of *Black and White*. What does she hope the audience members experience from the music?

12. The women have difficulties with Dorothy and her unfiltered outbursts. Have you ever had a friendship where the effort to preserve it made you question if it was worthwhile?

13. Nora backed away from motherhood because of the way she was treated throughout her life. What advice might she have for her goddaughter Isla about being a part of two worlds?

14. James wonders if Nora loves him more or the music they create. What do you think?

15. Takami reminds Nora that their father wanted them to have purpose and meaning in their lives. He tells Nora she has achieved the purpose. What does she later discover as the meaning?

Song of the Pearl and Oyster 244

Made in the USA
Columbia, SC
08 June 2023